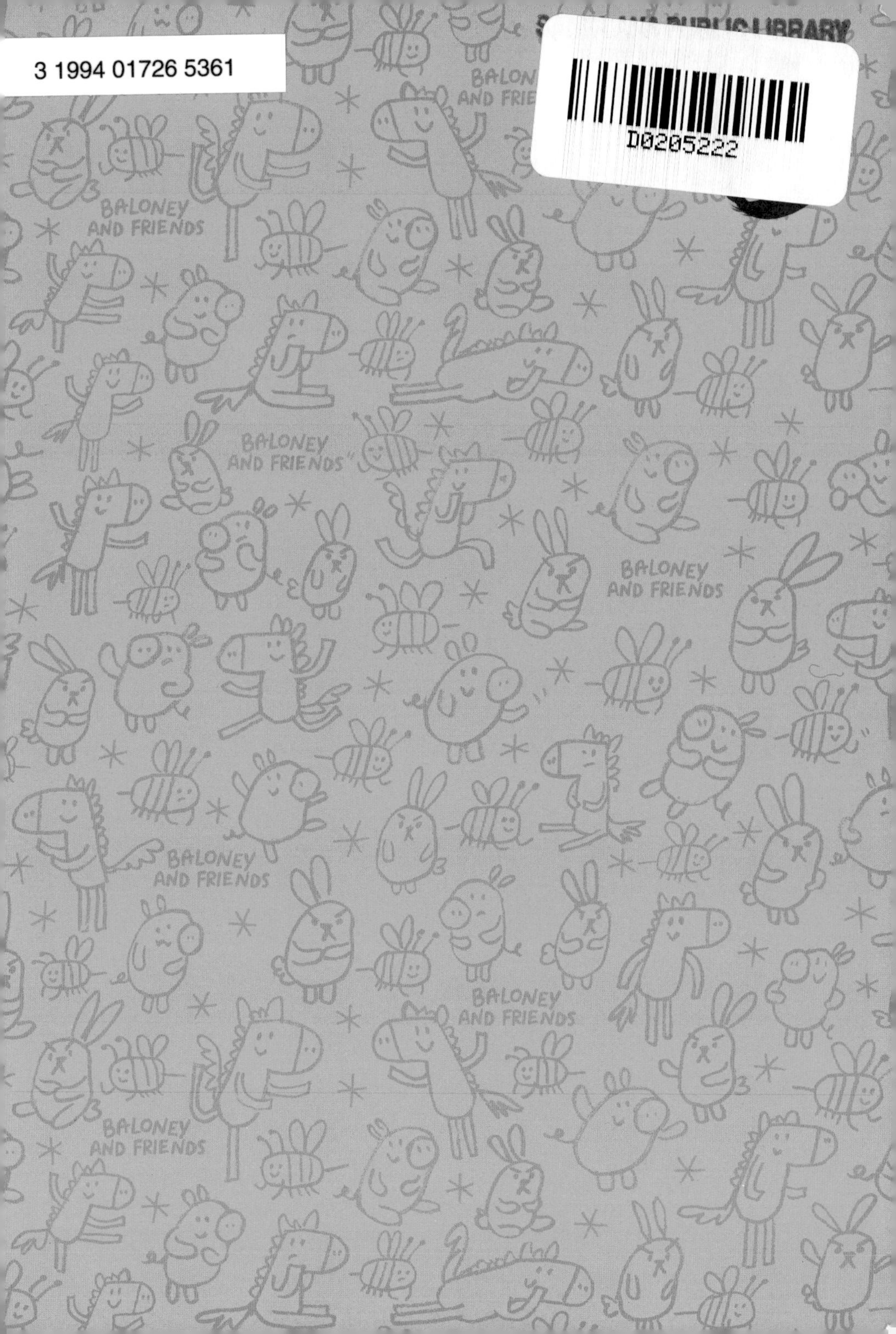
BALONEY
AND FRIENDS

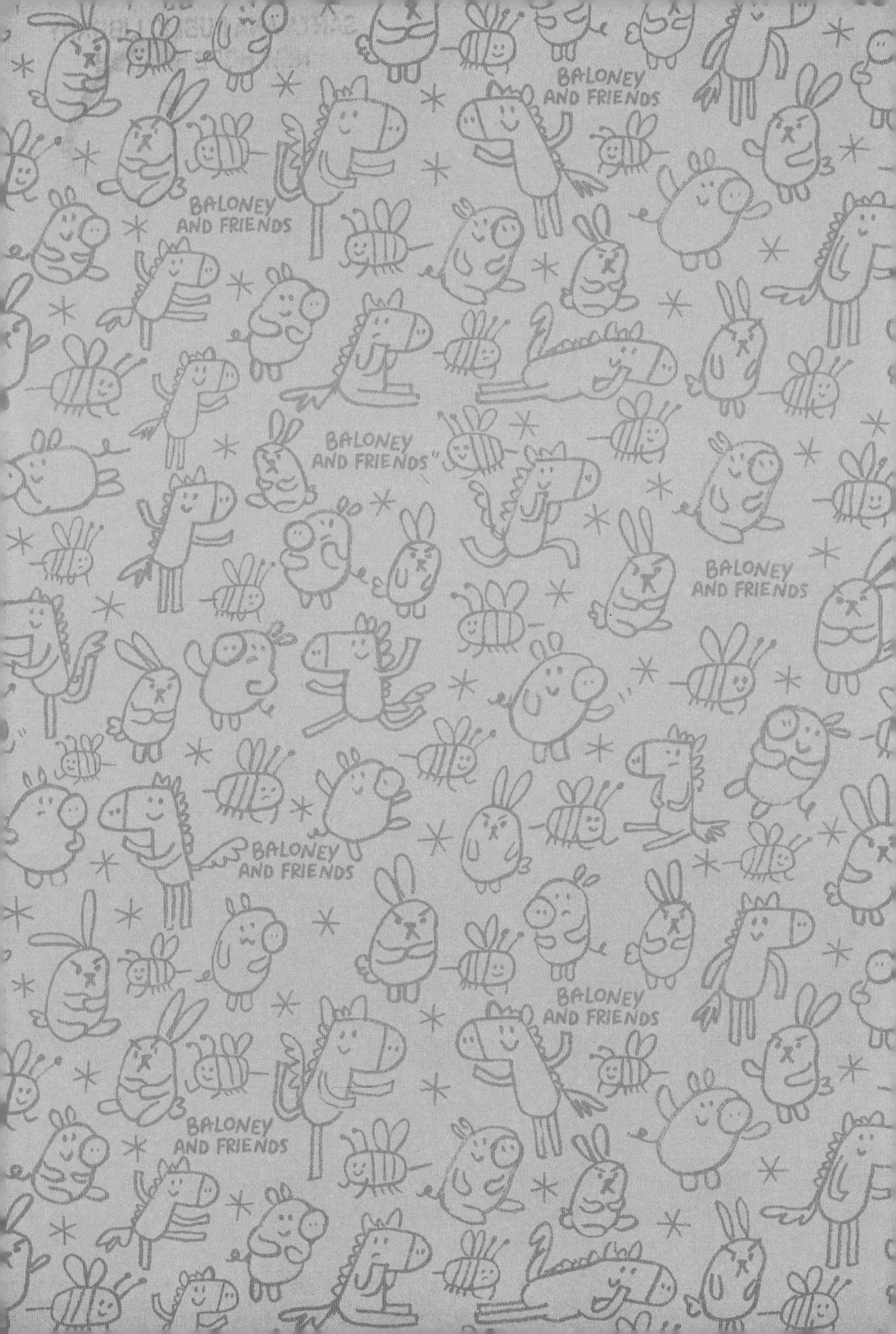
BALONEY AND FRIENDS

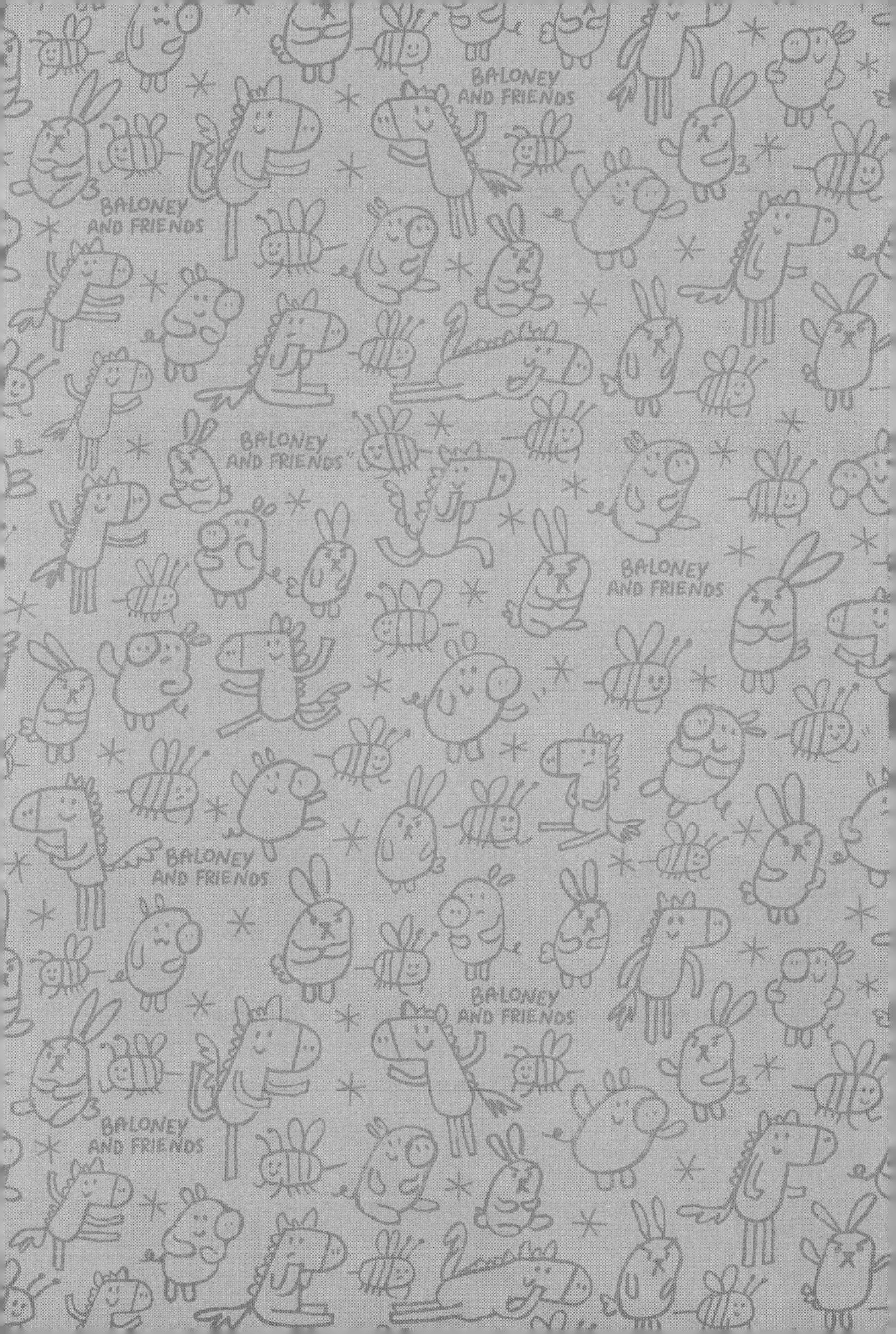
BALONEY AND FRIENDS
BALONEY AND FRIENDS
BALONEY AND FRIENDS
BALONEY AND FRIENDS
BALONEY AND FRIENDS
BALONEY AND FRIENDS
BALONEY AND FRIENDS

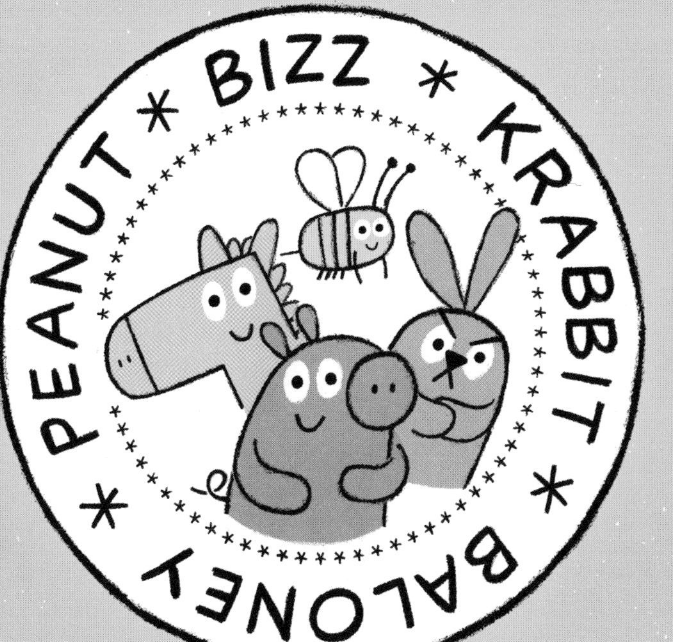
PEANUT * BIZZ * KRABBIT * BALONEY *

FOR ELINE, ANDY, MILO, AND ILYA

Special thanks to my editor, Rotem; to my art director, Joann; to Dina, Heather, Tracey, and all my friends at Disney • Hyperion; to my wife, Kay, for patiently reading every draft; to Andrea for encouraging me to "just start"; to Steve for telling me to "keep going"; and to Dav, Ryan, and Patrick for their kindness along the way. And extra special thanks go to the Lower School Girls of Springside Chestnut Hill Academy, who saw the book in early sketches and were very helpful.

 • Little, Brown and Company • Hachette Book Group • 1290 Avenue of the Americas, New York, NY 10104 • Visit us at LBYR.com • Originally published in paper over board by Disney • Hyperion, an imprint of Disney Book Group, in April 2020 • First Trade Paperback Edition: April 2021 • Little, Brown and Company is a division of Hachette Book Group, Inc. The Little, Brown name and logo are trademarks of Hachette Book Group, Inc. • The publisher is not responsible for websites (or their content) that are not owned by the publisher. • The Library of Congress has cataloged the paper over board edition as follows: 2019945148 • ISBNs: 978-0-7595-5469-6 (pbk.), 978-1-368-06172-8 (ebook), 978-0-316-70370-3 (ebook), 978-0-316-70387-1 (ebook) • PRINTED IN CHINA • APS • 10 9 8 7 6 5 4 3 2 1

BALONEY
AND FRIENDS

GREG PIZZOLI

LITTLE, BROWN AND COMPANY

New York   Boston

TABLE OF CONTENTS

BALONEY + FRIENDS

GET STARTED

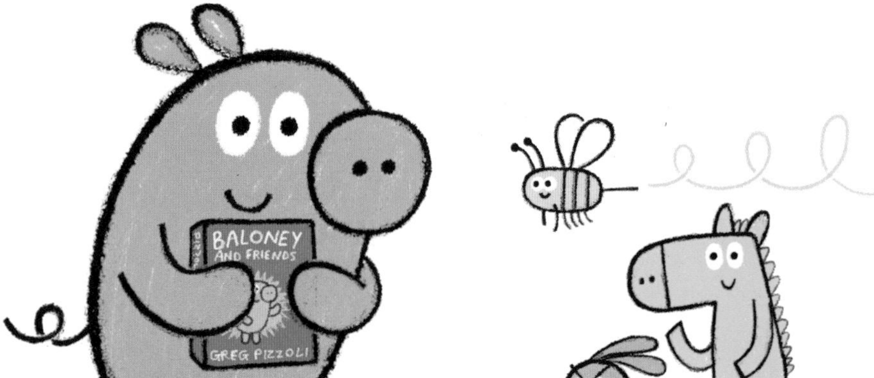
BALONEY
AND FRIENDS
GREG PIZZOLI

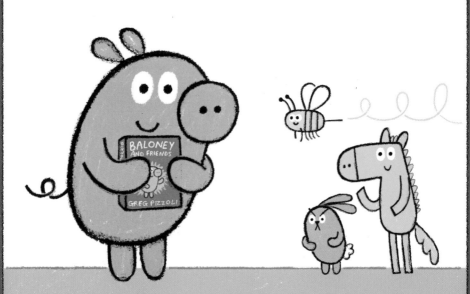

(AN INTRODUCTION OF SORTS)

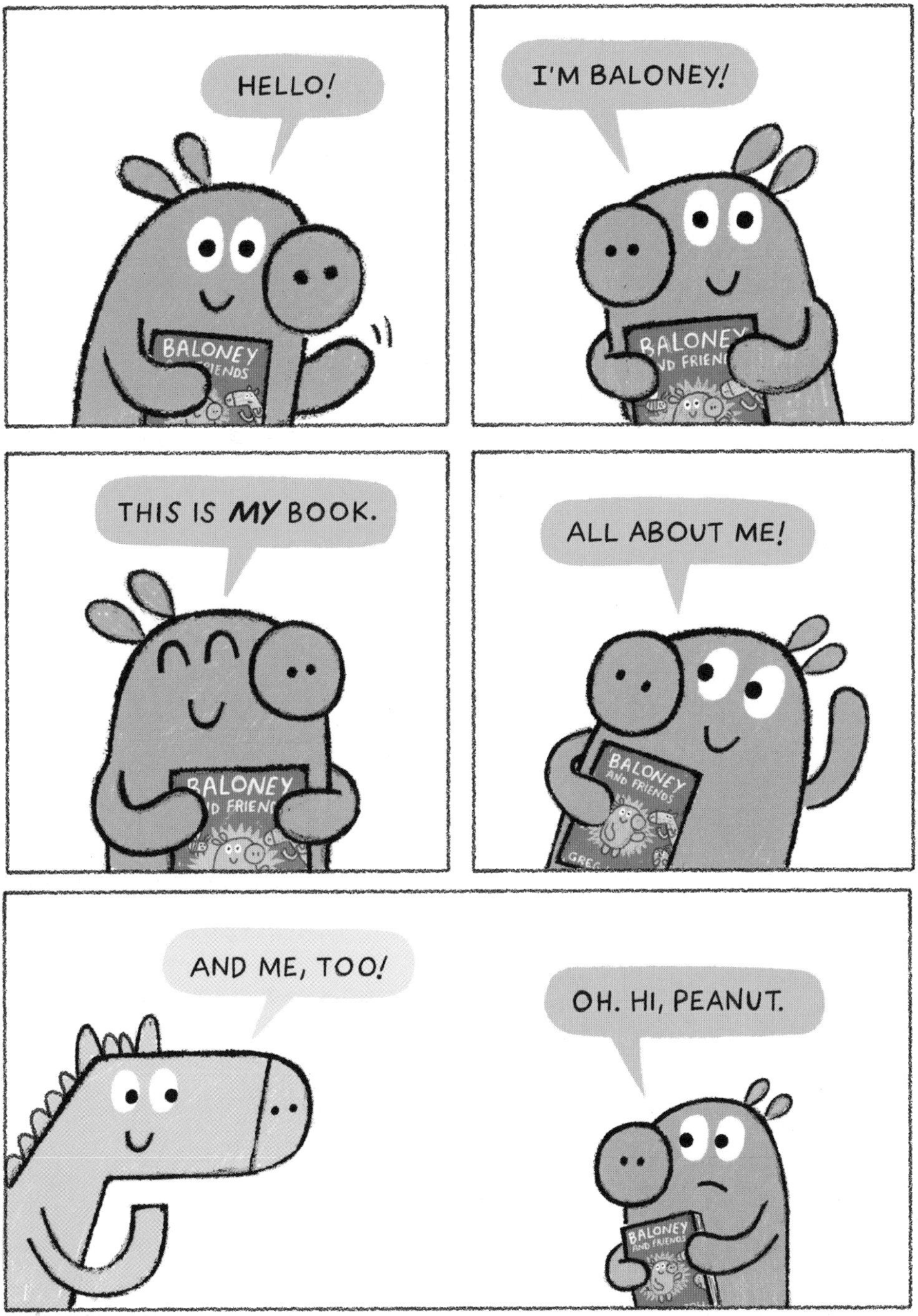
HELLO!
I'M BALONEY!
THIS IS *MY* BOOK.
ALL ABOUT ME!
AND ME, TOO!
OH. HI, PEANUT.

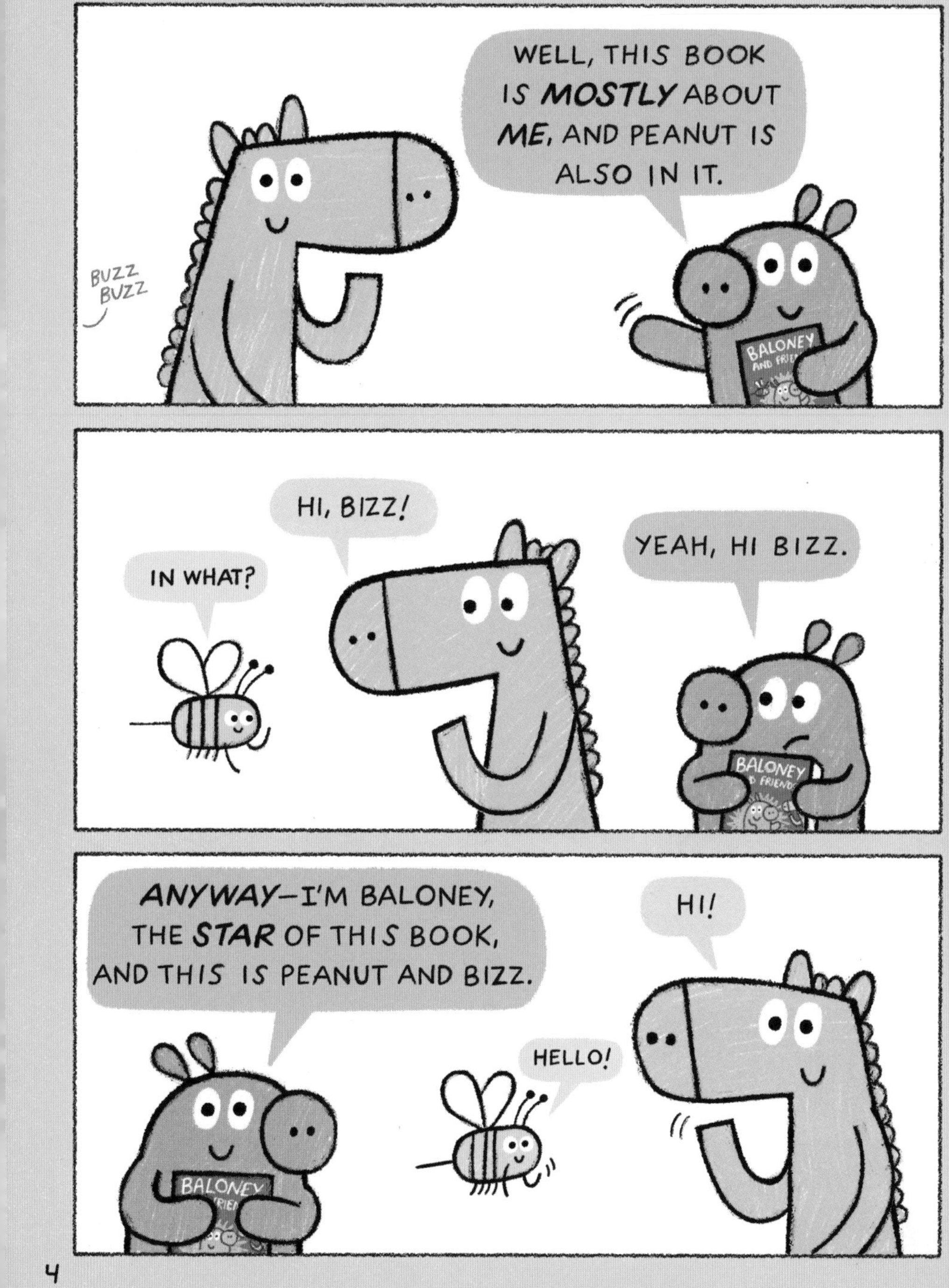
BUZZ BUZZ
WELL, THIS BOOK IS MOSTLY ABOUT ME, AND PEANUT IS ALSO IN IT.
IN WHAT?
HI, BIZZ!
YEAH, HI BIZZ.
ANYWAY—I'M BALONEY, THE STAR OF THIS BOOK, AND THIS IS PEANUT AND BIZZ.
HI!
HELLO!

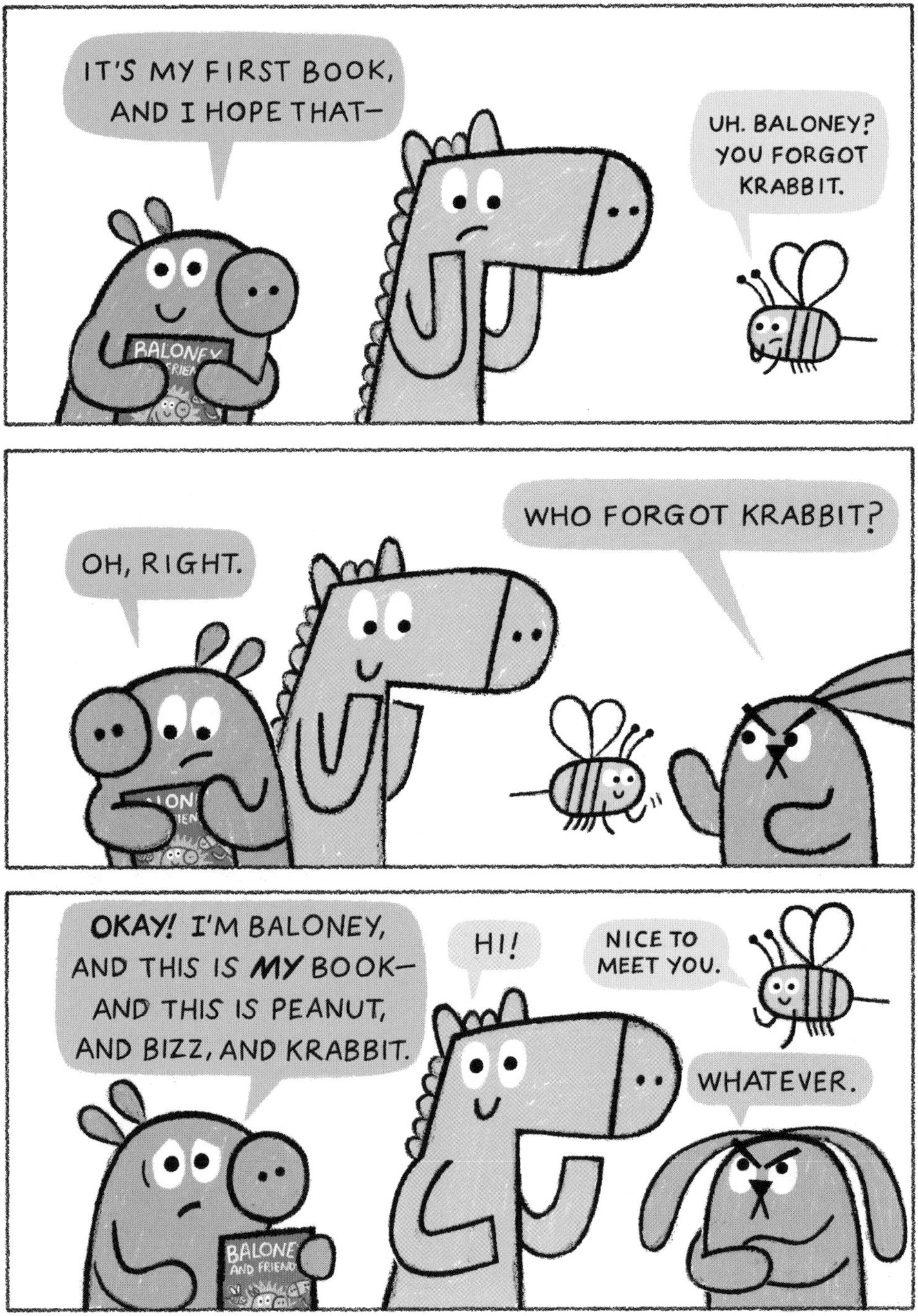
IT'S MY FIRST BOOK, AND I HOPE THAT—
UH. BALONEY? YOU FORGOT KRABBIT.
BALONEY
OH, RIGHT.
WHO FORGOT KRABBIT?
OKAY! I'M BALONEY, AND THIS IS MY BOOK— AND THIS IS PEANUT, AND BIZZ, AND KRABBIT.
HI!
NICE TO MEET YOU.
WHATEVER.
BALONEY AND FRIENDS

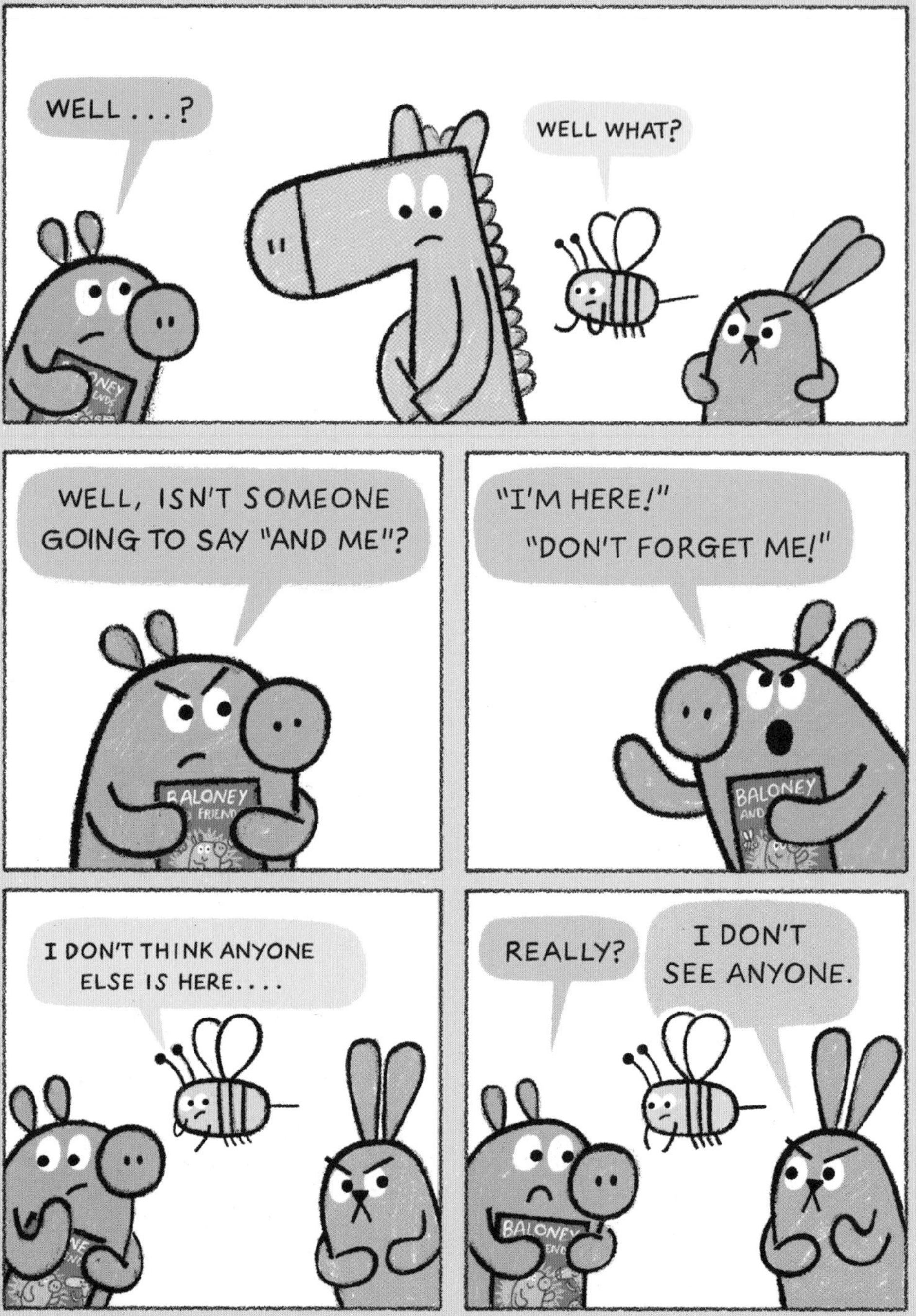
WELL . . . ?
WELL WHAT?
WELL, ISN'T SOMEONE GOING TO SAY "AND ME"?
"I'M HERE!"
"DON'T FORGET ME!"
I DON'T THINK ANYONE ELSE IS HERE. . . .
REALLY?
I DON'T SEE ANYONE.

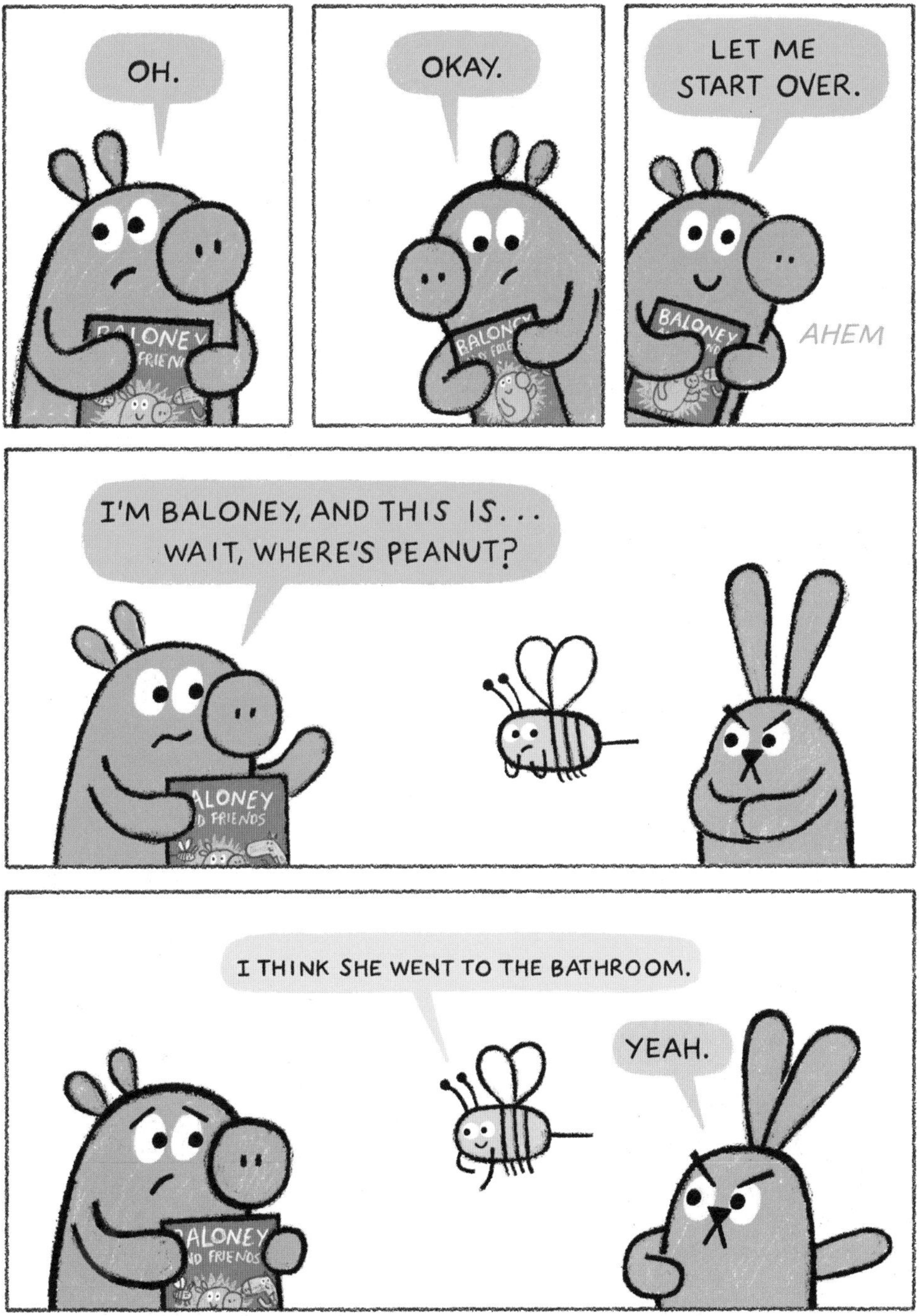
OH.
OKAY.
LET ME START OVER.
AHEM
I'M BALONEY, AND THIS IS . . . WAIT, WHERE'S PEANUT?
I THINK SHE WENT TO THE BATHROOM.
YEAH.

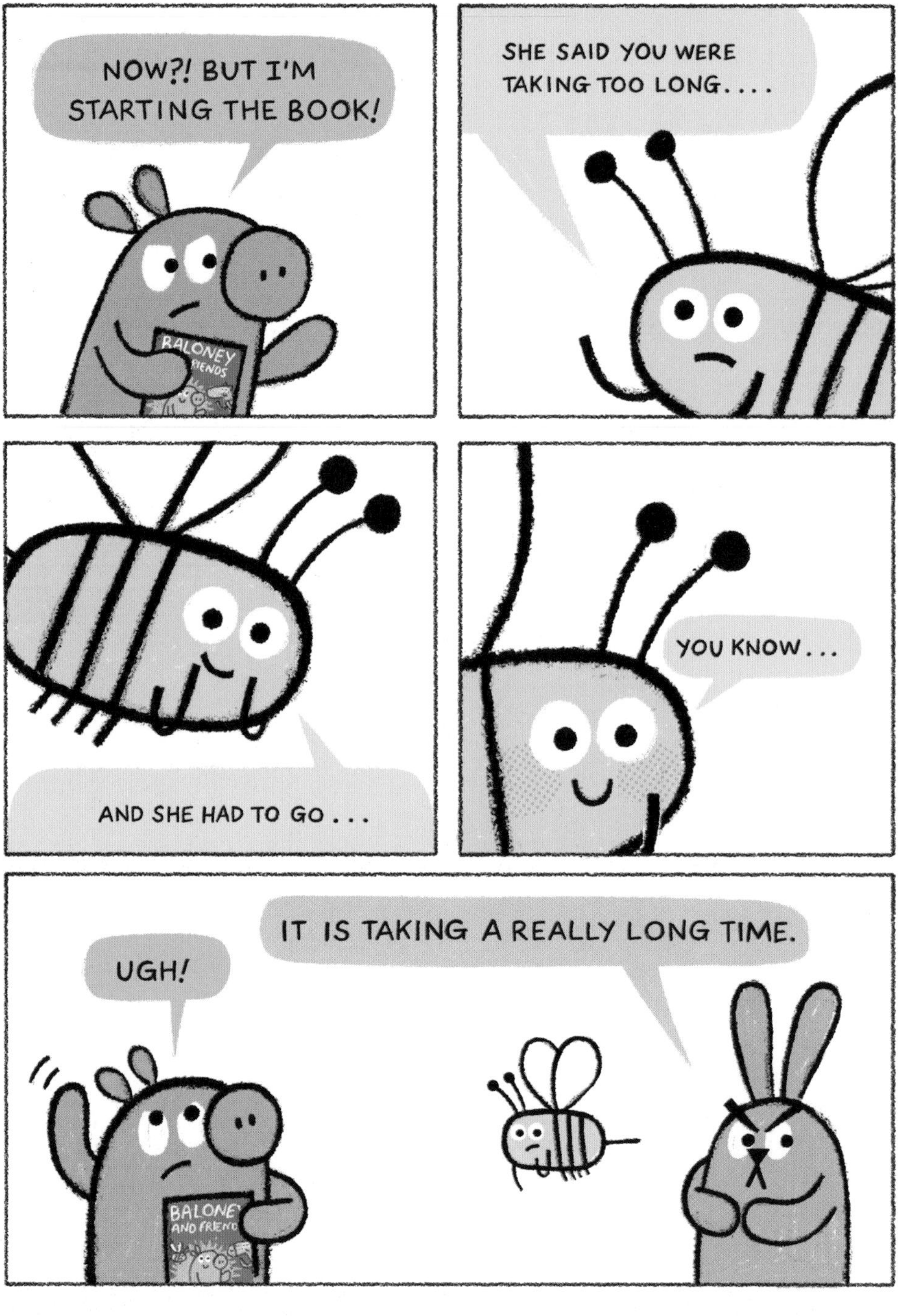
NOW?! BUT I'M STARTING THE BOOK!
BALONEY FRIENDS
SHE SAID YOU WERE TAKING TOO LONG....
AND SHE HAD TO GO...
YOU KNOW...
UGH!
IT IS TAKING A REALLY LONG TIME.
BALONEY AND FRIENDS

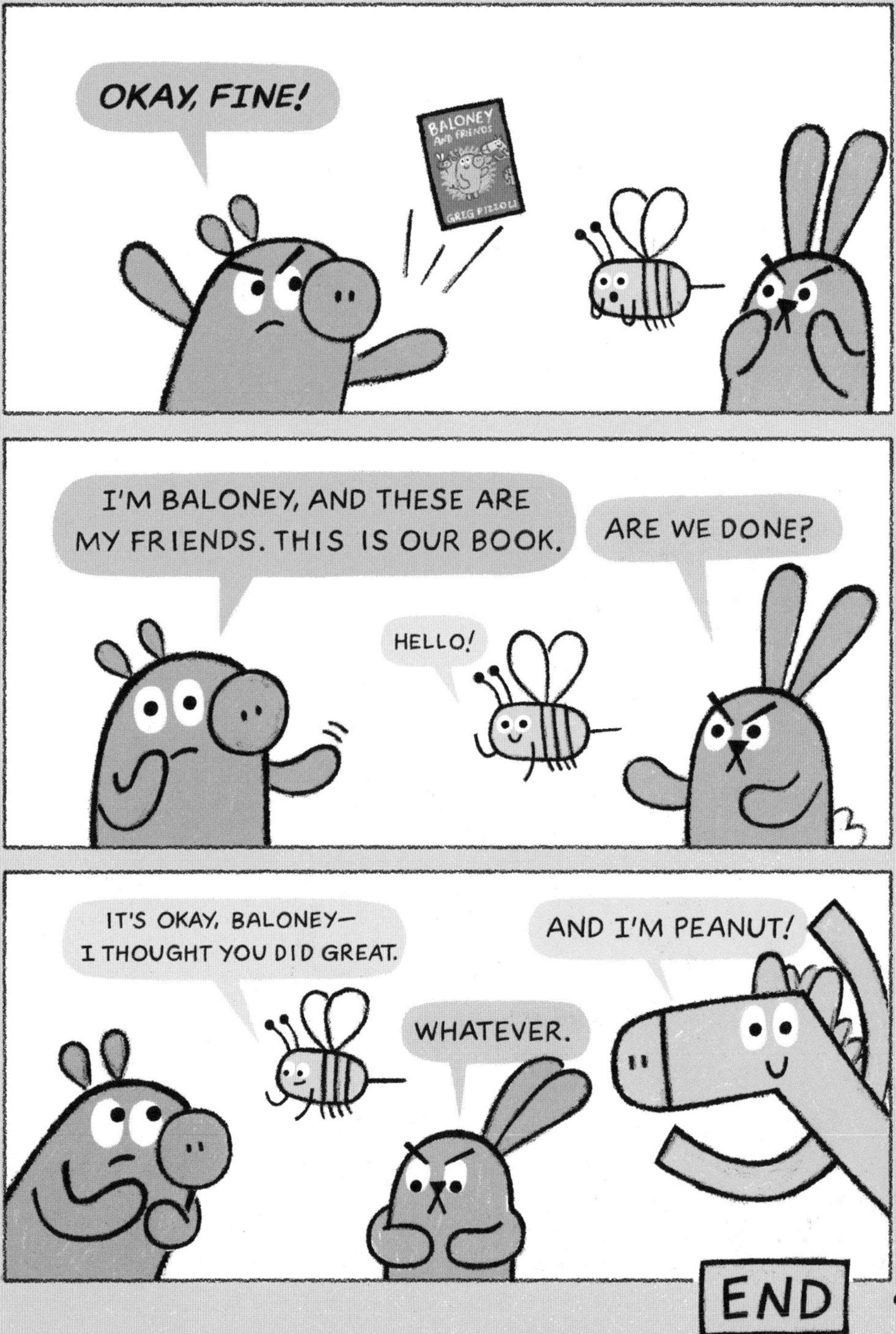
OKAY, FINE!
BALONEY AND FRIENDS
GREG PIZZOLI
I'M BALONEY, AND THESE ARE MY FRIENDS. THIS IS OUR BOOK.
HELLO!
ARE WE DONE?
IT'S OKAY, BALONEY— I THOUGHT YOU DID GREAT.
WHATEVER.
AND I'M PEANUT!
END

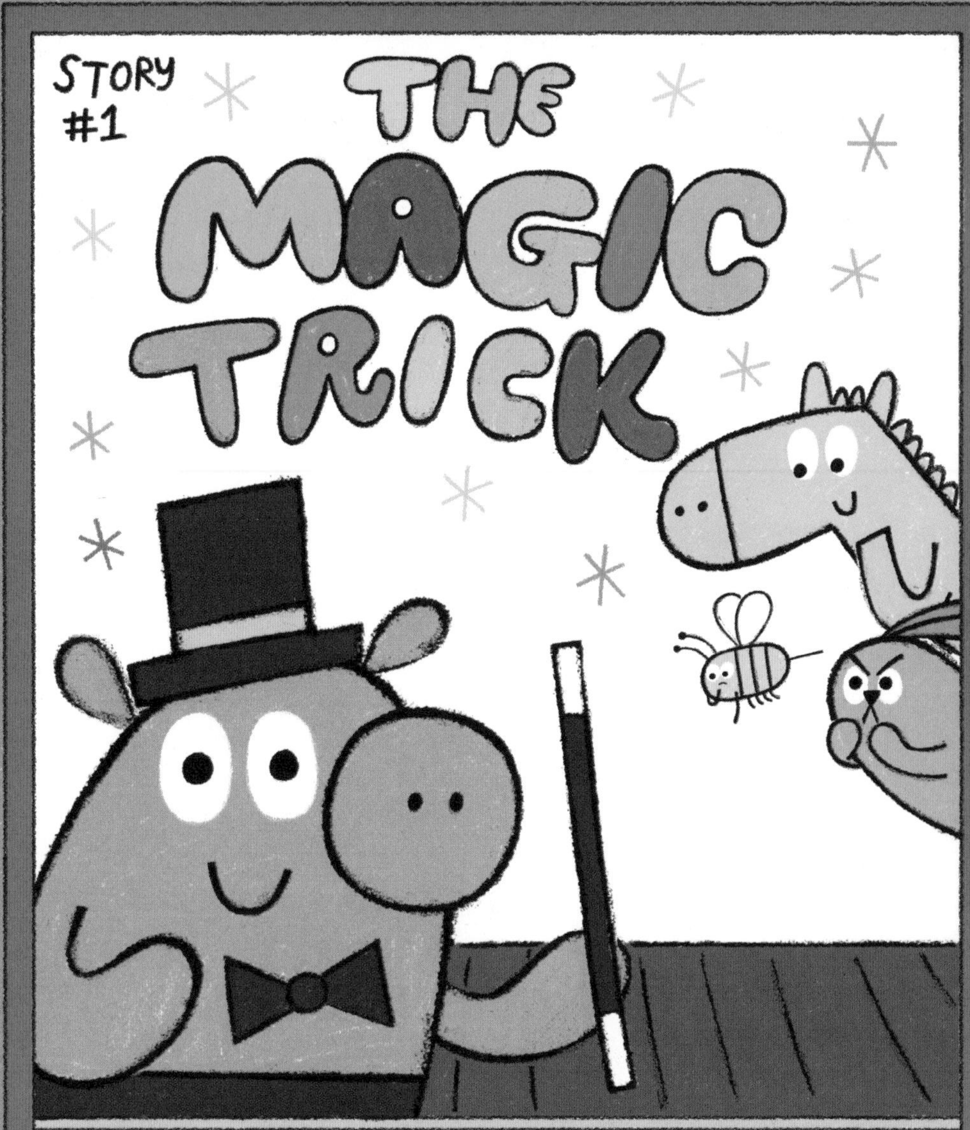
STORY #1
THE MAGIC TRICK
STARRING BALONEY
WITH GUEST STARS PEANUT, BIZZ, AND KRABBIT

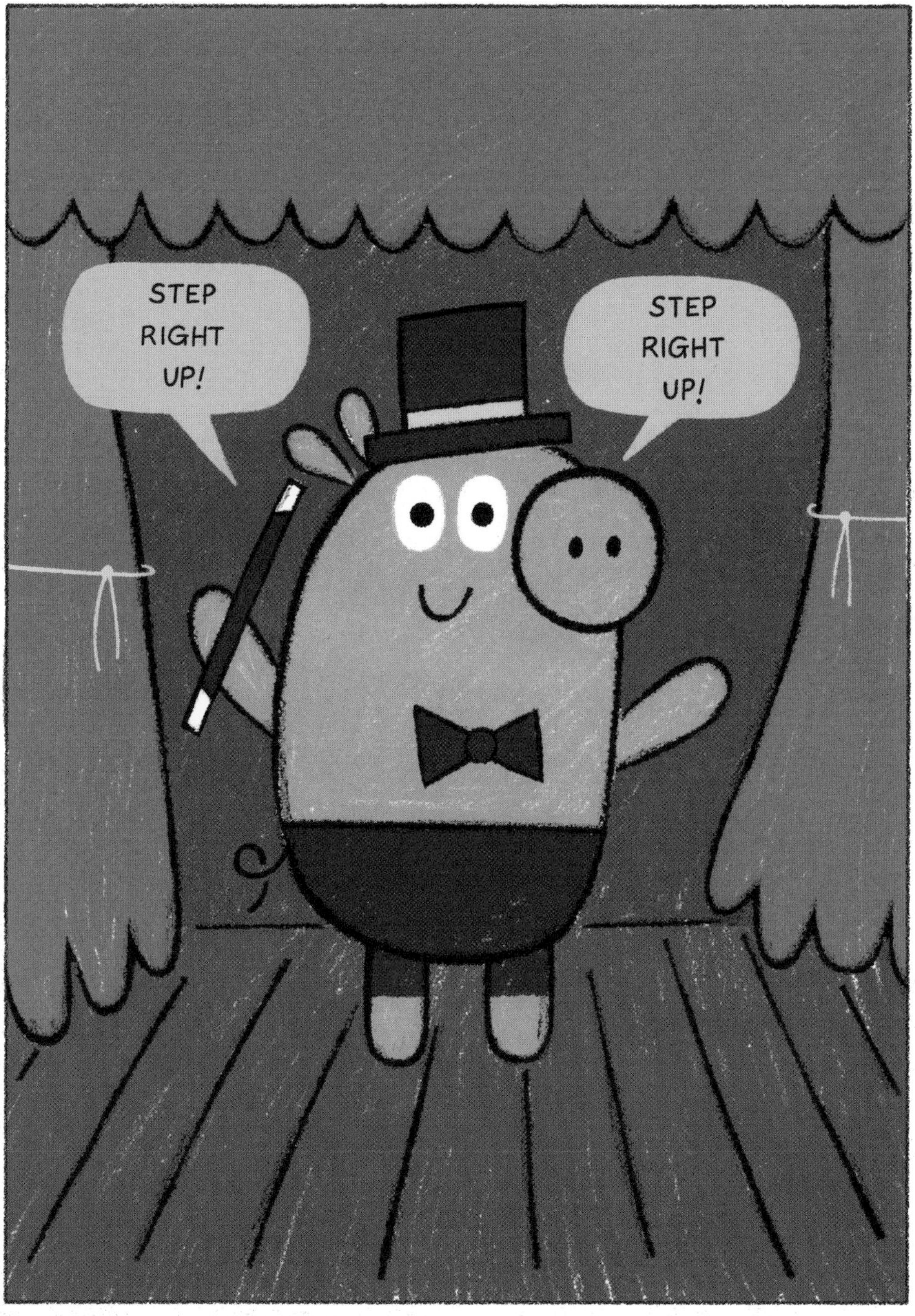
STEP RIGHT UP!
STEP RIGHT UP!

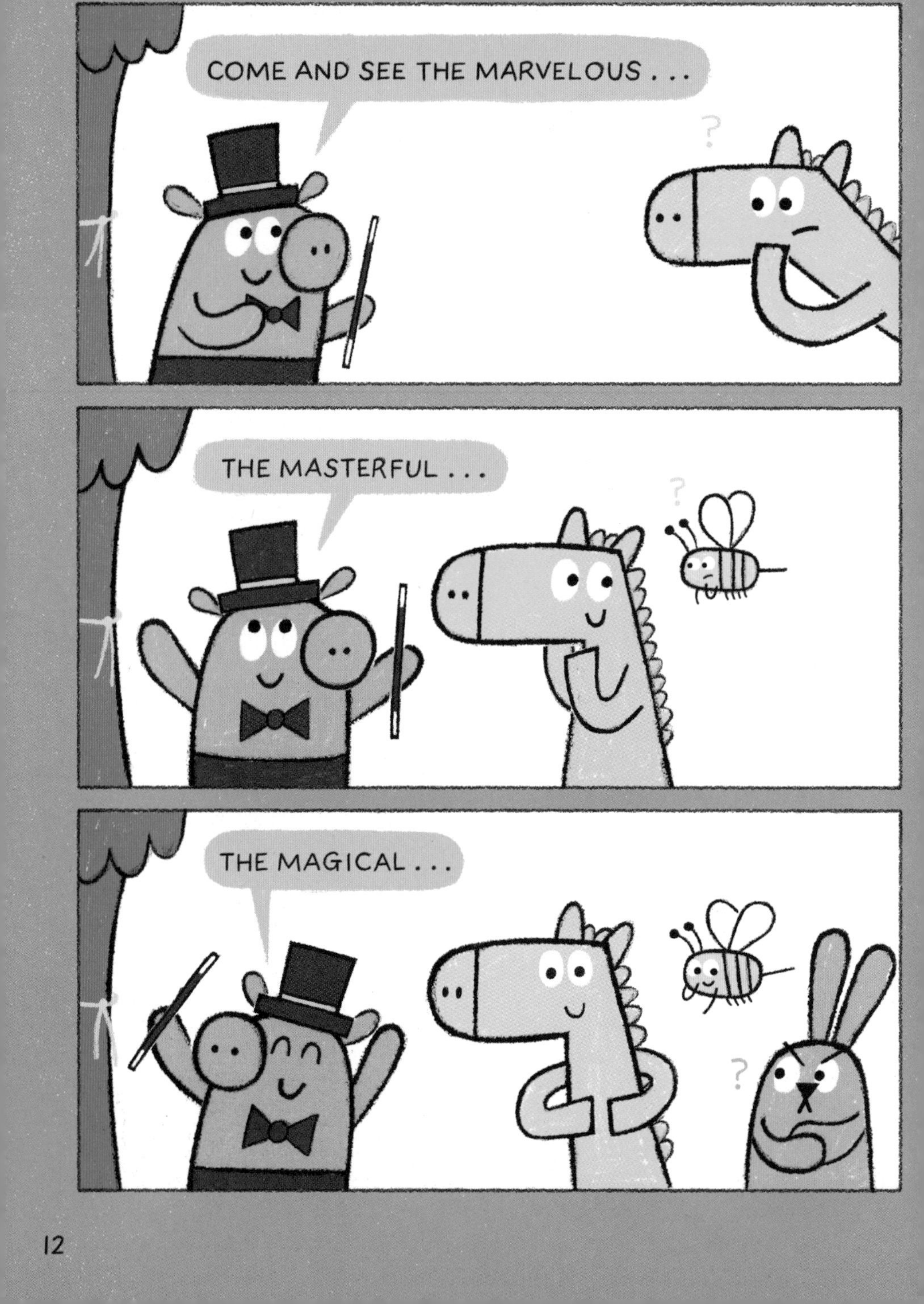
COME AND SEE THE MARVELOUS . . .
?
THE MASTERFUL . . .
?
THE MAGICAL . . .
?

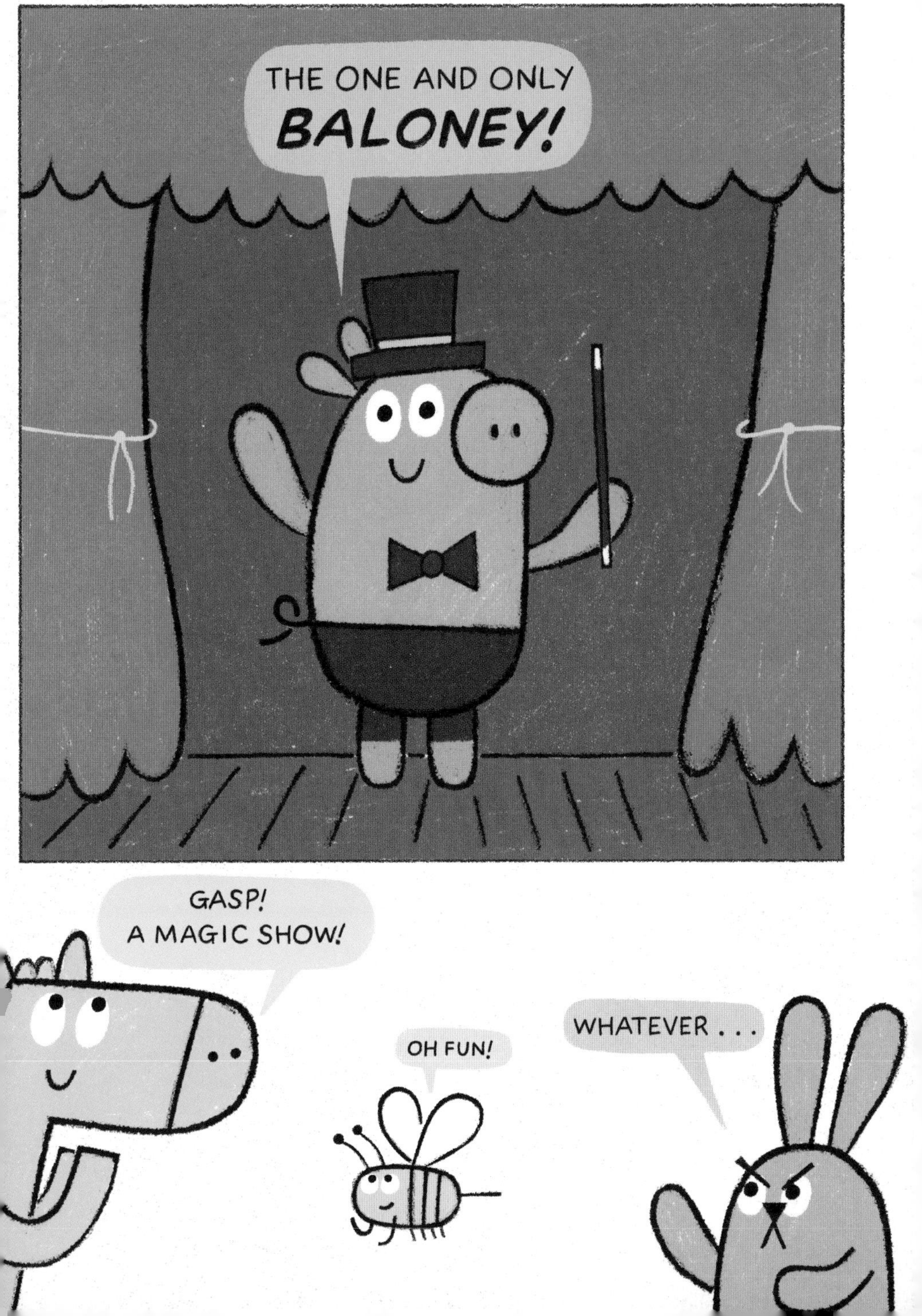
THE ONE AND ONLY
BALONEY!
GASP!
A MAGIC SHOW!
OH FUN!
WHATEVER . . .

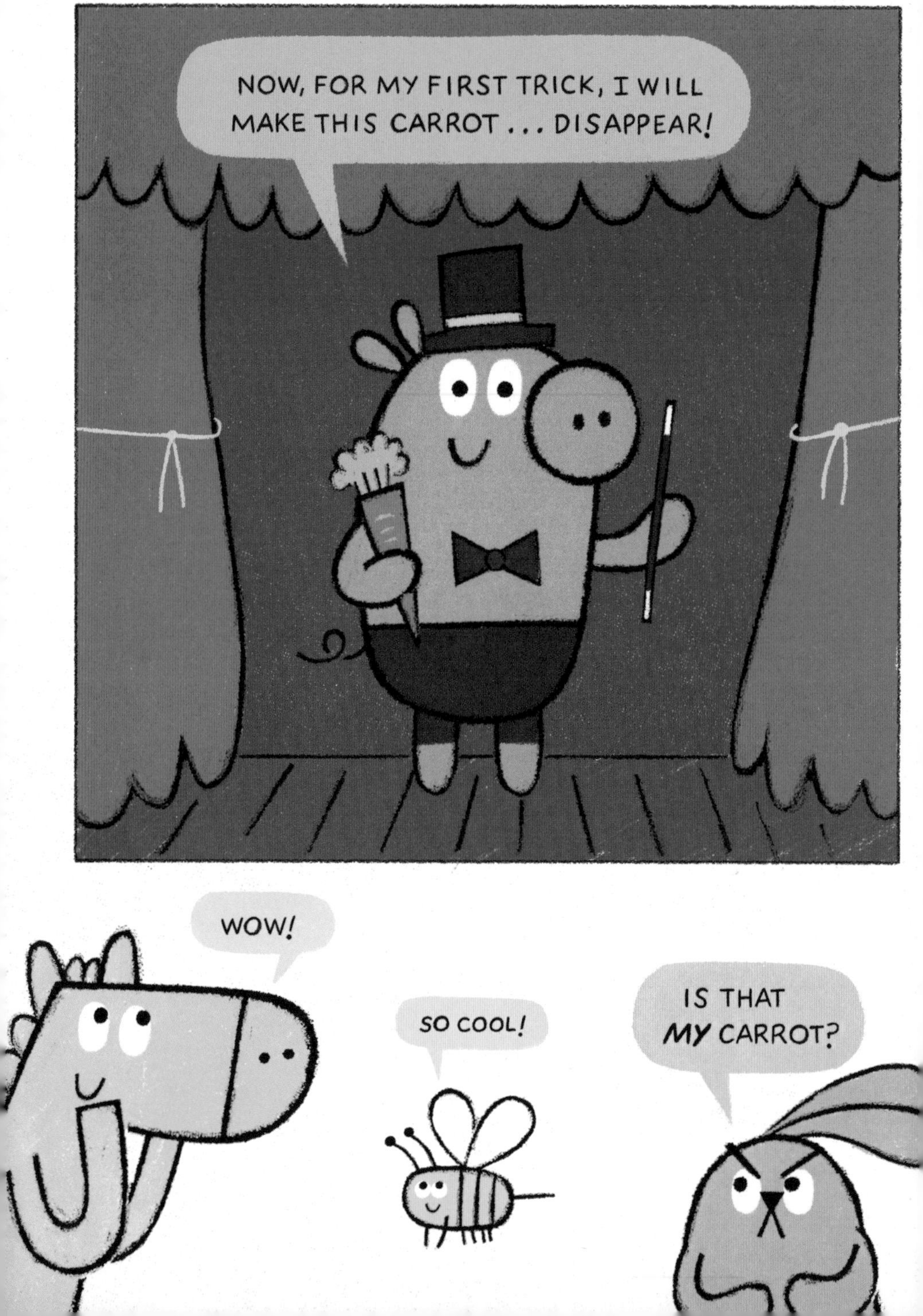
NOW, FOR MY FIRST TRICK, I WILL MAKE THIS CARROT . . . DISAPPEAR!
WOW!
SO COOL!
IS THAT *MY* CARROT?

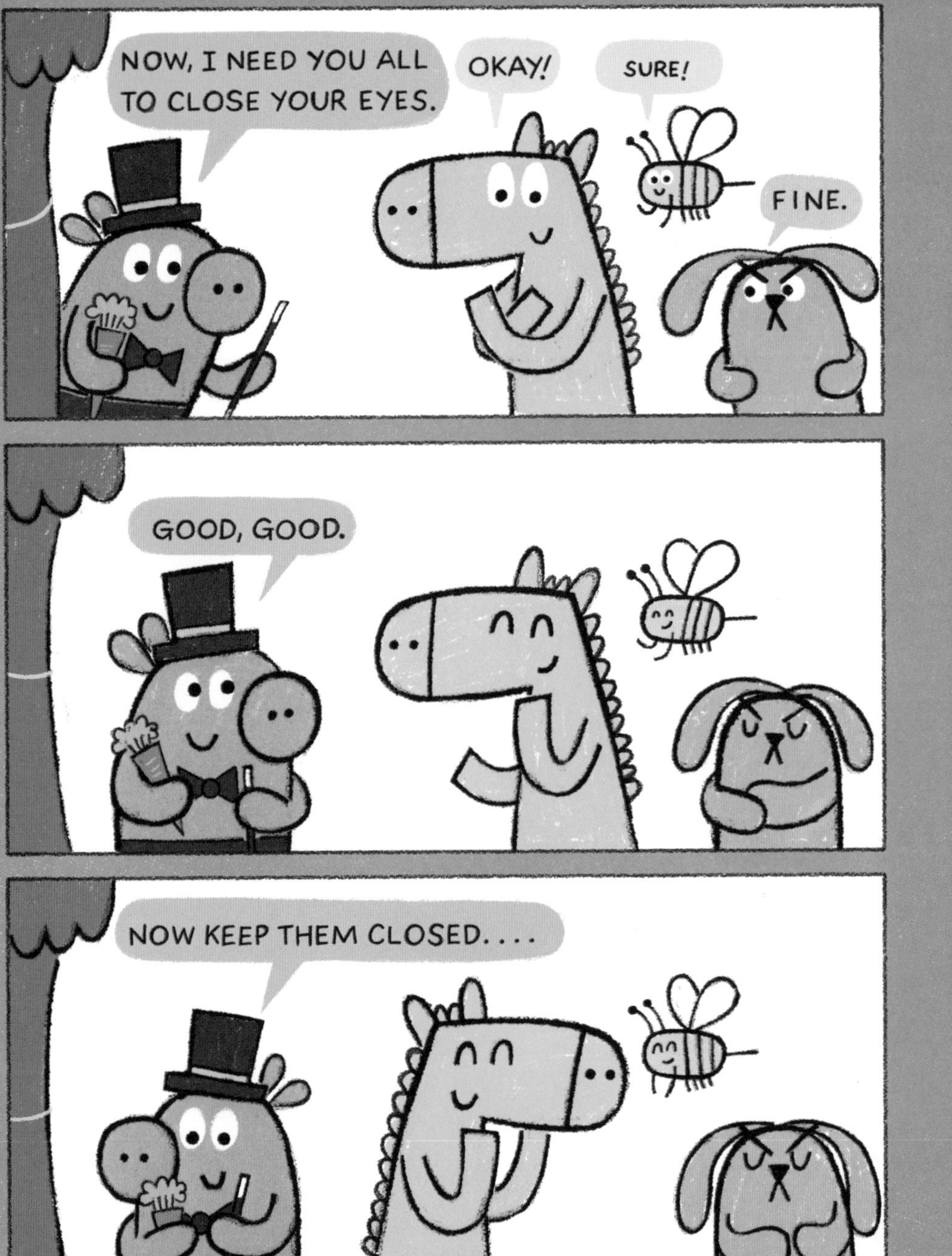
NOW, I NEED YOU ALL TO CLOSE YOUR EYES.
OKAY!
SURE!
FINE.
GOOD, GOOD.
NOW KEEP THEM CLOSED....

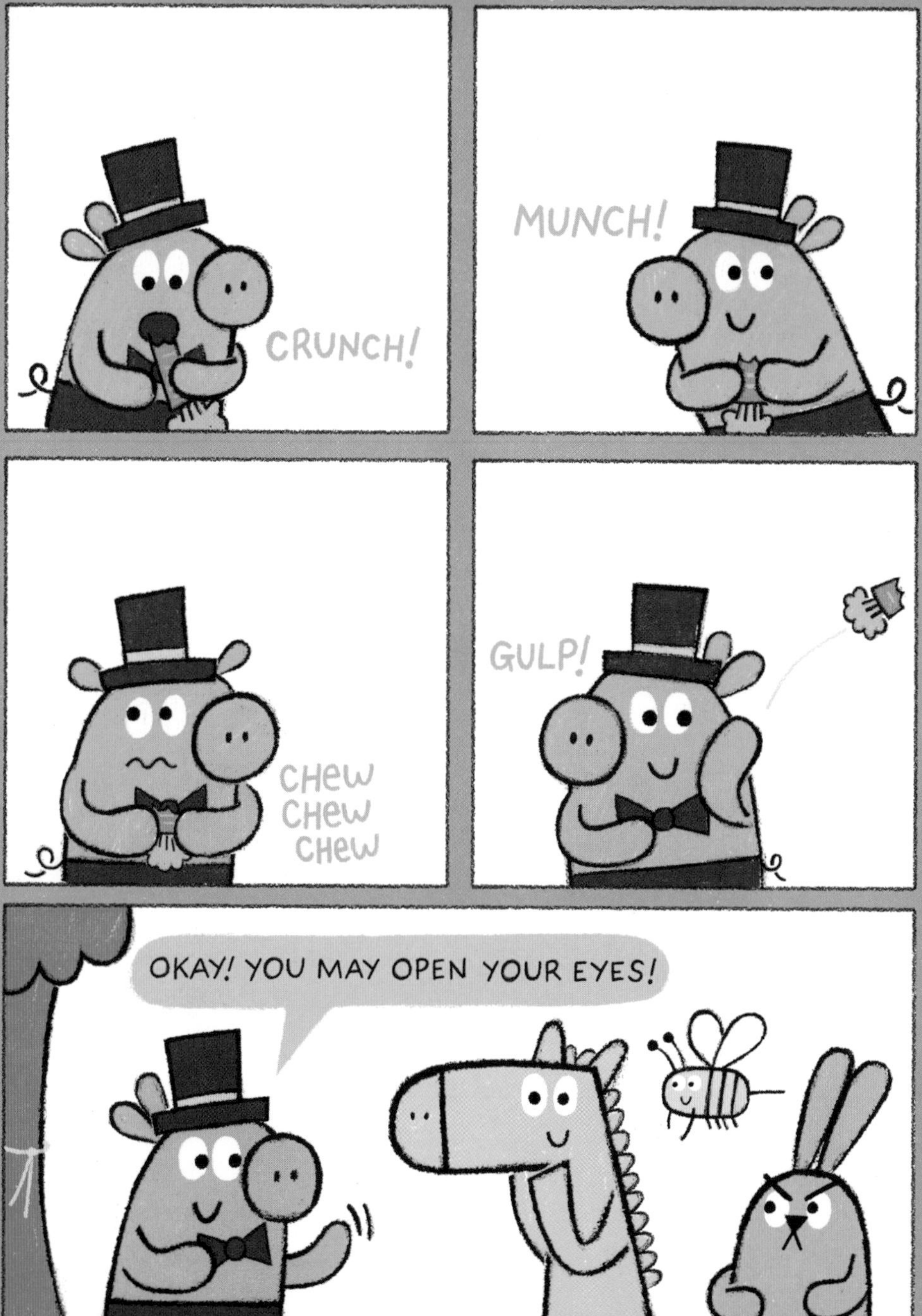
CRUNCH!
MUNCH!
CHEW
CHEW
CHEW
GULP!
OKAY! YOU MAY OPEN YOUR EYES!

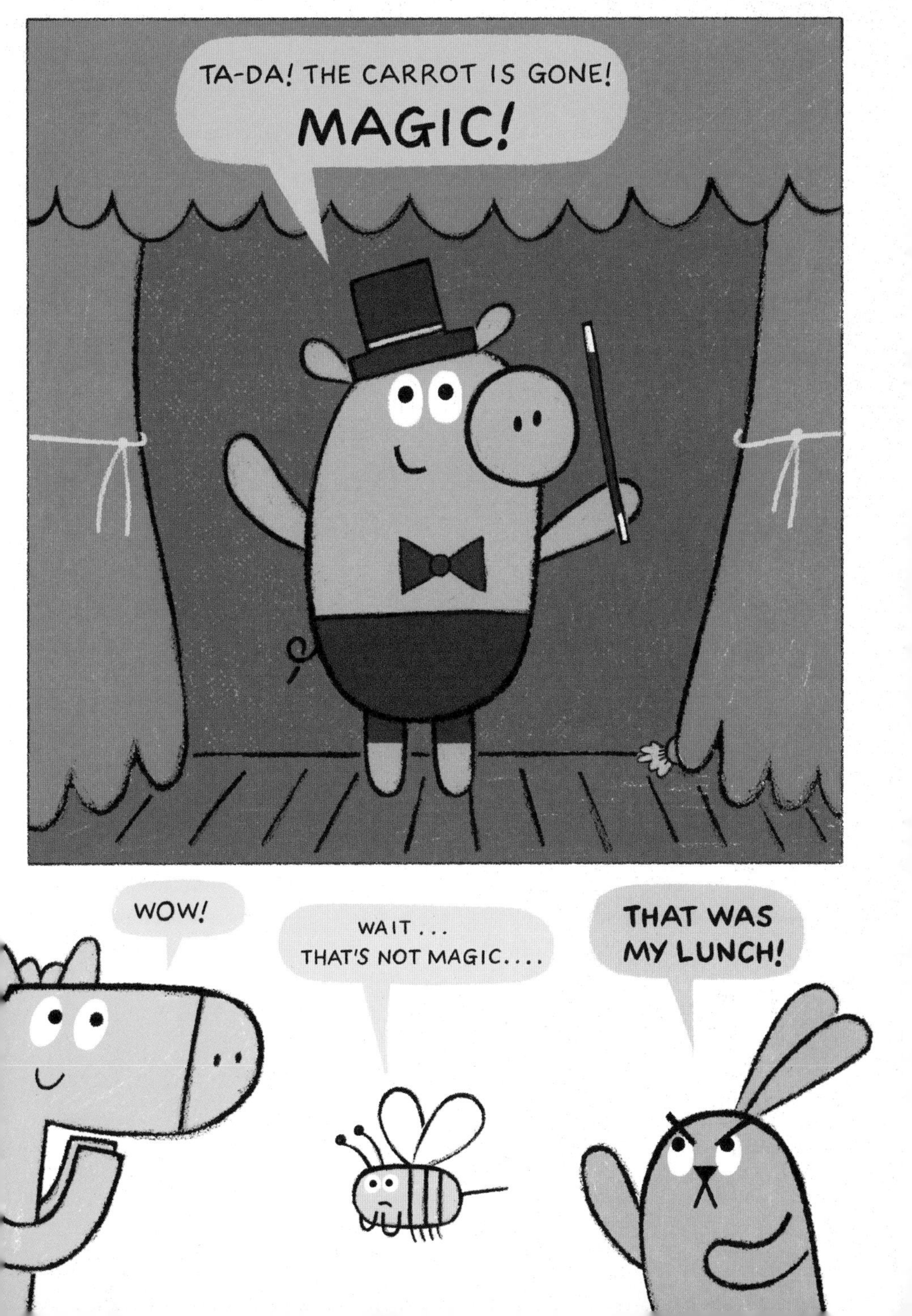
TA-DA! THE CARROT IS GONE!
MAGIC!
WOW!
WAIT . . .
THAT'S NOT MAGIC. . . .
THAT WAS MY LUNCH!

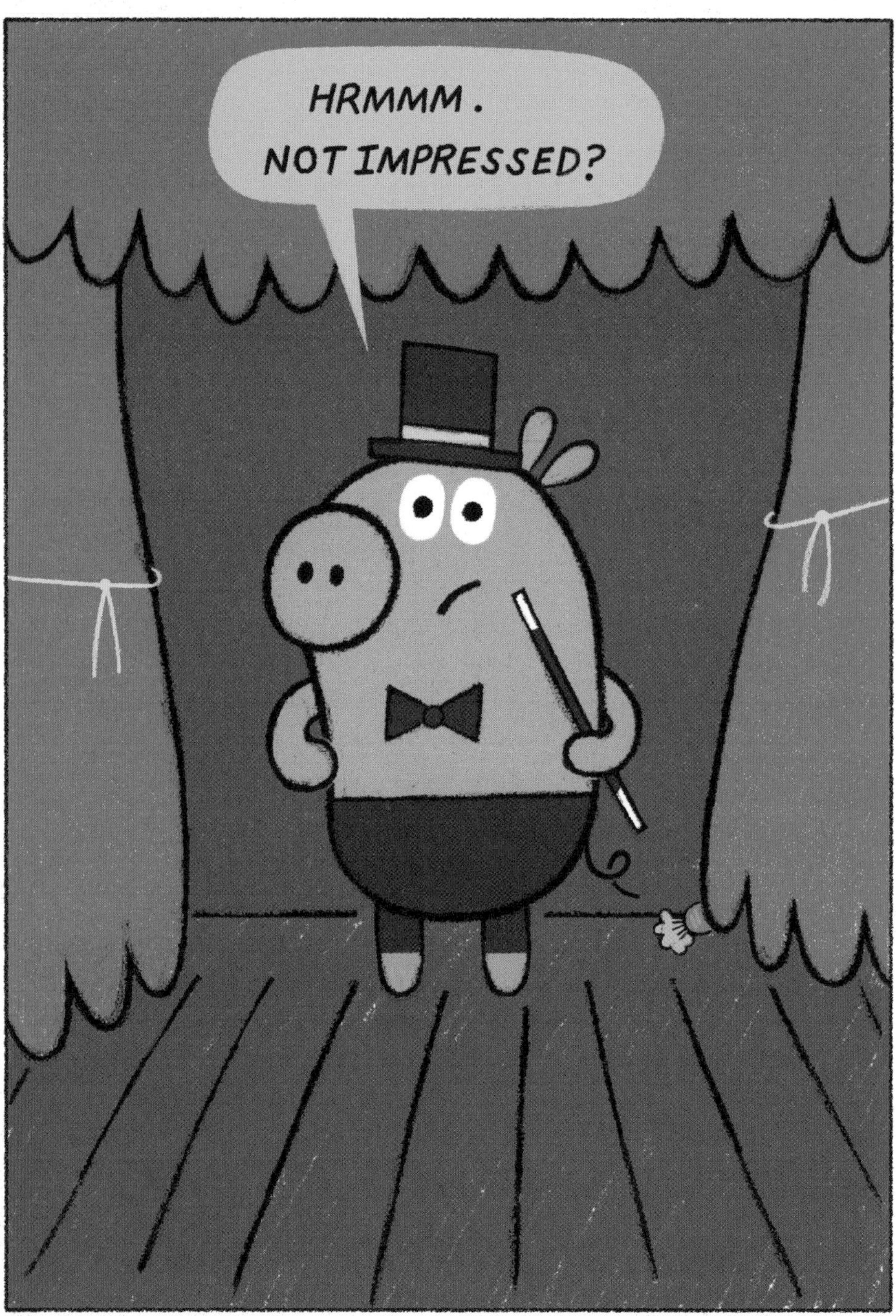
HRMMM.
NOT IMPRESSED?

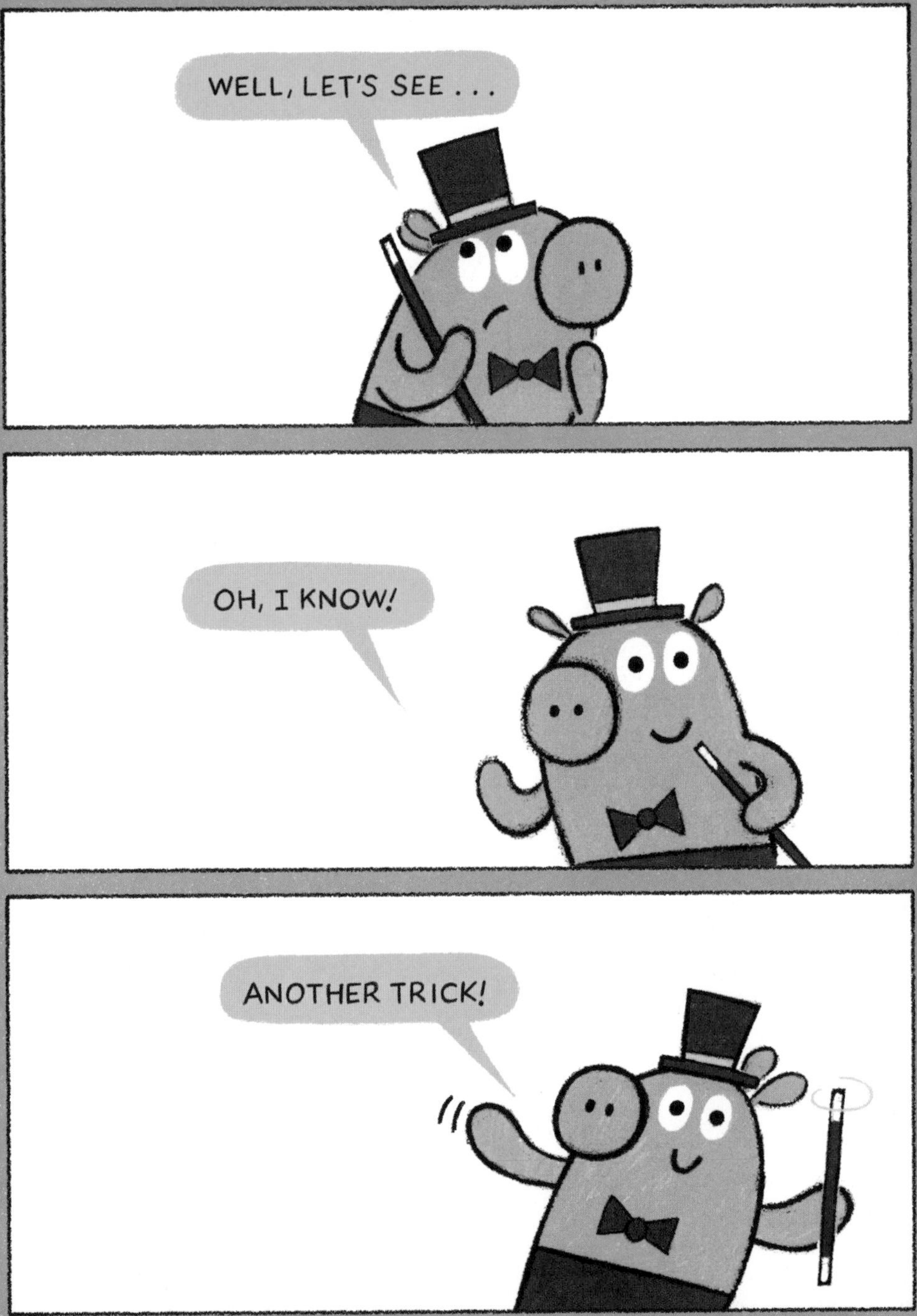
WELL, LET'S SEE . . .
OH, I KNOW!
ANOTHER TRICK!

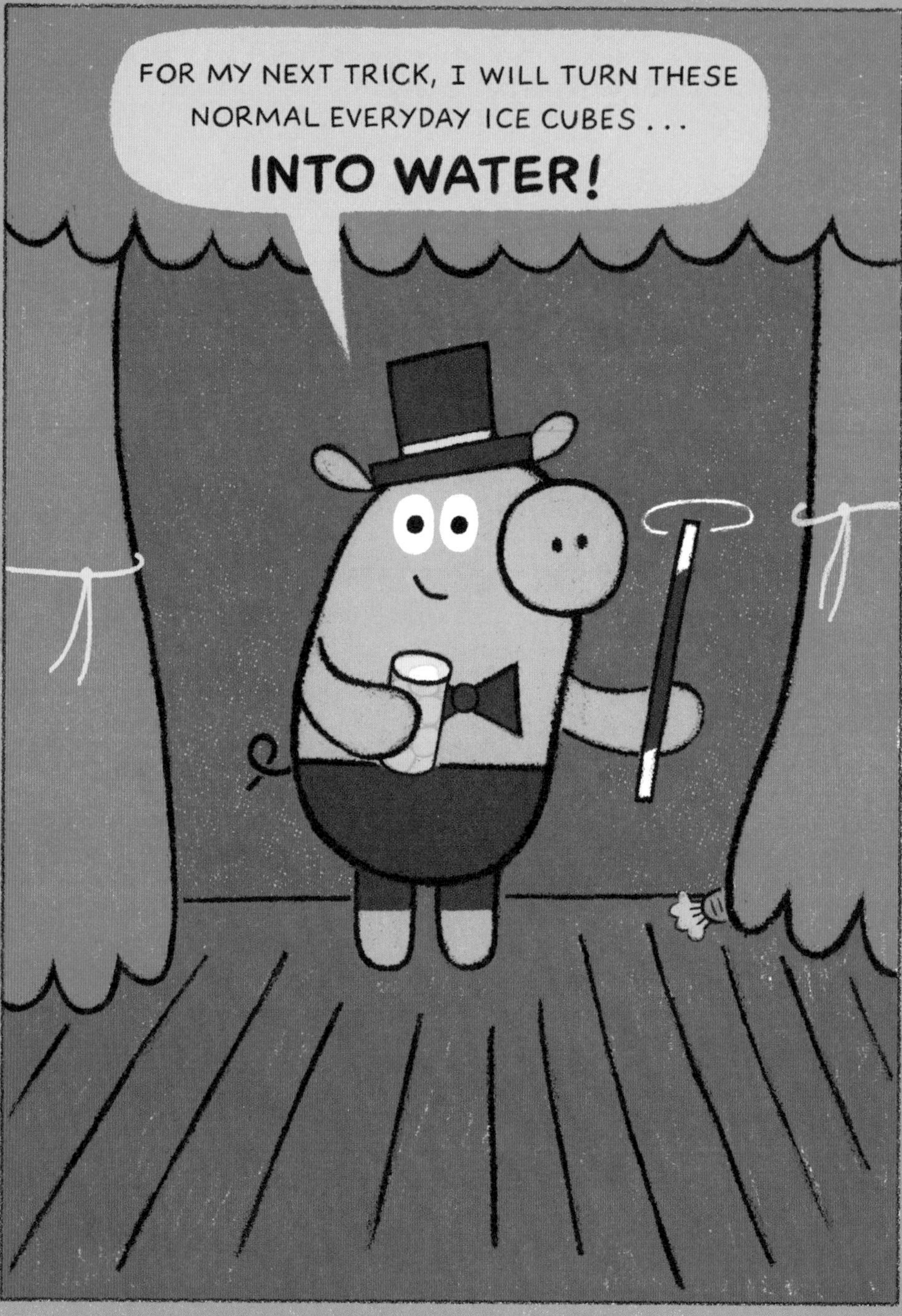
FOR MY NEXT TRICK, I WILL TURN THESE NORMAL EVERYDAY ICE CUBES . . .
INTO WATER!

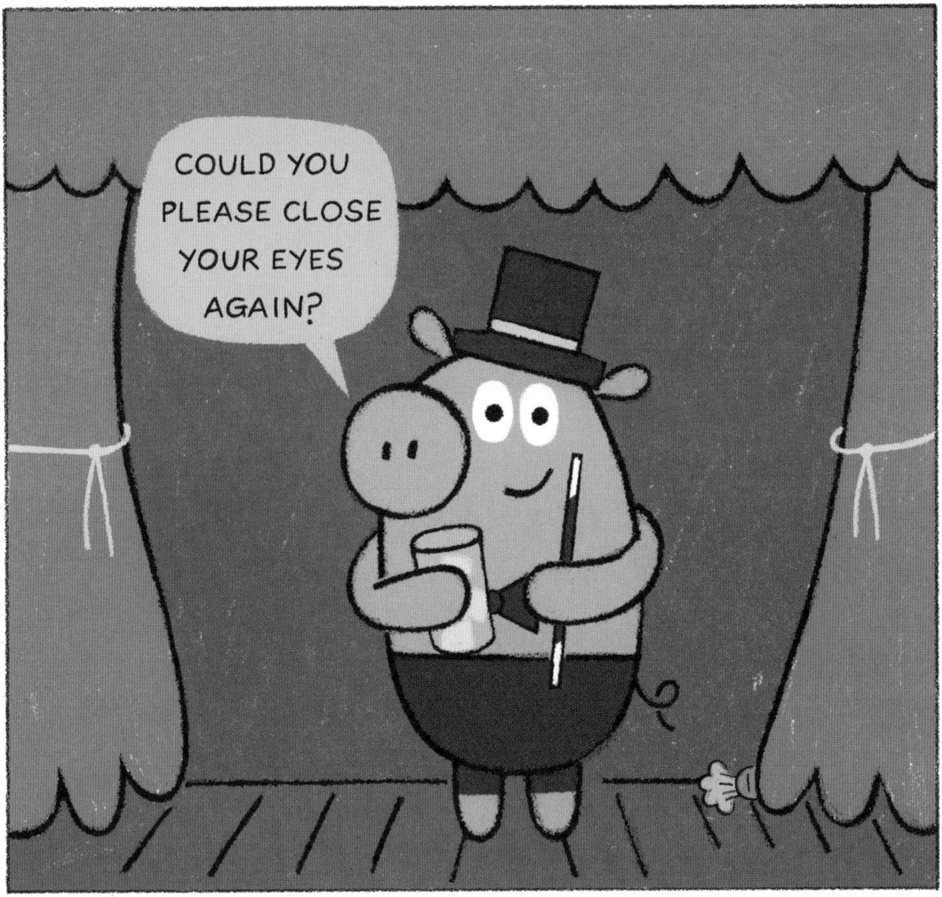
COULD YOU PLEASE CLOSE YOUR EYES AGAIN?

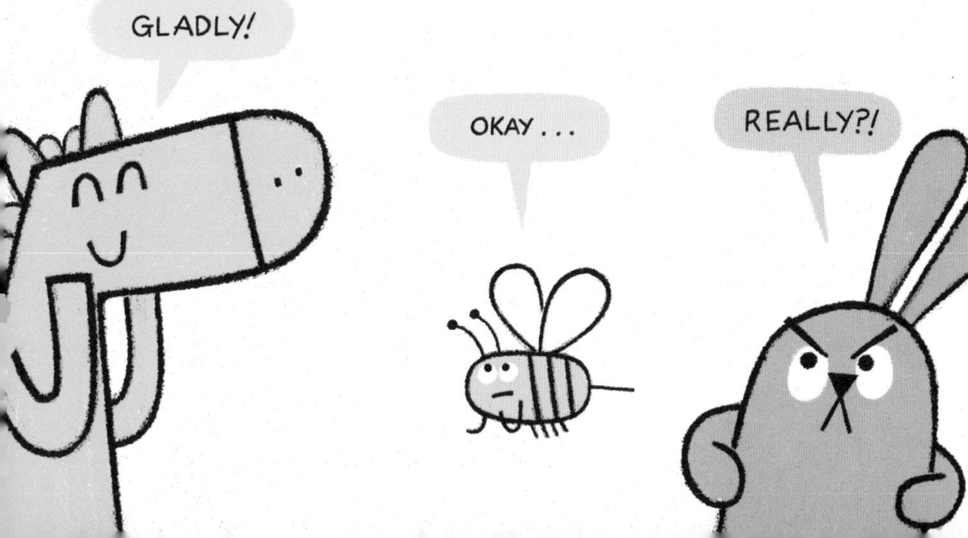
GLADLY!
OKAY . . .
REALLY?!

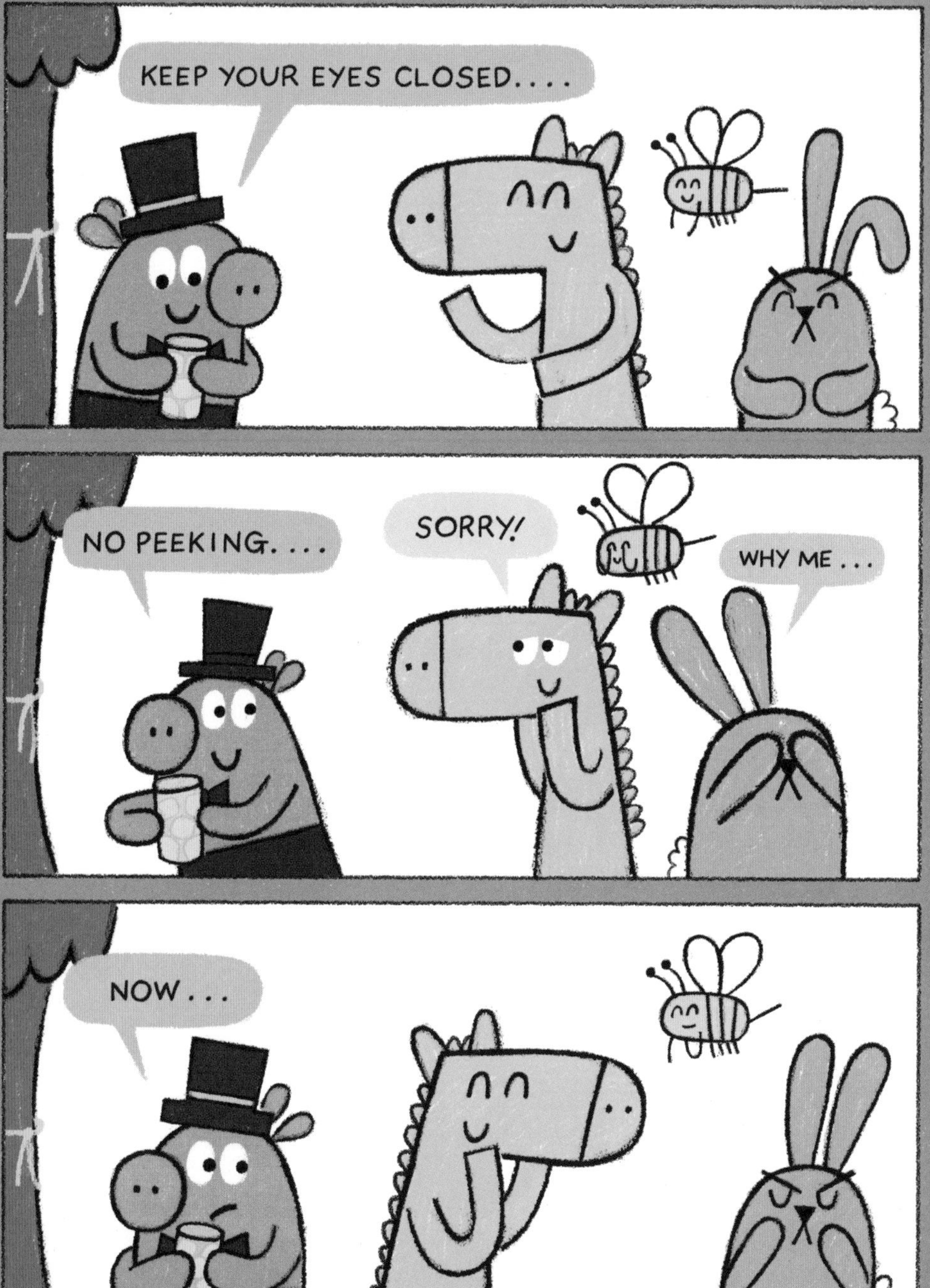
KEEP YOUR EYES CLOSED....
NO PEEKING....
SORRY!
WHY ME...
NOW...

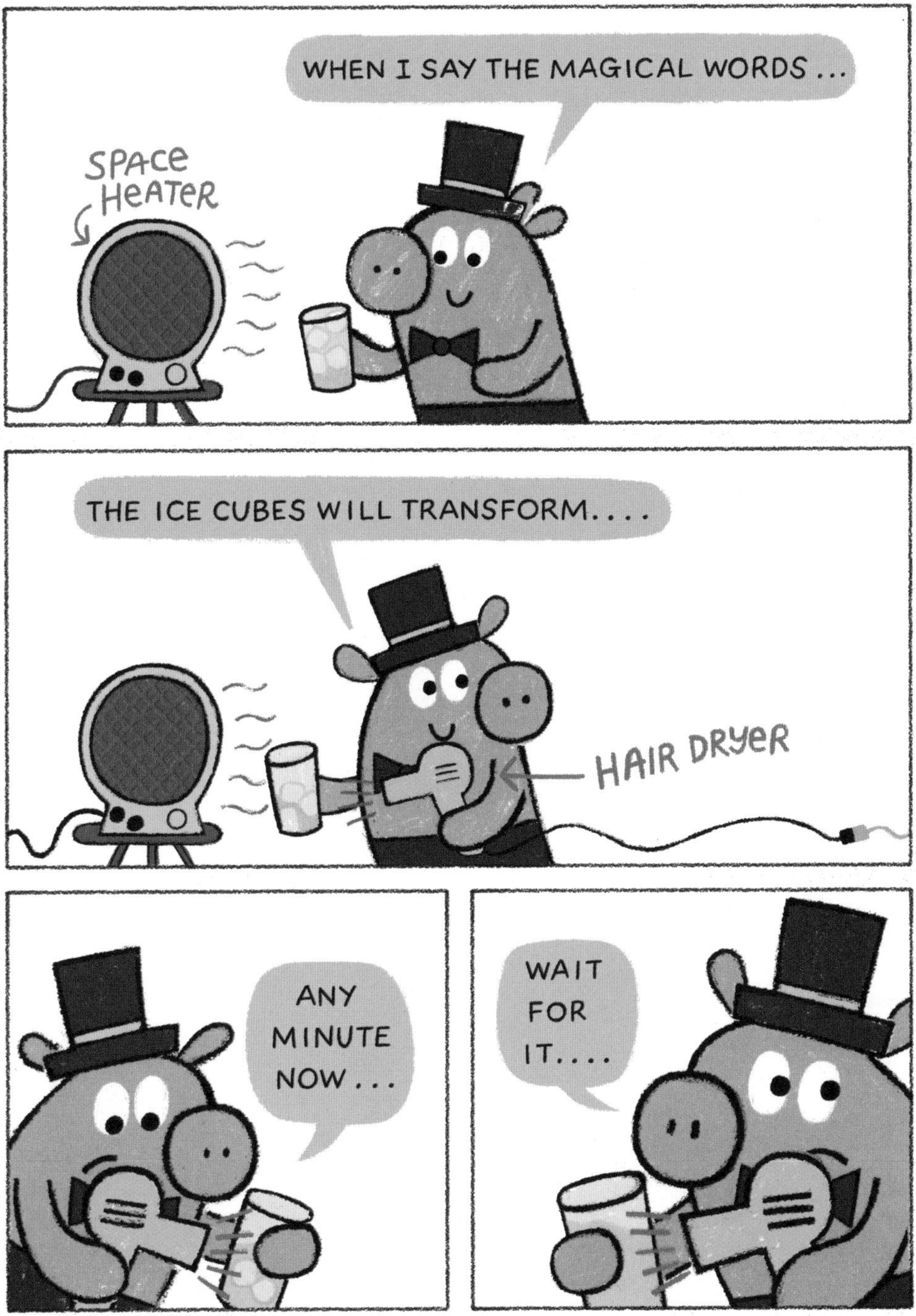
WHEN I SAY THE MAGICAL WORDS . . .
SPACE HEATER
THE ICE CUBES WILL TRANSFORM. . . .
HAIR DRYER
ANY MINUTE NOW . . .
WAIT FOR IT. . . .

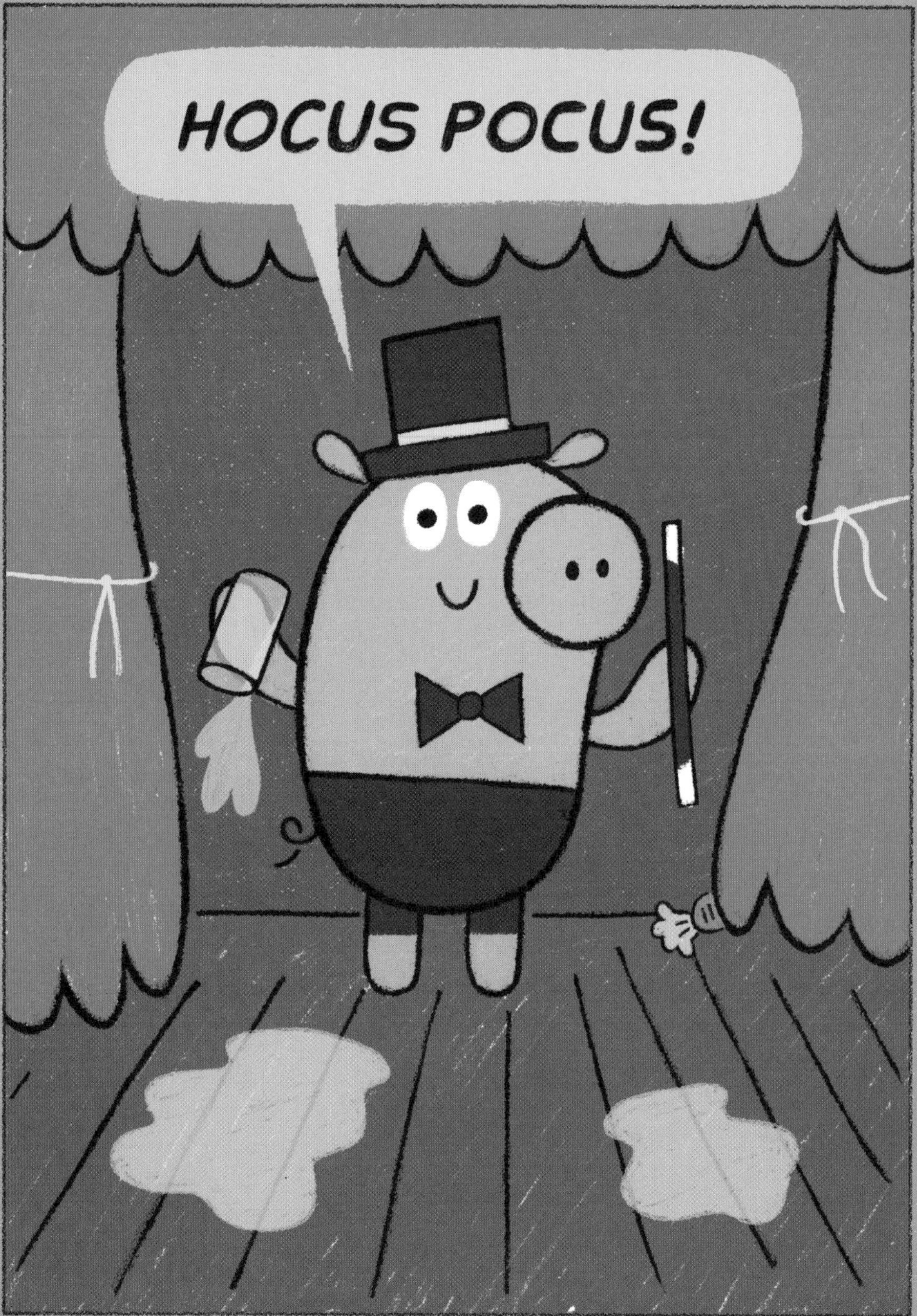
HOCUS POCUS!

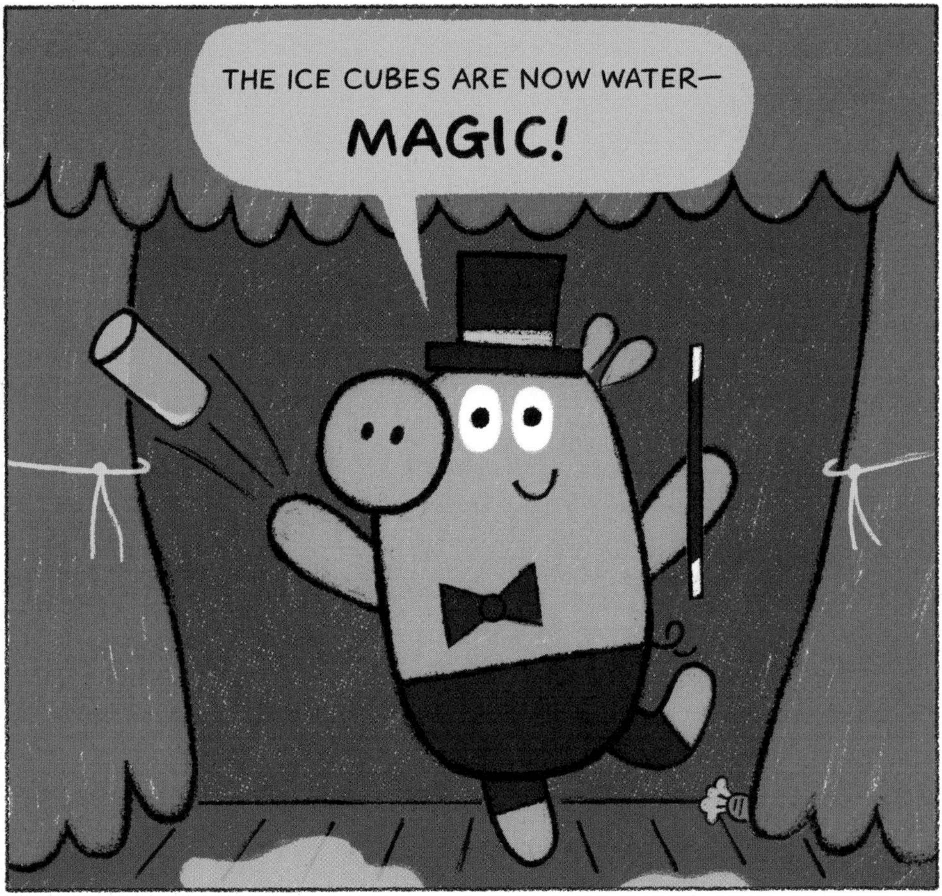
THE ICE CUBES ARE NOW WATER—
MAGIC!

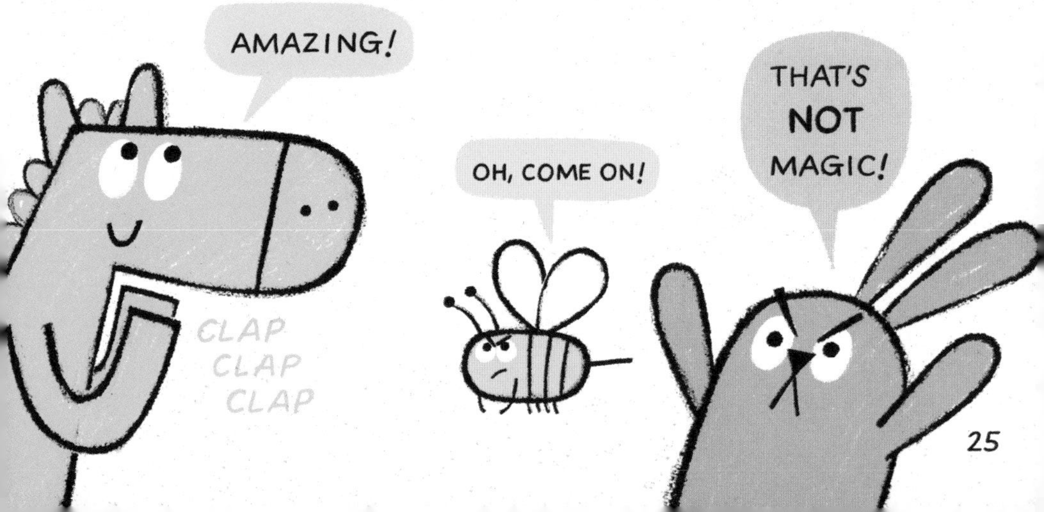
AMAZING!
CLAP CLAP CLAP
OH, COME ON!
THAT'S NOT MAGIC!

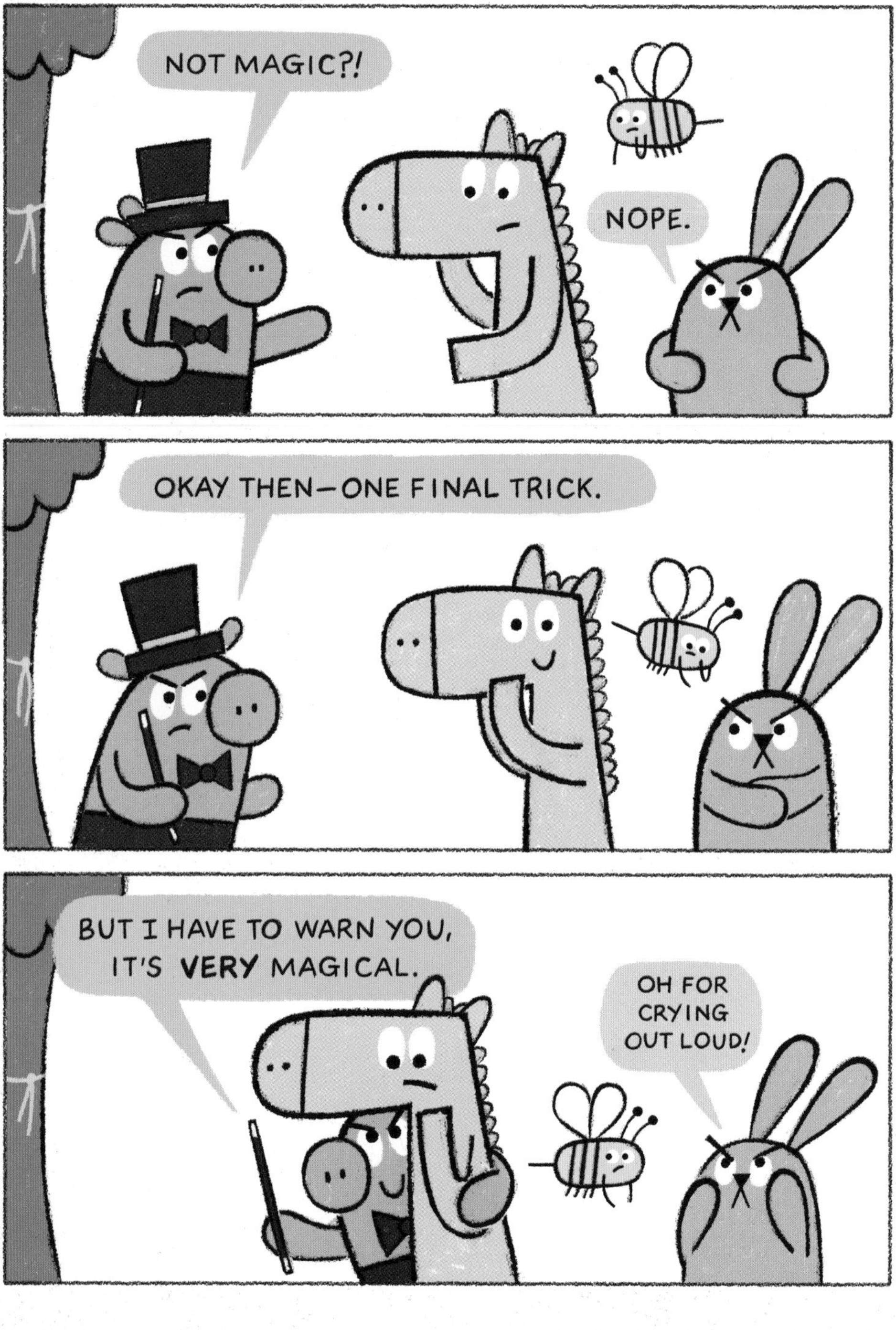
NOT MAGIC?!
NOPE.
OKAY THEN—ONE FINAL TRICK.
BUT I HAVE TO WARN YOU, IT'S **VERY** MAGICAL.
OH FOR CRYING OUT LOUD!

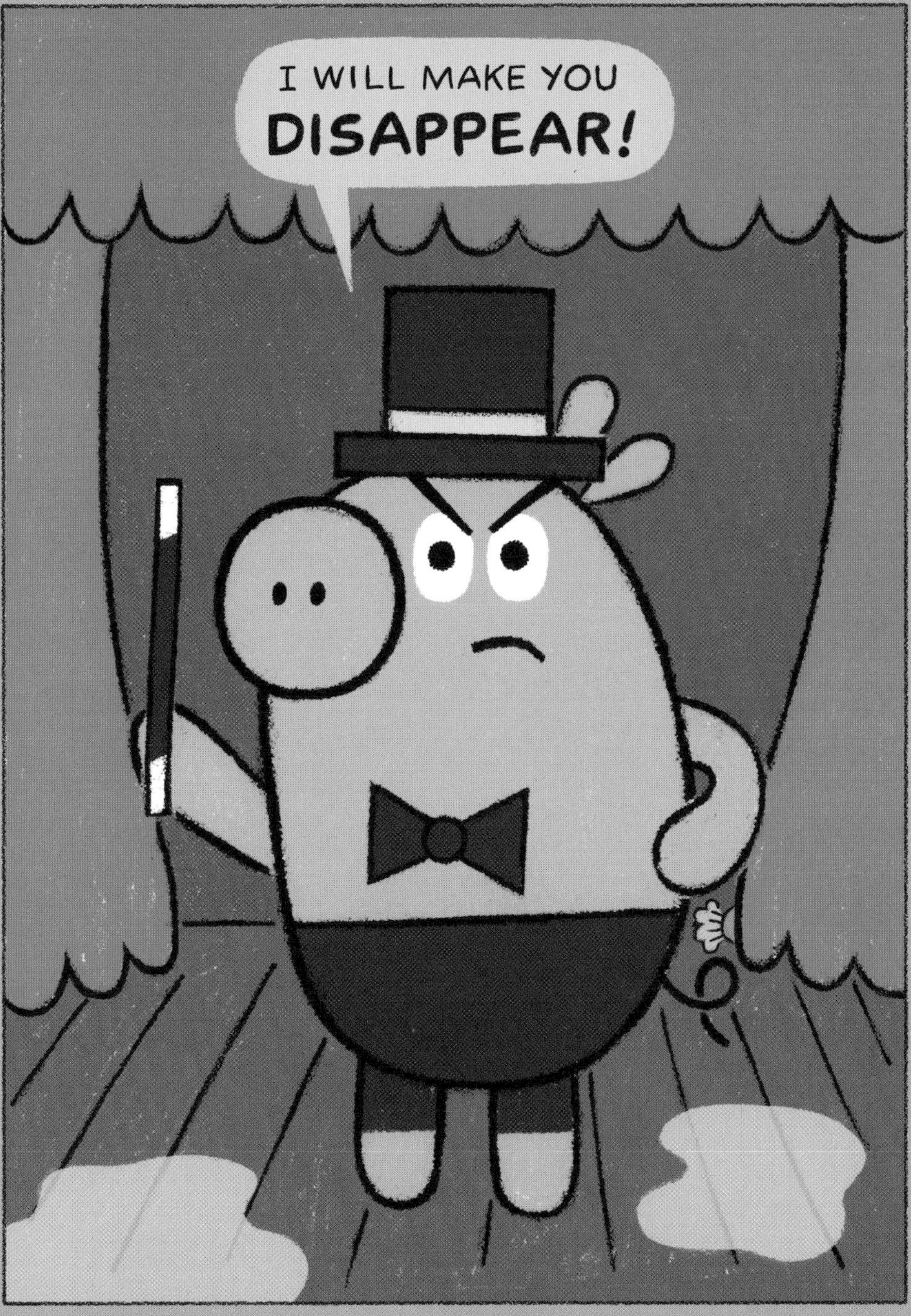
I WILL MAKE YOU DISAPPEAR!

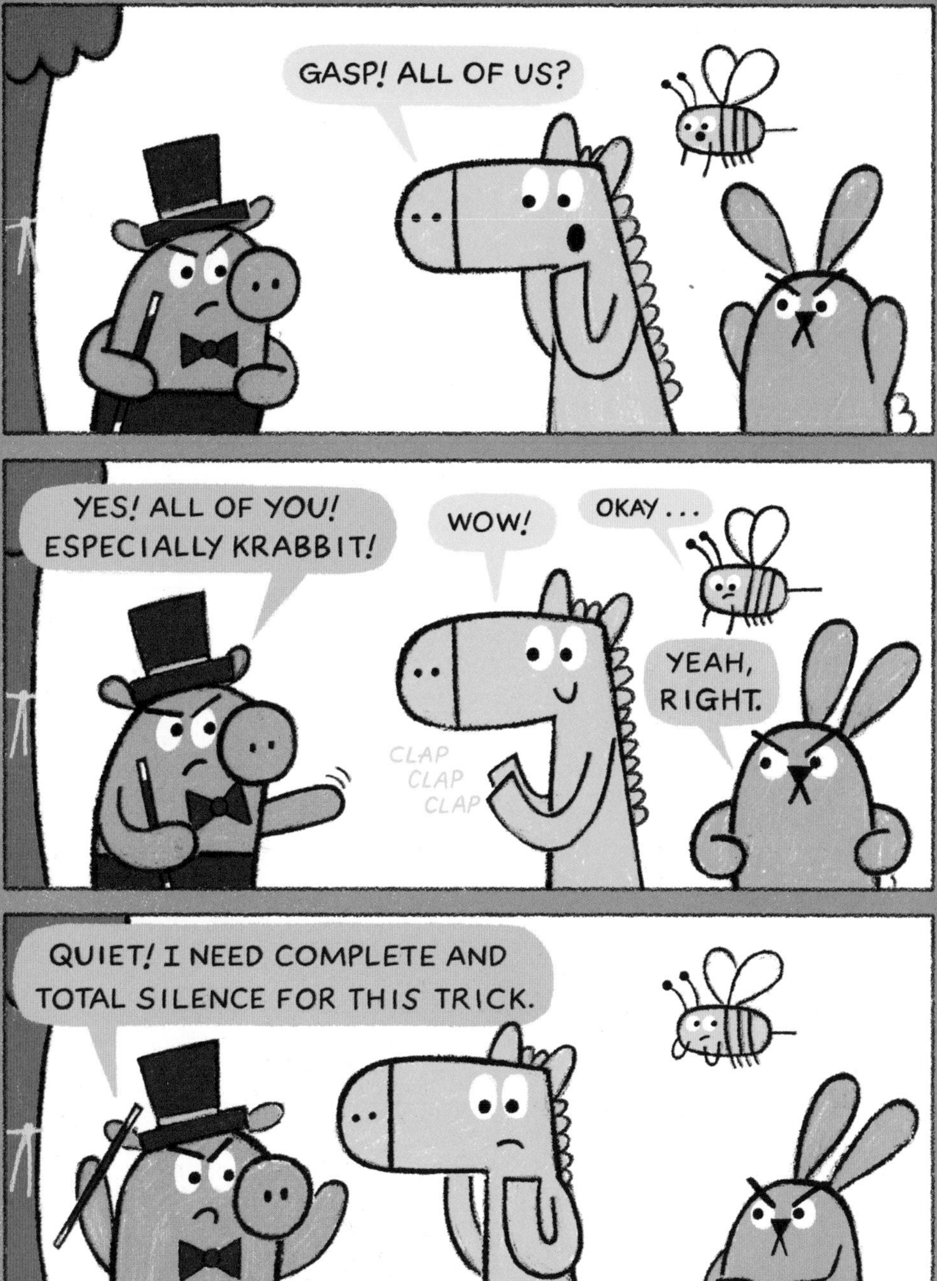
GASP! ALL OF US?
YES! ALL OF YOU! ESPECIALLY KRABBIT!
WOW!
OKAY . . .
YEAH, RIGHT.
CLAP CLAP CLAP
QUIET! I NEED COMPLETE AND TOTAL SILENCE FOR THIS TRICK.

BANK OF AMERICA

New! Zelle(R) QR codes in our app
Learn more at bofa.com/zelle

06/19/22   09:11   ICAH2435
XXXXXXXX7121
HARBOR-EDINGER
FOUNTAIN VALL   CA

Ser. No. 8676
Withdrawal $300.00
From PRIMARY   Checking
Available Balance $123,004.48

Member FDIC

Next time use your phone instead of your card.
Visit bankofamerica.com/CardlessATM

BANK OF AMERICA

New! Zelle(R) QR codes in our app
Learn more at bofa.com/zelle

XXXXXXXX7121
*HARBOR-EDINGER
Withdrawal

Member FDIC

ATM

Next time use your phone instead of your card.
Visit bankofamerica.com/CardlessATM

00-14-3675B (06-2006)
September 2021

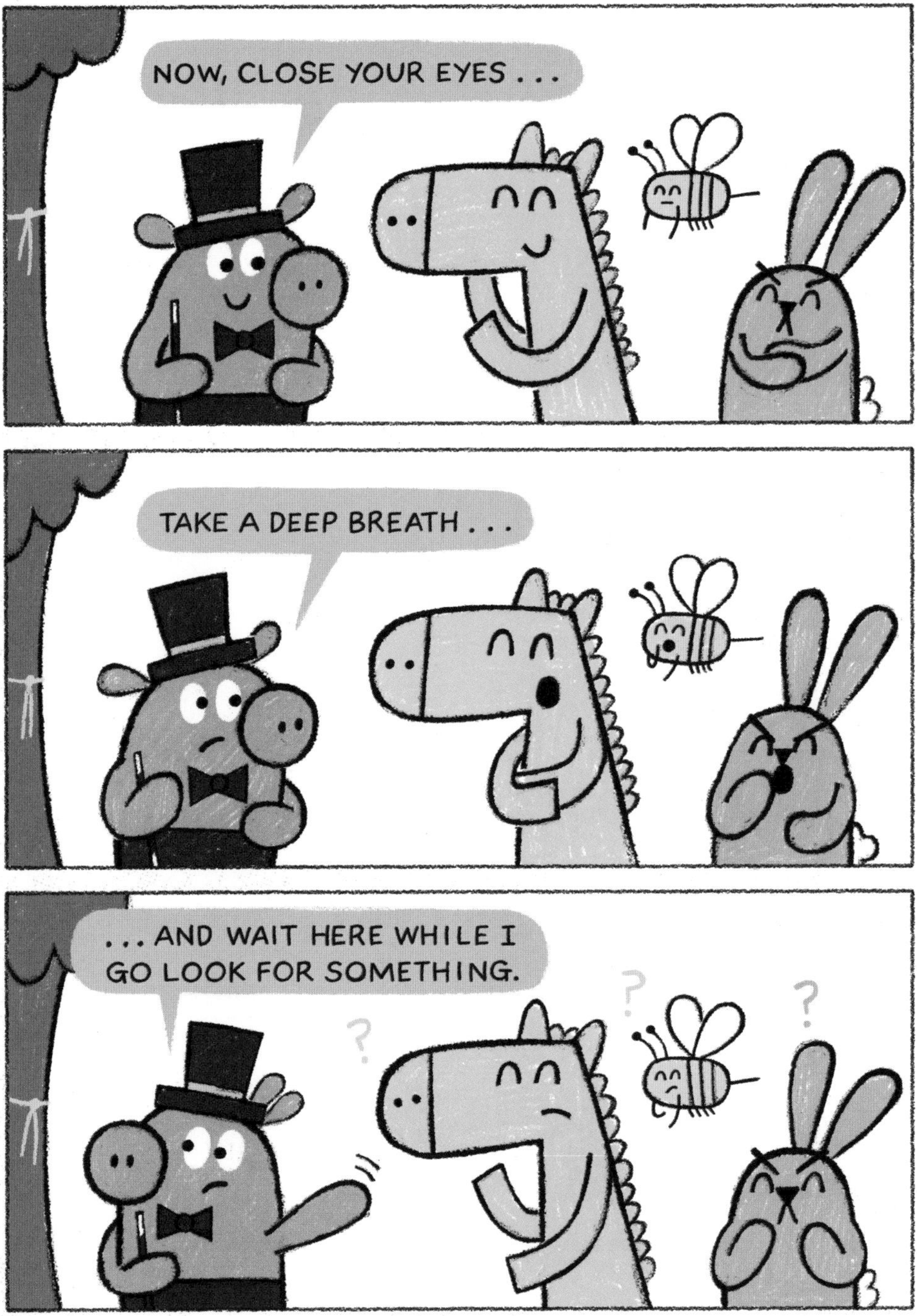
NOW, CLOSE YOUR EYES . . .
TAKE A DEEP BREATH . . .
. . . AND WAIT HERE WHILE I GO LOOK FOR SOMETHING.
?
?
?

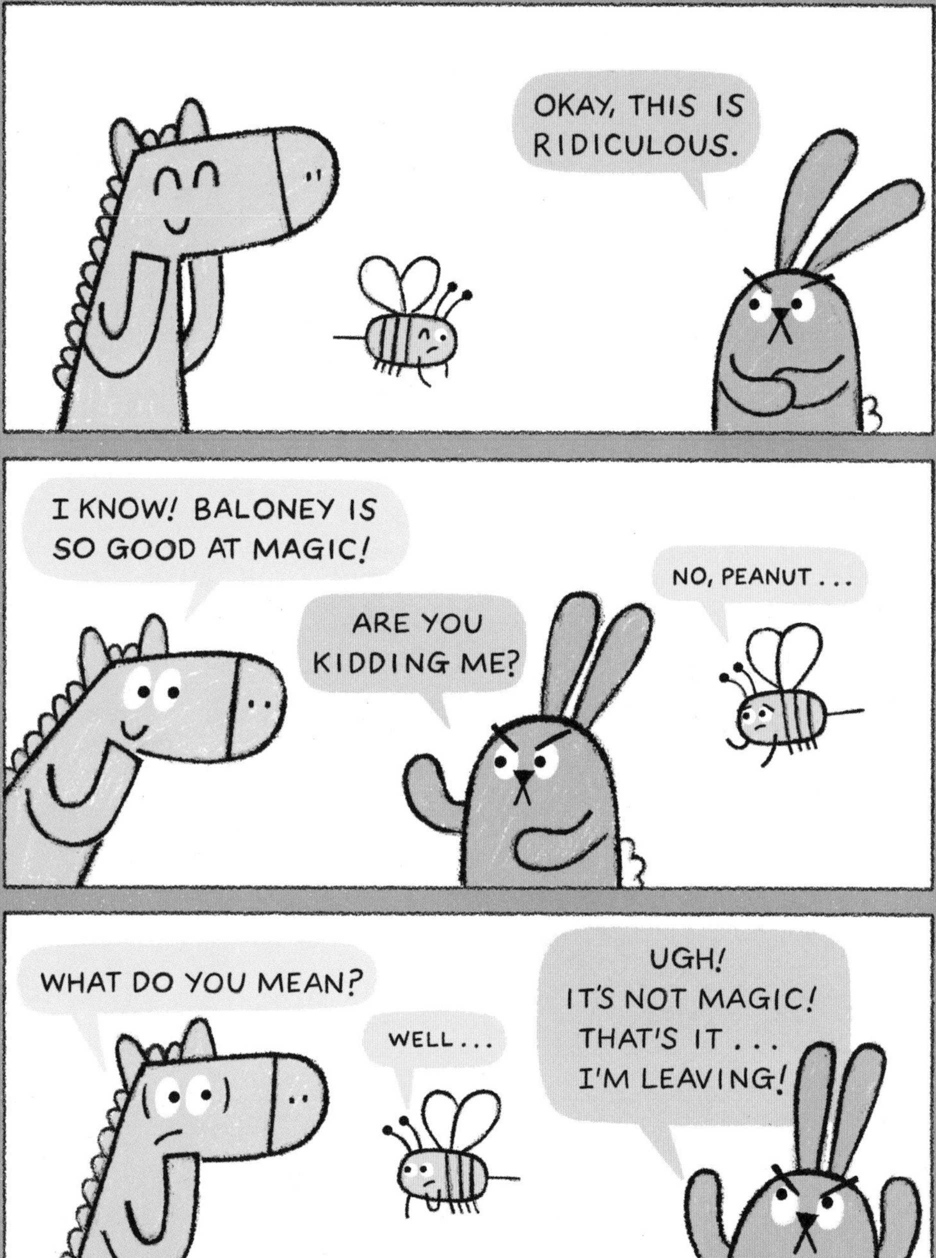
OKAY, THIS IS RIDICULOUS.
I KNOW! BALONEY IS SO GOOD AT MAGIC!
ARE YOU KIDDING ME?
NO, PEANUT . . .
WHAT DO YOU MEAN?
WELL . . .
UGH! IT'S NOT MAGIC! THAT'S IT . . . I'M LEAVING!

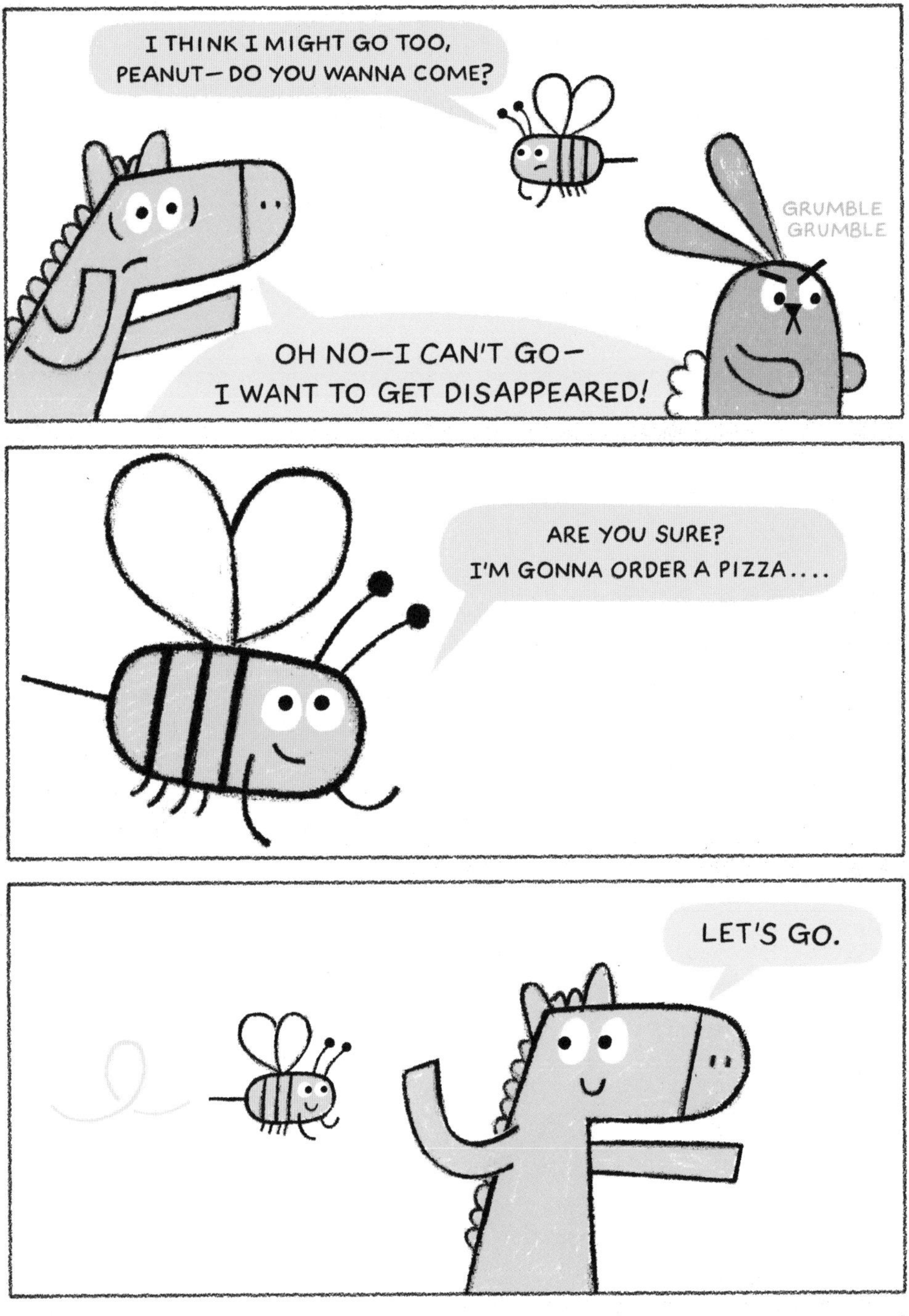
I THINK I MIGHT GO TOO, PEANUT—DO YOU WANNA COME?
GRUMBLE GRUMBLE
OH NO—I CAN'T GO—I WANT TO GET DISAPPEARED!
ARE YOU SURE? I'M GONNA ORDER A PIZZA....
LET'S GO.

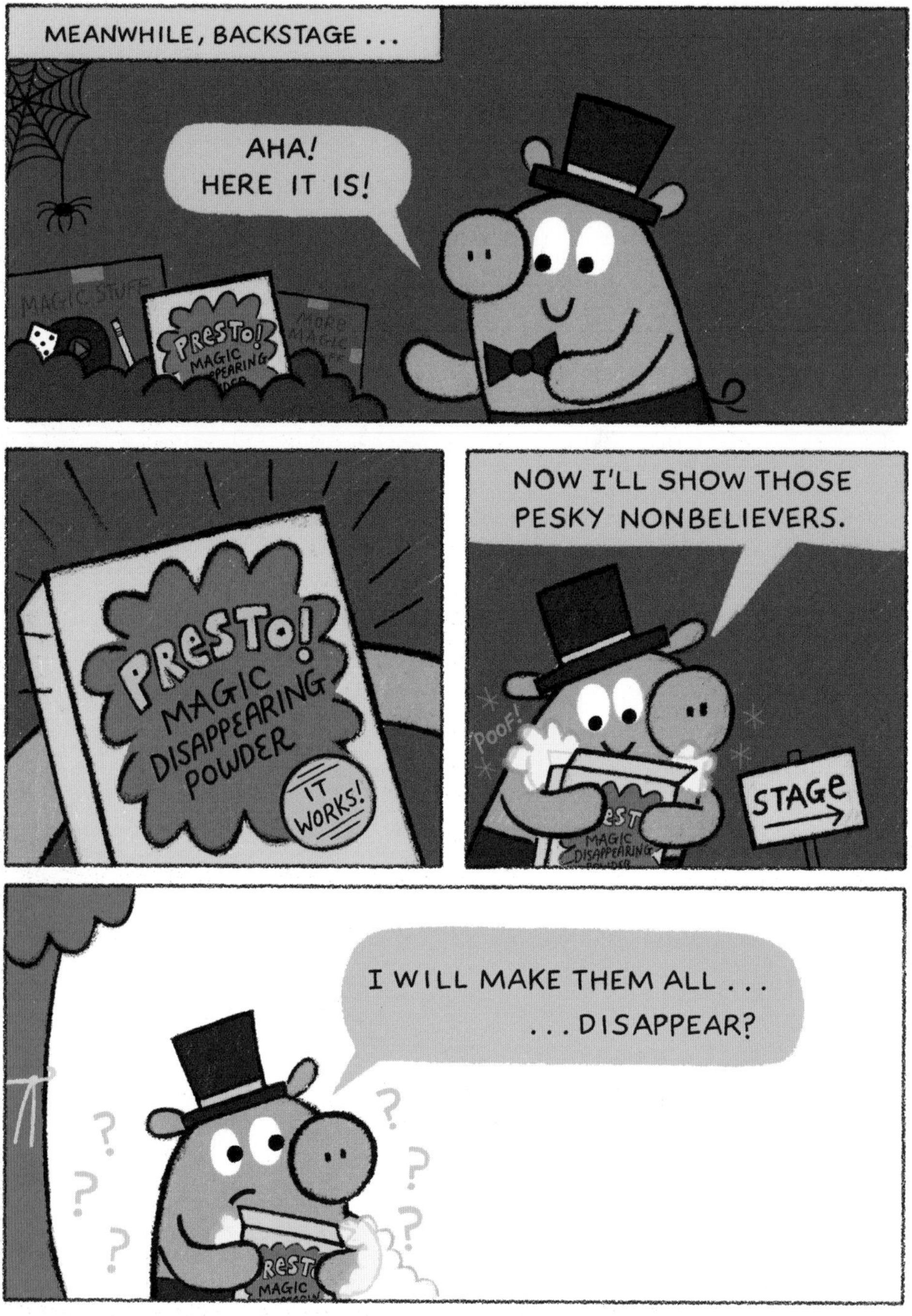
MEANWHILE, BACKSTAGE . . .
AHA!
HERE IT IS!
MAGIC STUFF
PRESTO!
MAGIC
DISAPPEARING
POWDER
IT WORKS!
NOW I'LL SHOW THOSE
PESKY NONBELIEVERS.
POOF!
STAGE
I WILL MAKE THEM ALL . . .
. . . DISAPPEAR?

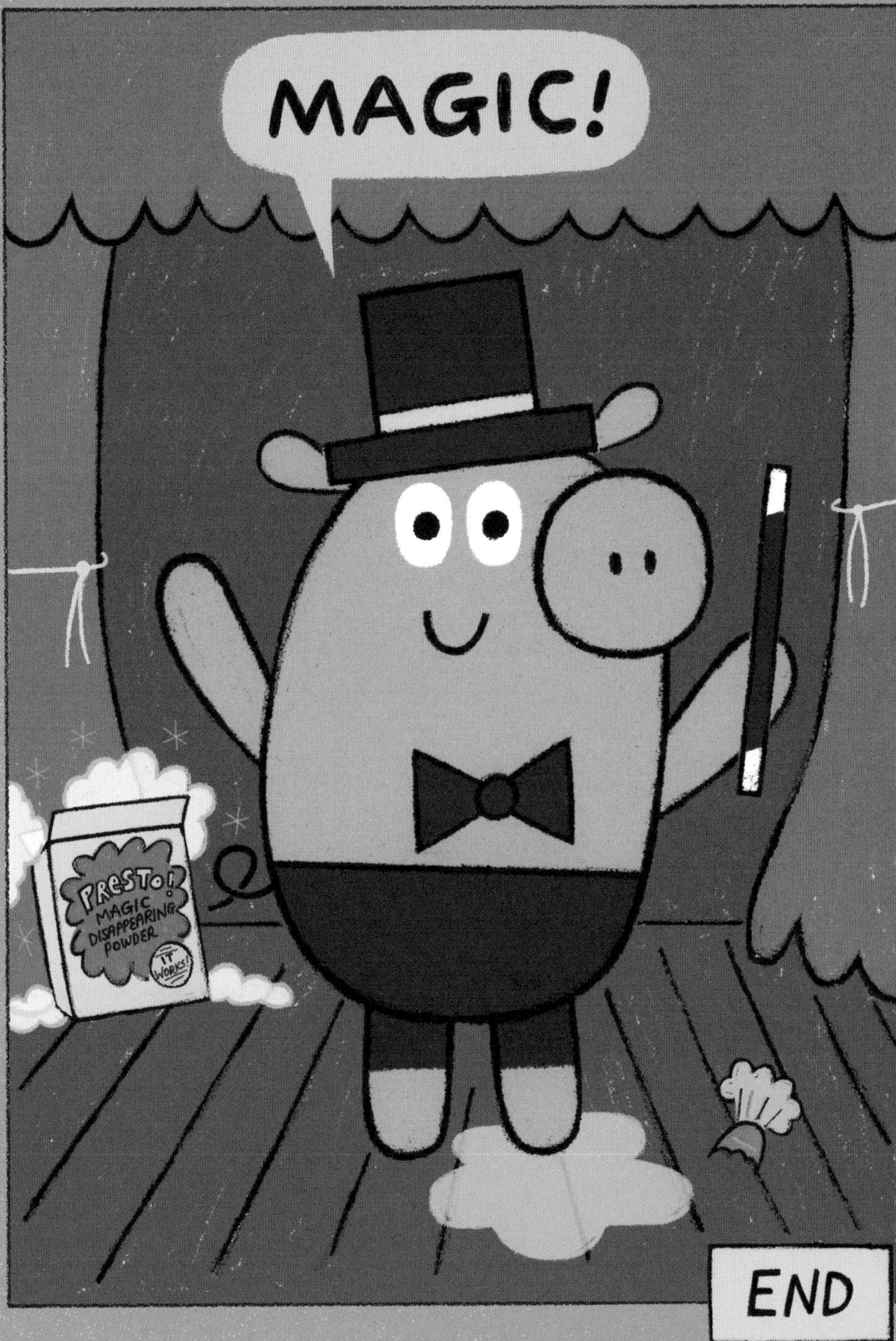
MAGIC!
PRESTO!
MAGIC
DISAPPEARING
POWDER
IT WORKS!
END

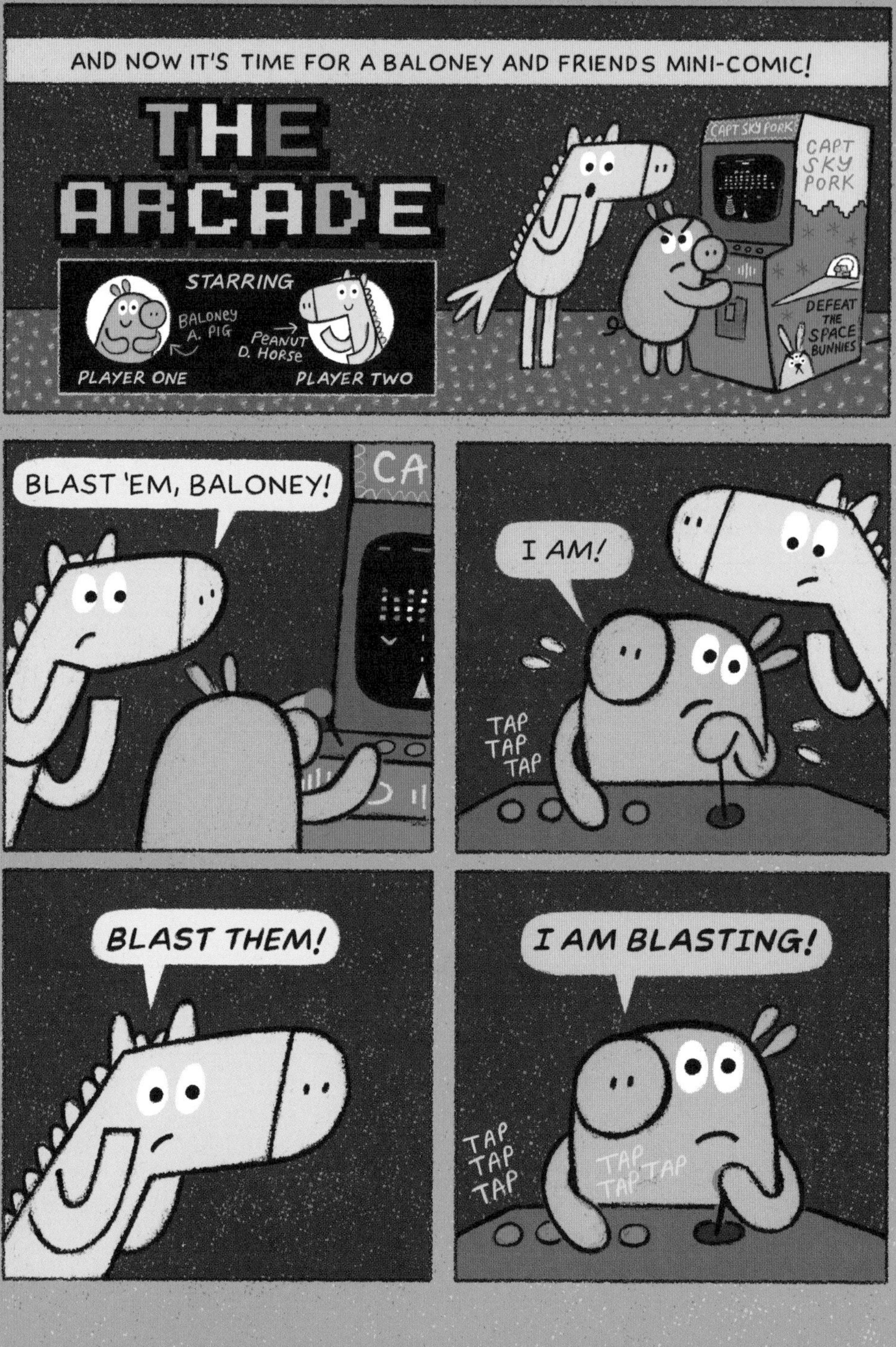

AND NOW IT'S TIME FOR A BALONEY AND FRIENDS MINI-COMIC!
THE ARCADE
CAPT SKY PORK
CAPT SKY PORK
DEFEAT THE SPACE BUNNIES
STARRING
BALONEY A. PIG
PEANUT D. HORSE
PLAYER ONE
PLAYER TWO
BLAST 'EM, BALONEY!
CA
I AM!
TAP TAP TAP
BLAST THEM!
I AM BLASTING!
TAP TAP TAP
TAP TAP TAP

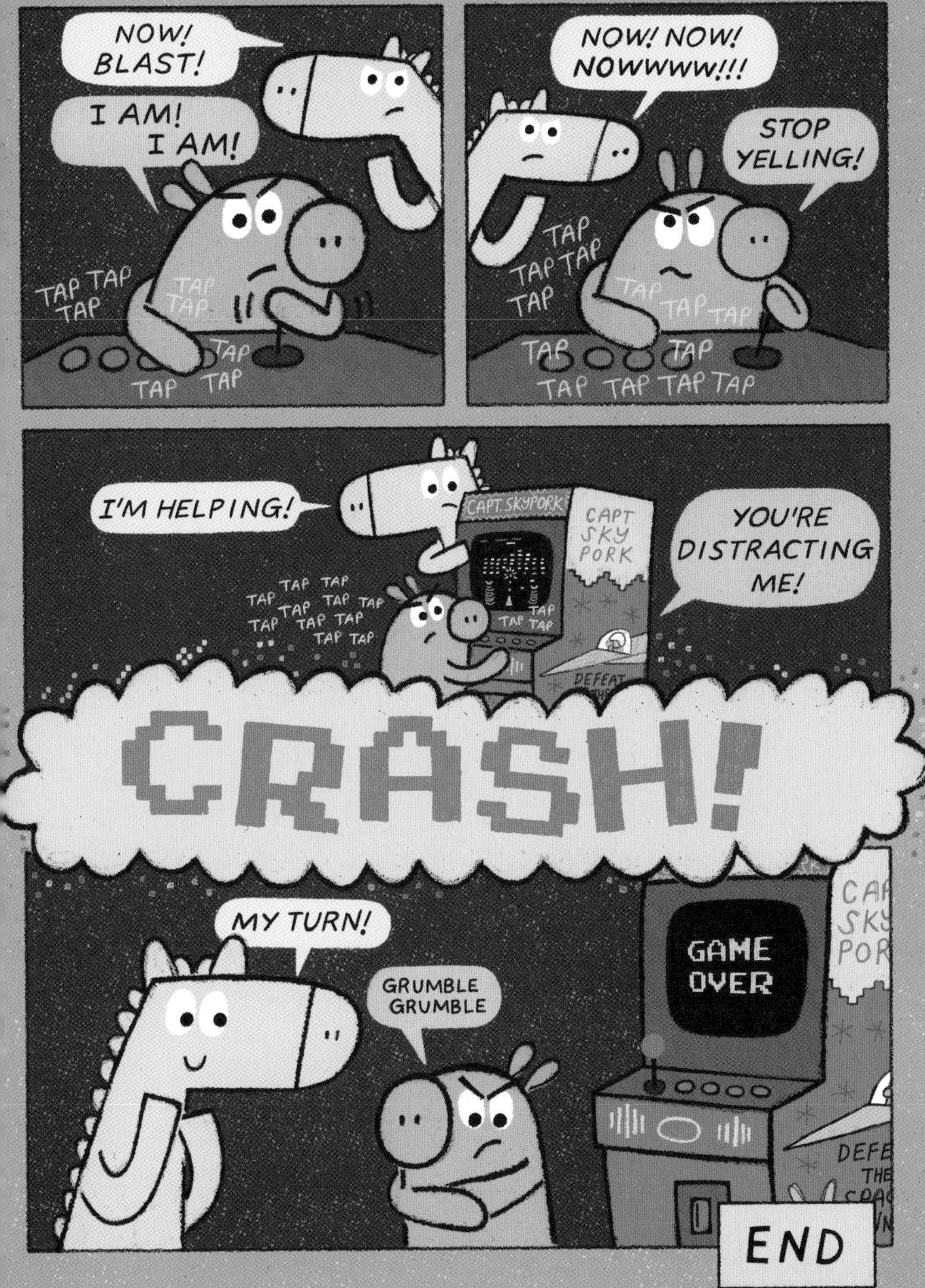
NOW! BLAST!
I AM! I AM!
TAP TAP TAP
TAP TAP
TAP
TAP TAP
NOW! NOW! NOWWWW!!!
STOP YELLING!
TAP TAP TAP TAP
TAP TAP TAP
TAP TAP
TAP TAP TAP TAP
I'M HELPING!
CAPT. SKYPORK
CAPT SKY PORK
YOU'RE DISTRACTING ME!
TAP TAP TAP TAP TAP TAP TAP TAP TAP TAP TAP
TAP TAP TAP
CRASH!
MY TURN!
GRUMBLE GRUMBLE
GAME OVER
END

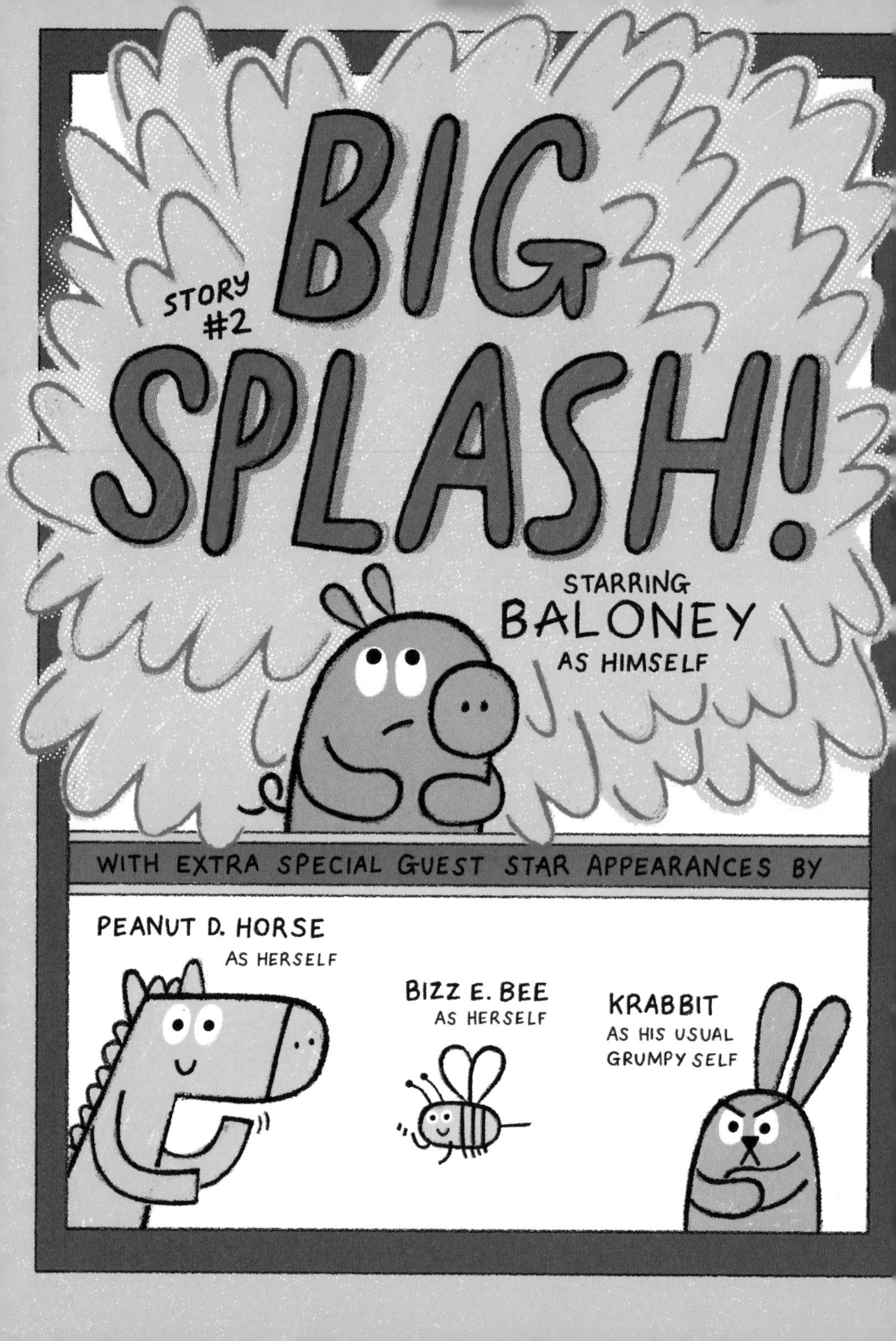
STORY #2
BIG SPLASH!
STARRING BALONEY AS HIMSELF
WITH EXTRA SPECIAL GUEST STAR APPEARANCES BY
PEANUT D. HORSE AS HERSELF
BIZZ E. BEE AS HERSELF
KRABBIT AS HIS USUAL GRUMPY SELF

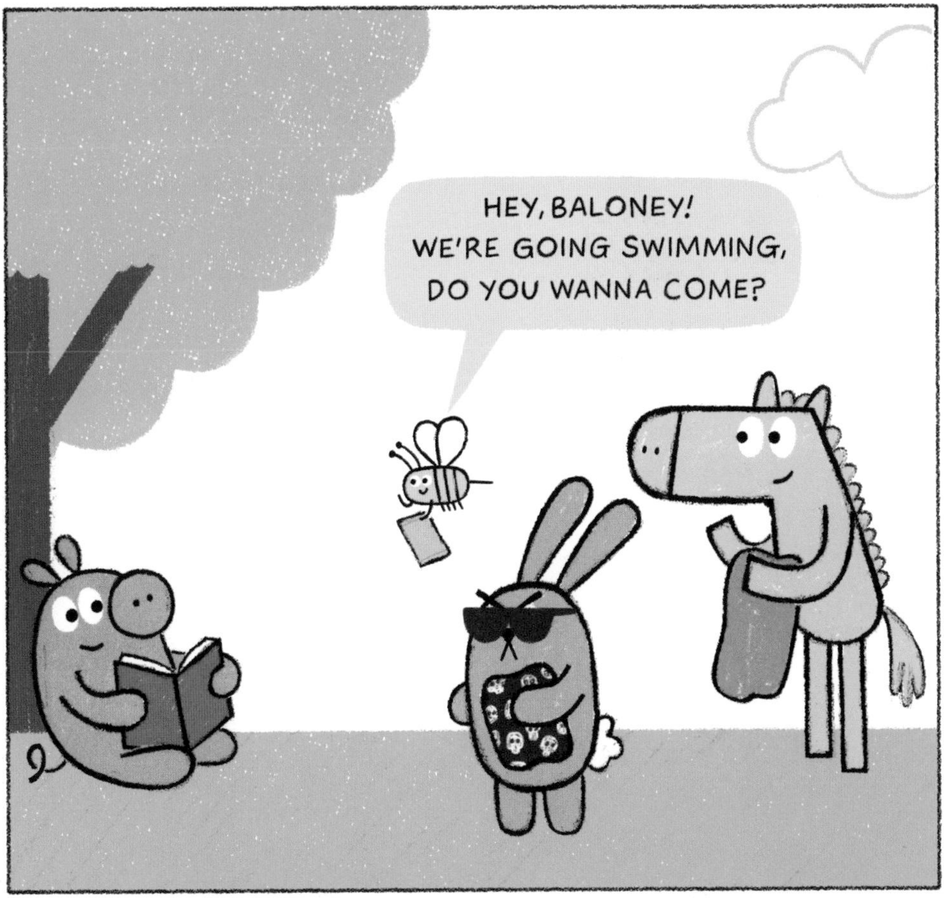
HEY, BALONEY!
WE'RE GOING SWIMMING,
DO YOU WANNA COME?

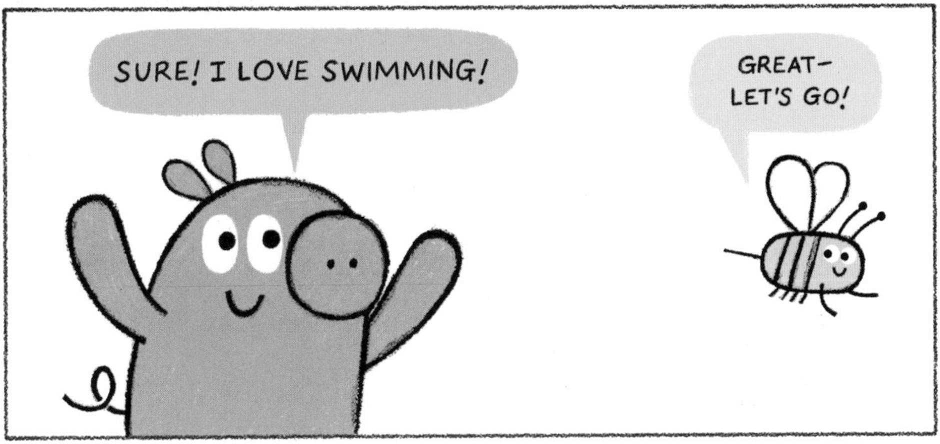
SURE! I LOVE SWIMMING!
GREAT–
LET'S GO!

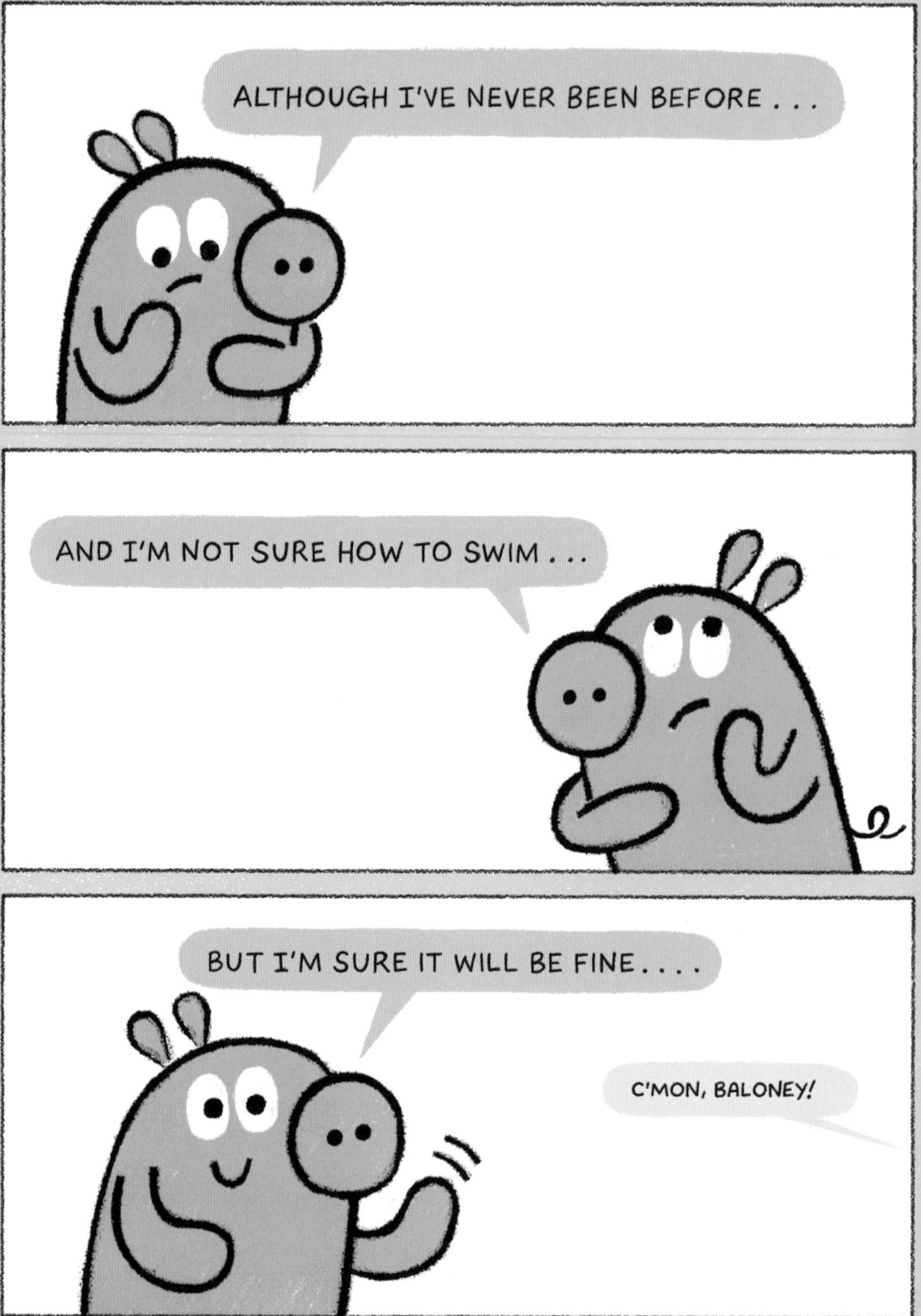
ALTHOUGH I'VE NEVER BEEN BEFORE . . .
AND I'M NOT SURE HOW TO SWIM . . .
BUT I'M SURE IT WILL BE FINE . . . .
C'MON, BALONEY!

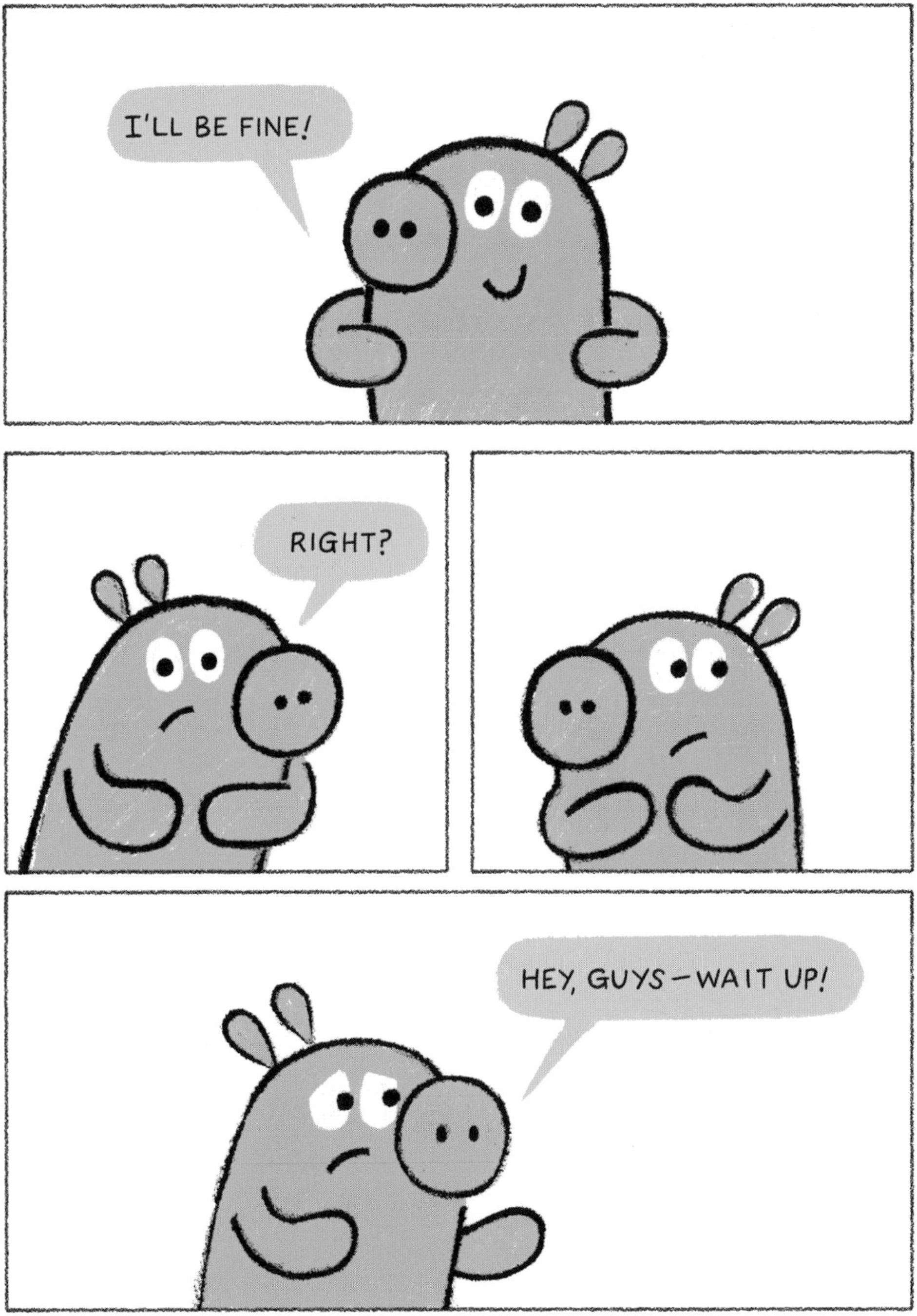
I'LL BE FINE!
RIGHT?
HEY, GUYS—WAIT UP!

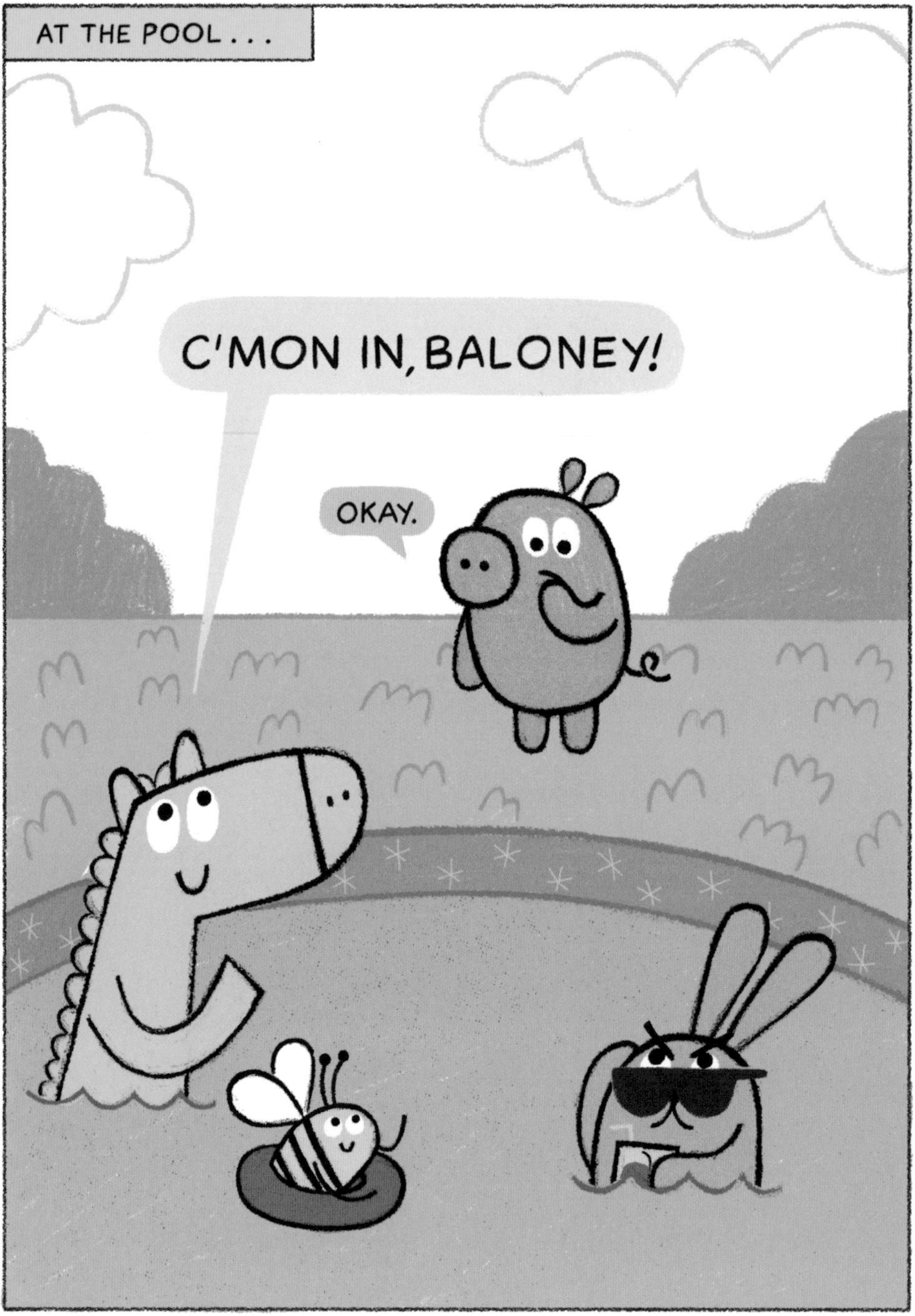
AT THE POOL . . .
C'MON IN, BALONEY!
OKAY.

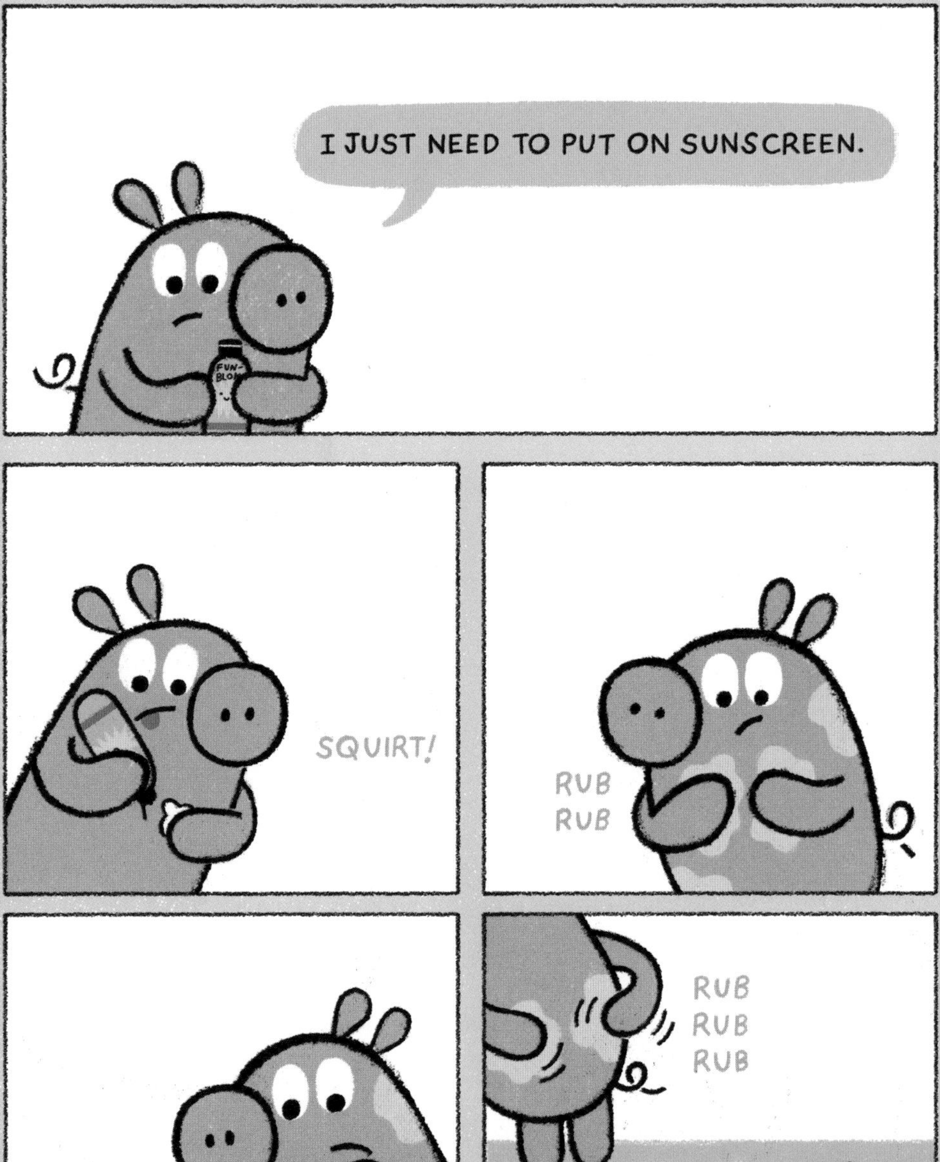
I JUST NEED TO PUT ON SUNSCREEN.
FUN-BLOK
SQUIRT!
RUB
RUB
SQUIRT!
FUN-BLOK
RUB
RUB
RUB
FUN-BLOK

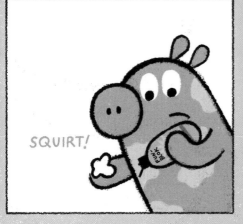

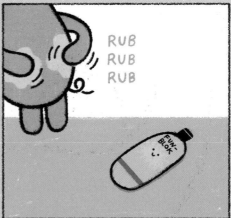

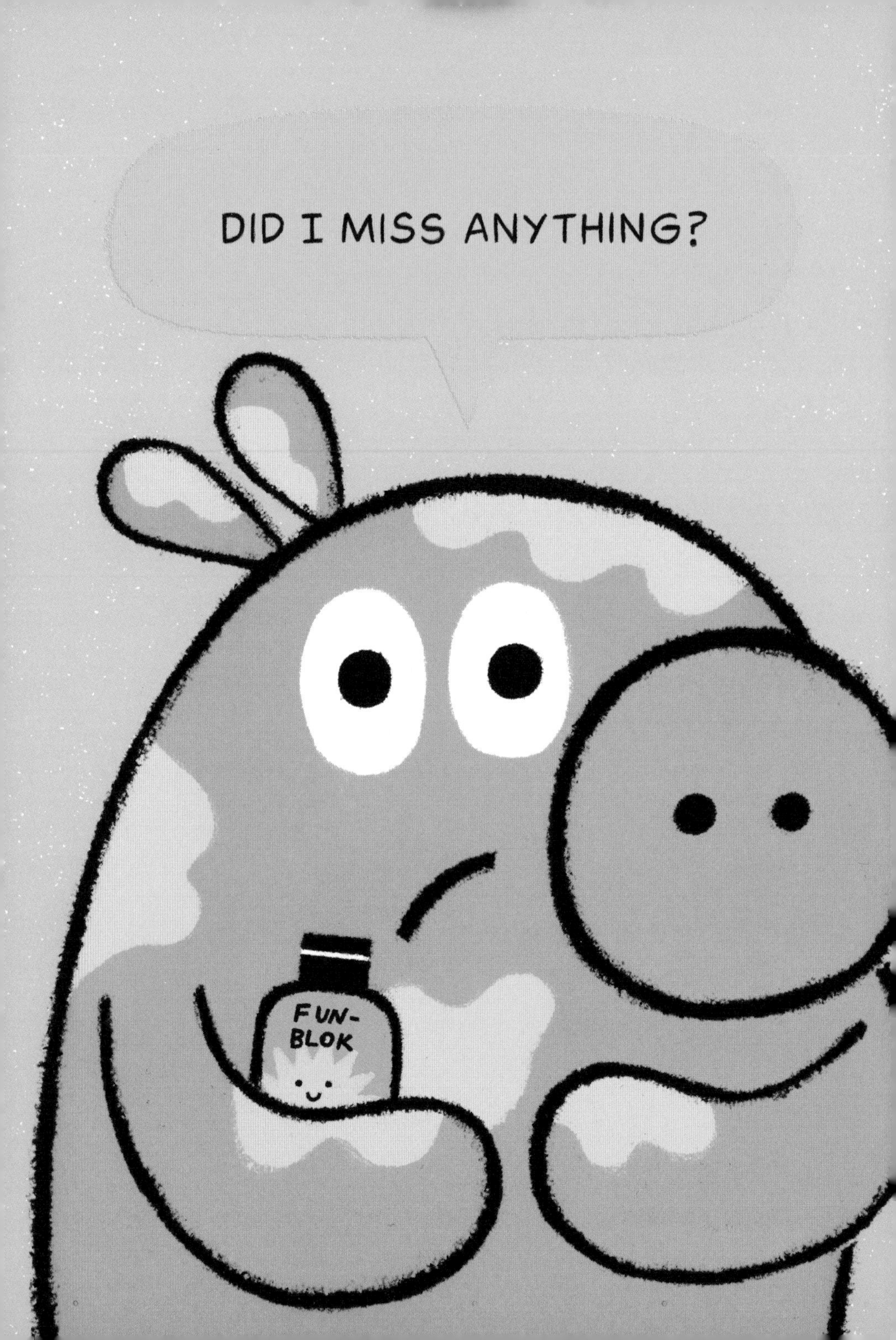
DID I MISS ANYTHING?
FUN-
BLOK

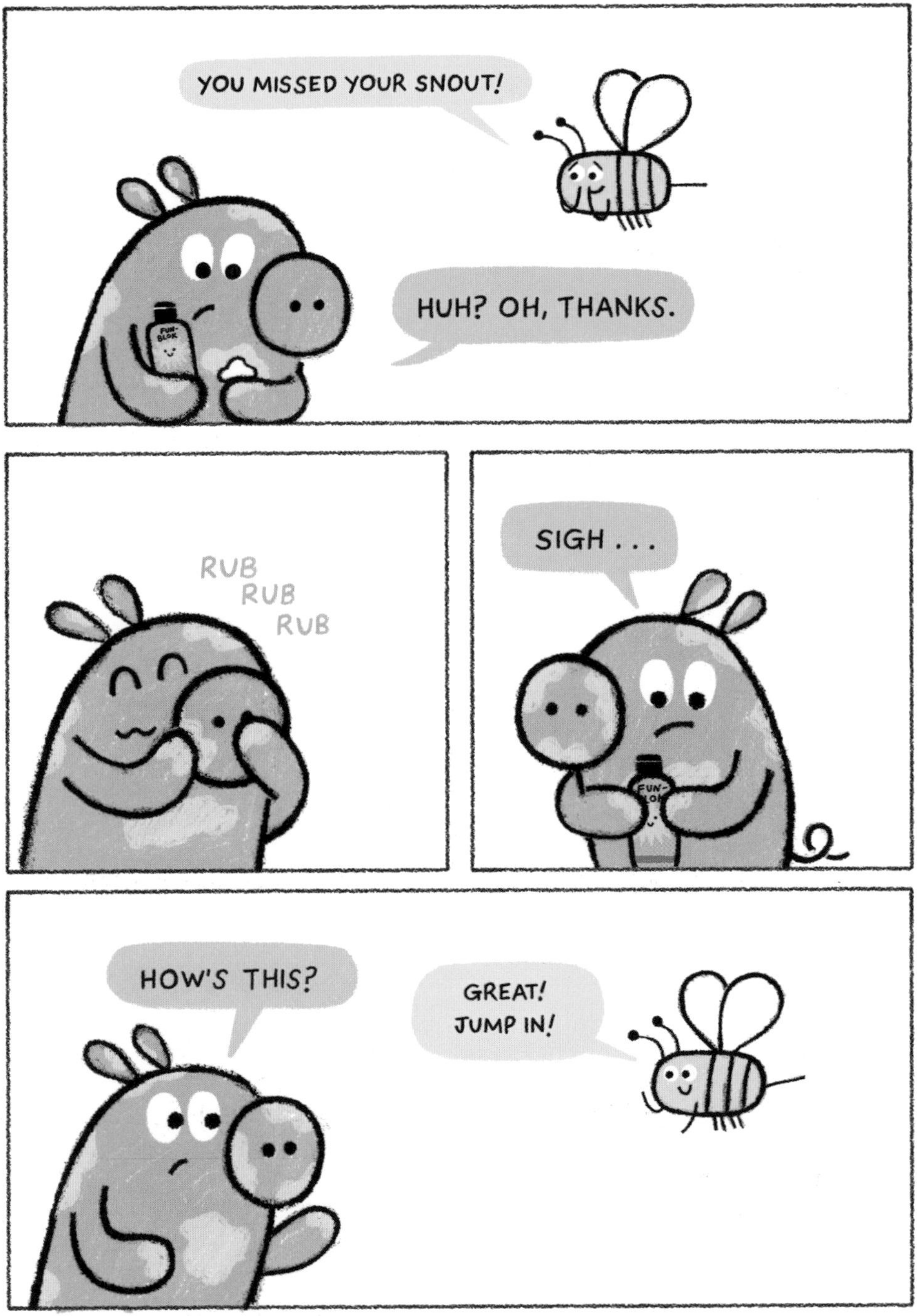
YOU MISSED YOUR SNOUT!
HUH? OH, THANKS.
RUB RUB RUB
SIGH . . .
HOW'S THIS?
GREAT! JUMP IN!

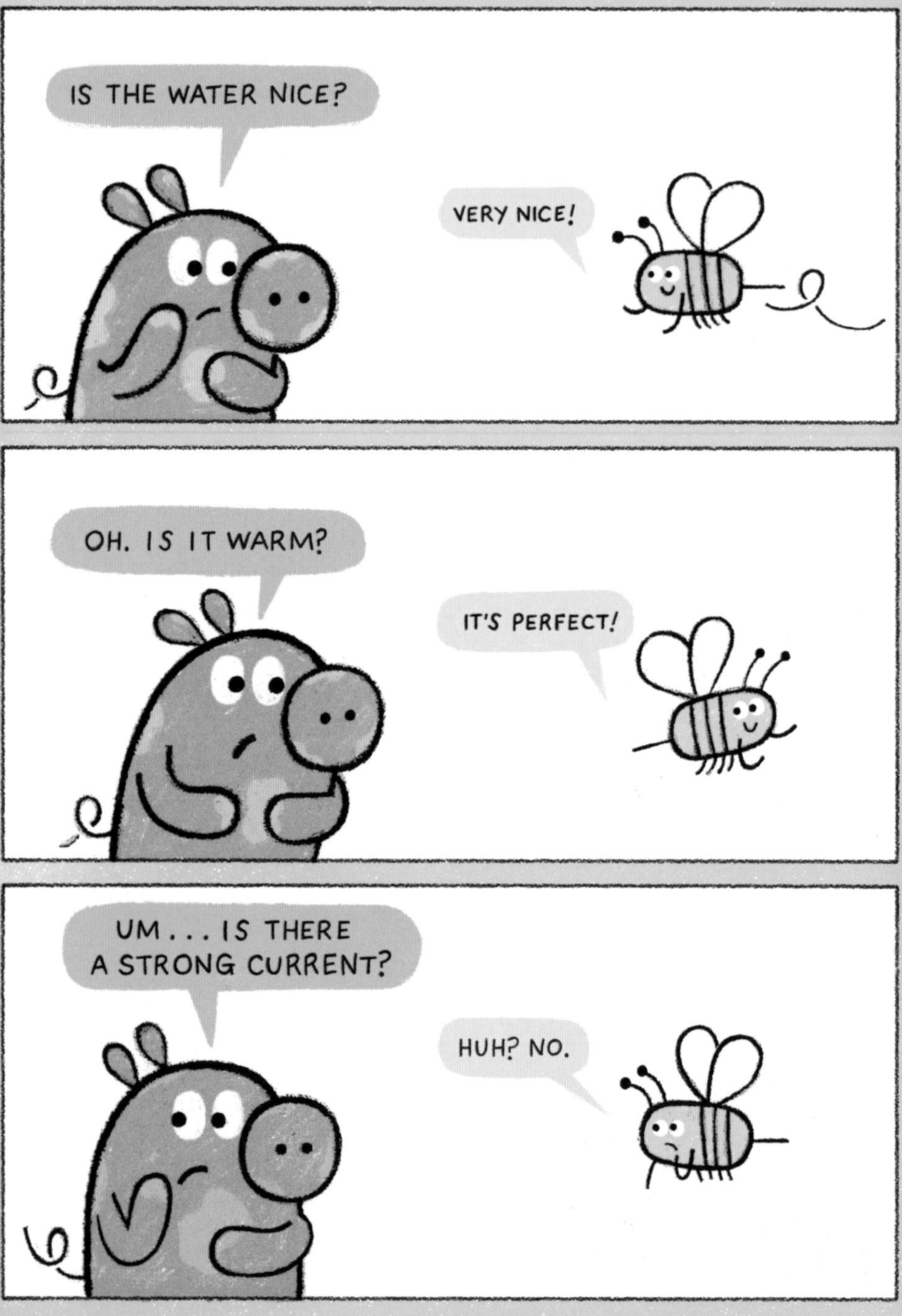
IS THE WATER NICE?
VERY NICE!
OH. IS IT WARM?
IT'S PERFECT!
UM . . . IS THERE A STRONG CURRENT?
HUH? NO.

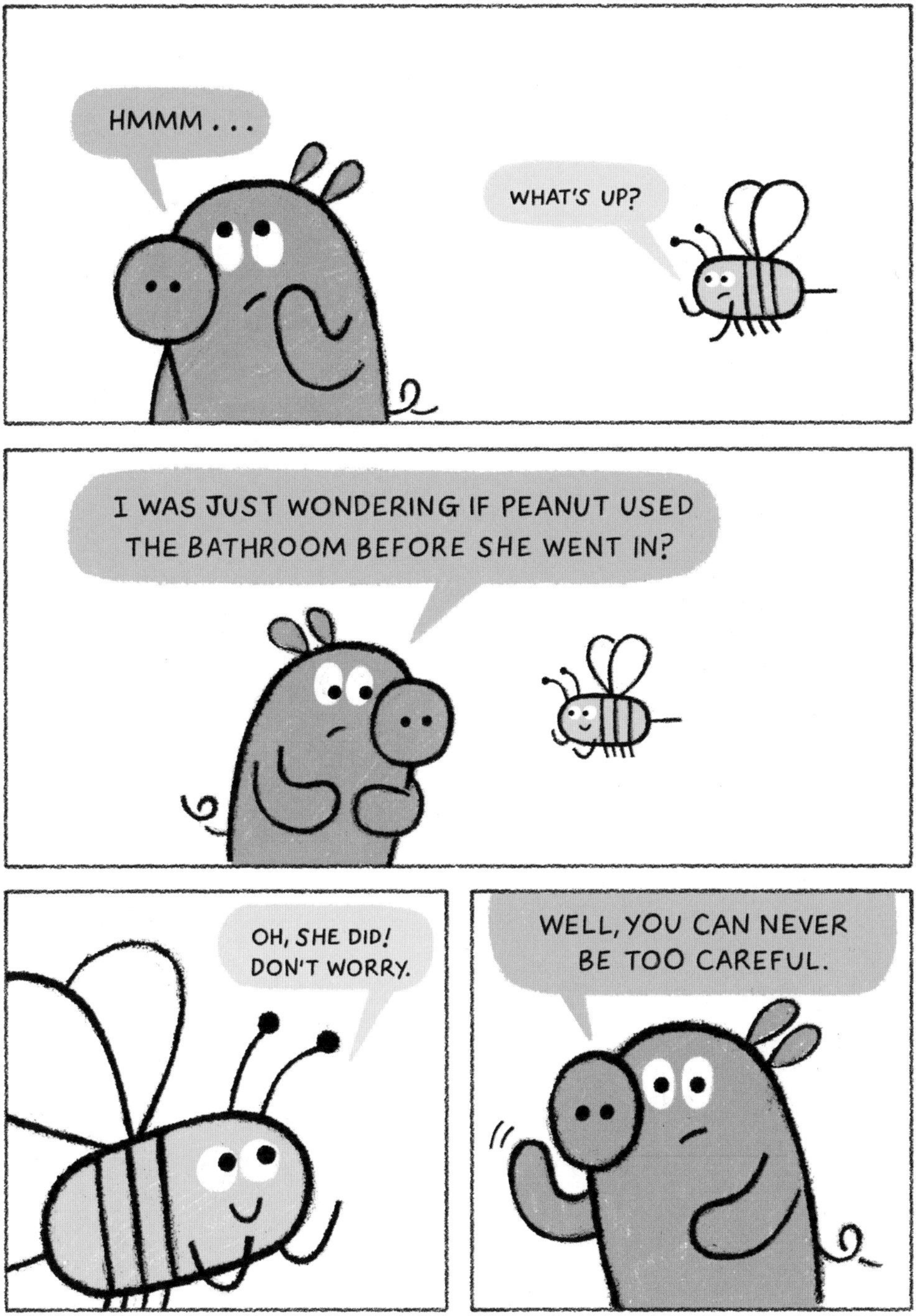
HMMM . . .
WHAT'S UP?
I WAS JUST WONDERING IF PEANUT USED THE BATHROOM BEFORE SHE WENT IN?
OH, SHE DID! DON'T WORRY.
WELL, YOU CAN NEVER BE TOO CAREFUL.

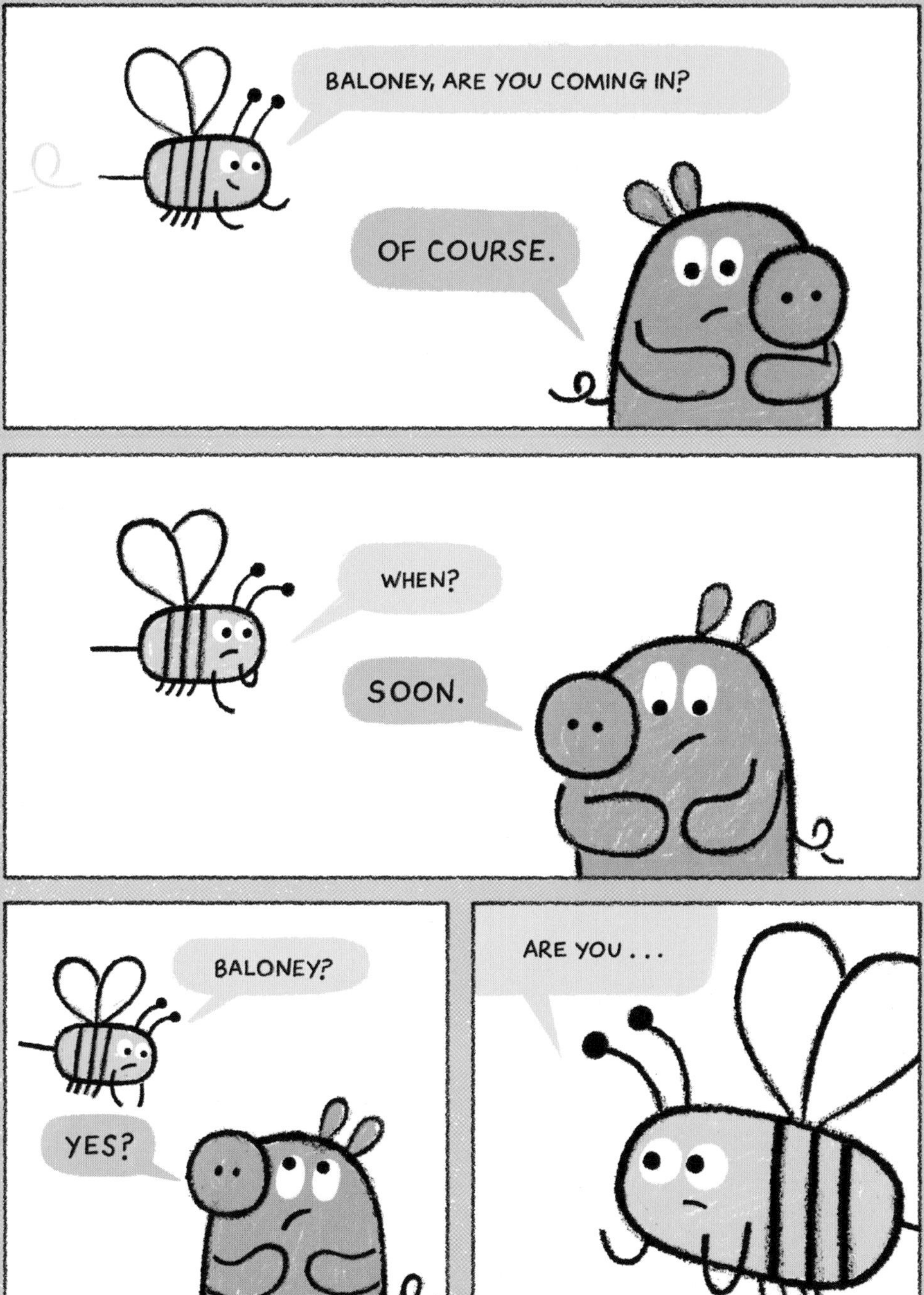
BALONEY, ARE YOU COMING IN?
OF COURSE.
WHEN?
SOON.
BALONEY?
YES?
ARE YOU . . .

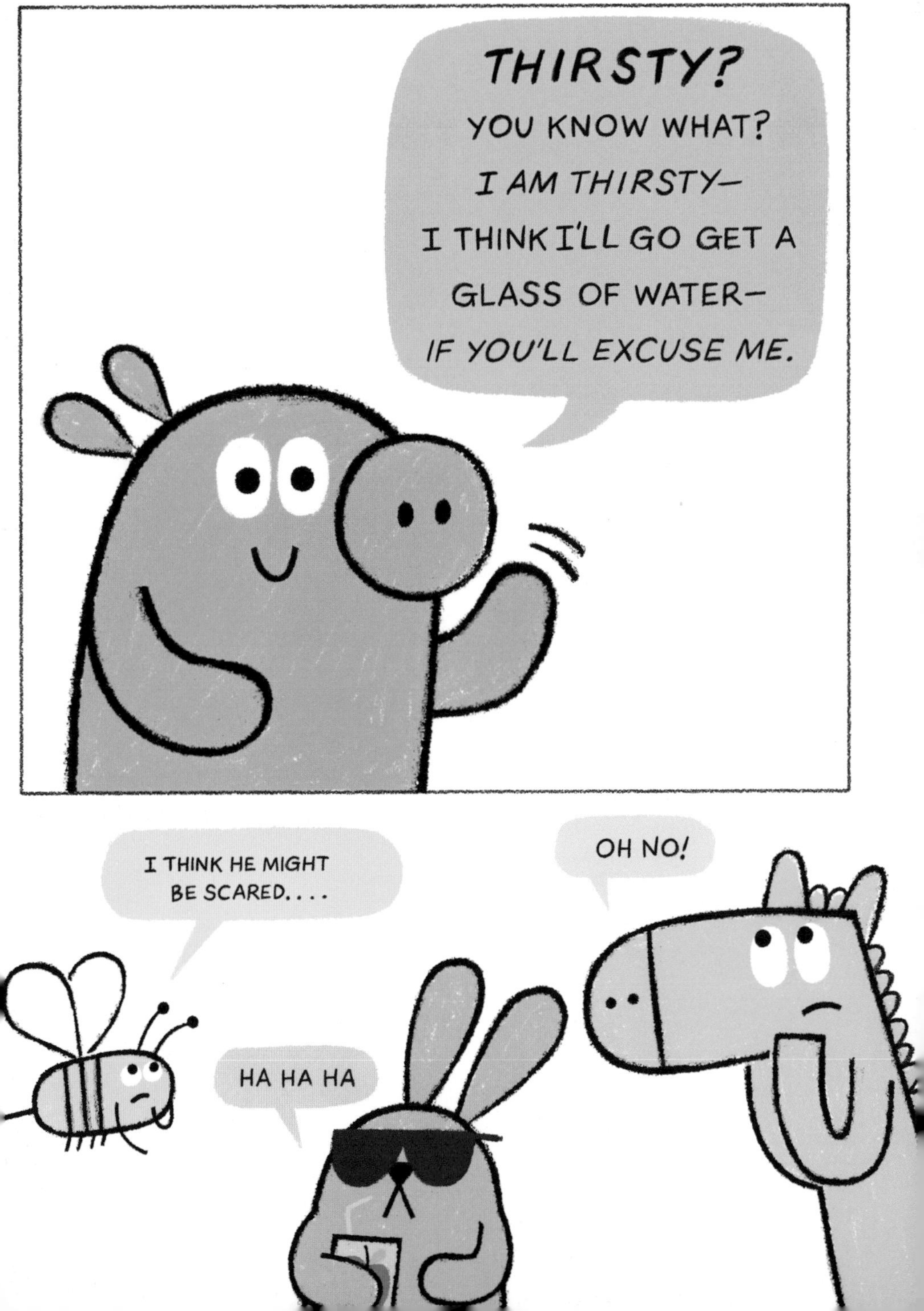
THIRSTY?
YOU KNOW WHAT?
I AM THIRSTY—
I THINK I'LL GO GET A
GLASS OF WATER—
IF YOU'LL EXCUSE ME.
I THINK HE MIGHT BE SCARED. . . .
HA HA HA
OH NO!

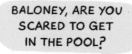

BALONEY, ARE YOU
SCARED TO GET
IN THE POOL?

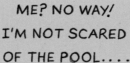
ME? NO WAY!
I'M NOT SCARED
OF THE POOL....

I AM, HOWEVER, A LITTLE CONCERNED
ABOUT THOSE STORM CLOUDS.

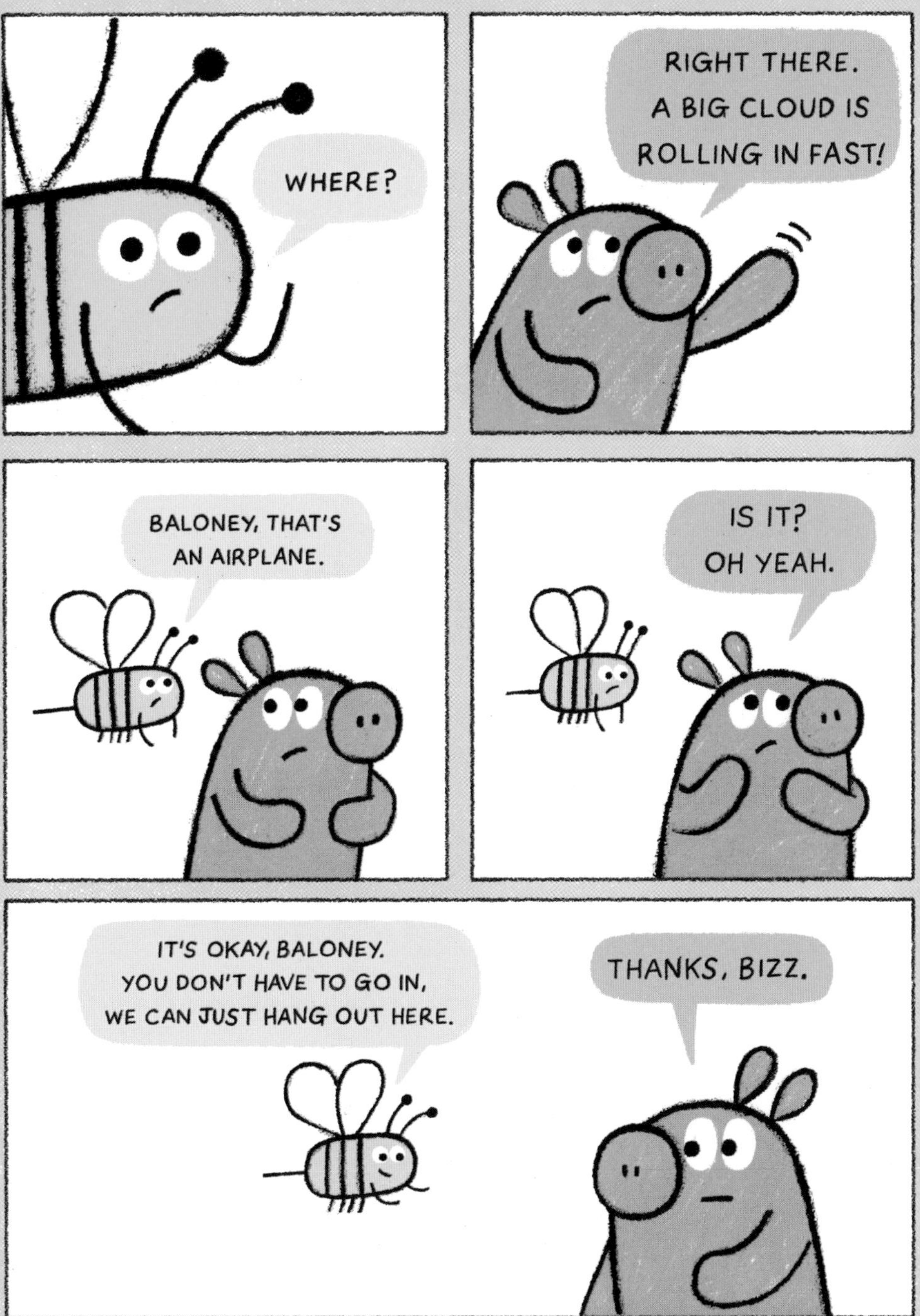
WHERE?
RIGHT THERE. A BIG CLOUD IS ROLLING IN FAST!
BALONEY, THAT'S AN AIRPLANE.
IS IT? OH YEAH.
IT'S OKAY, BALONEY. YOU DON'T HAVE TO GO IN, WE CAN JUST HANG OUT HERE.
THANKS, BIZZ.

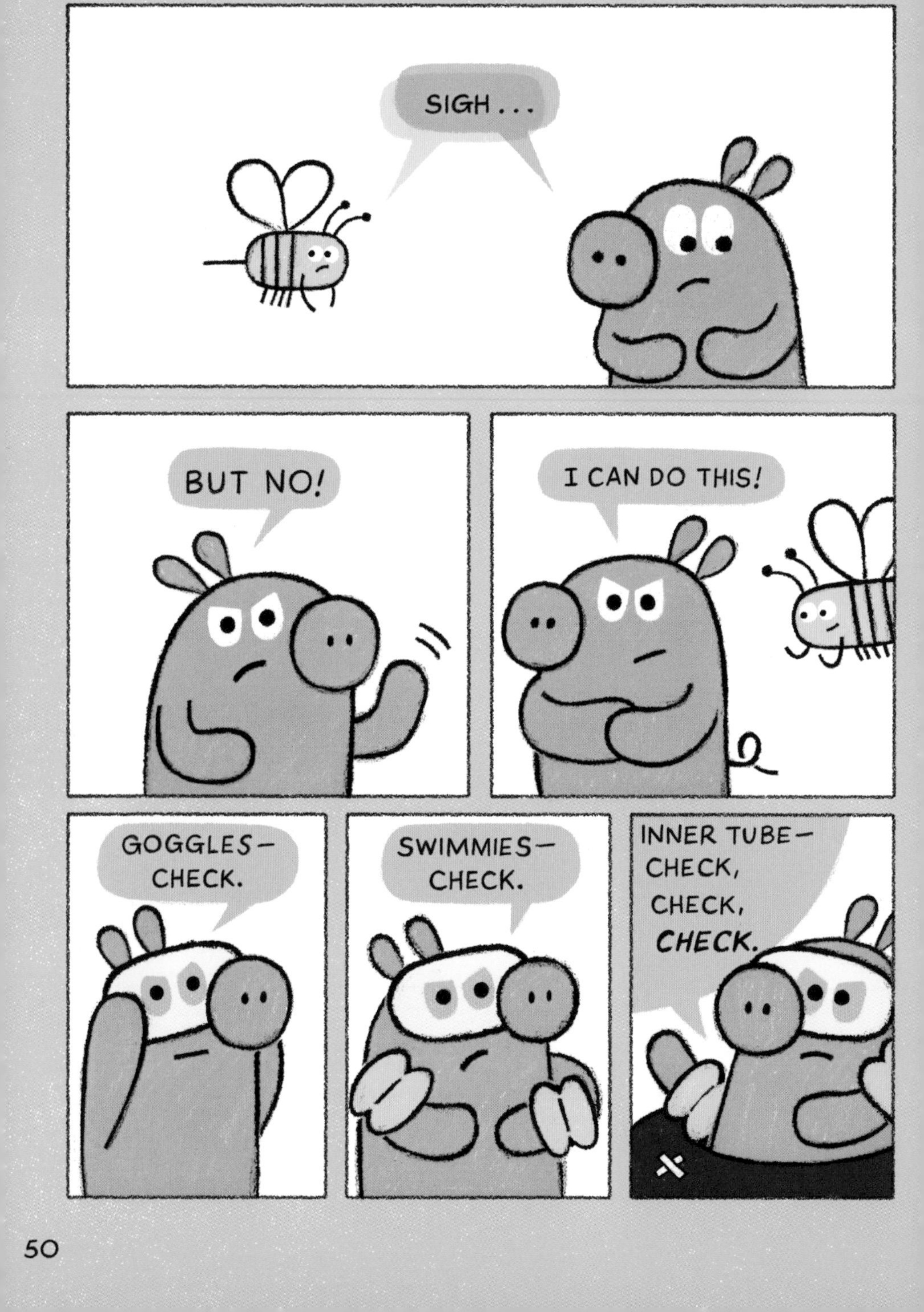
SIGH . . .
BUT NO!
I CAN DO THIS!
GOGGLES—
CHECK.
SWIMMIES—
CHECK.
INNER TUBE—
CHECK,
CHECK,
CHECK.

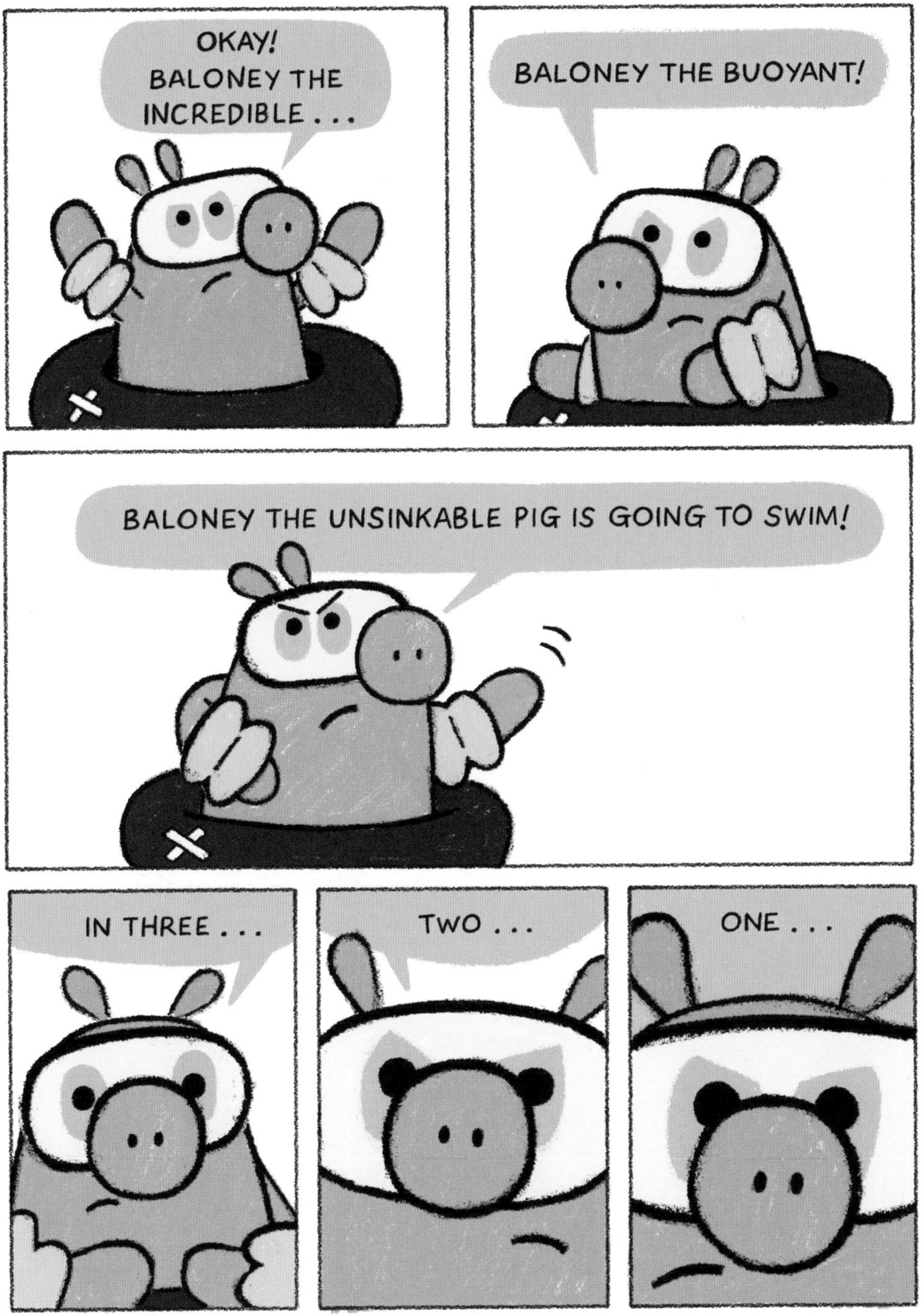
OKAY! BALONEY THE INCREDIBLE . . .
BALONEY THE BUOYANT!
BALONEY THE UNSINKABLE PIG IS GOING TO SWIM!
IN THREE . . .
TWO . . .
ONE . . .

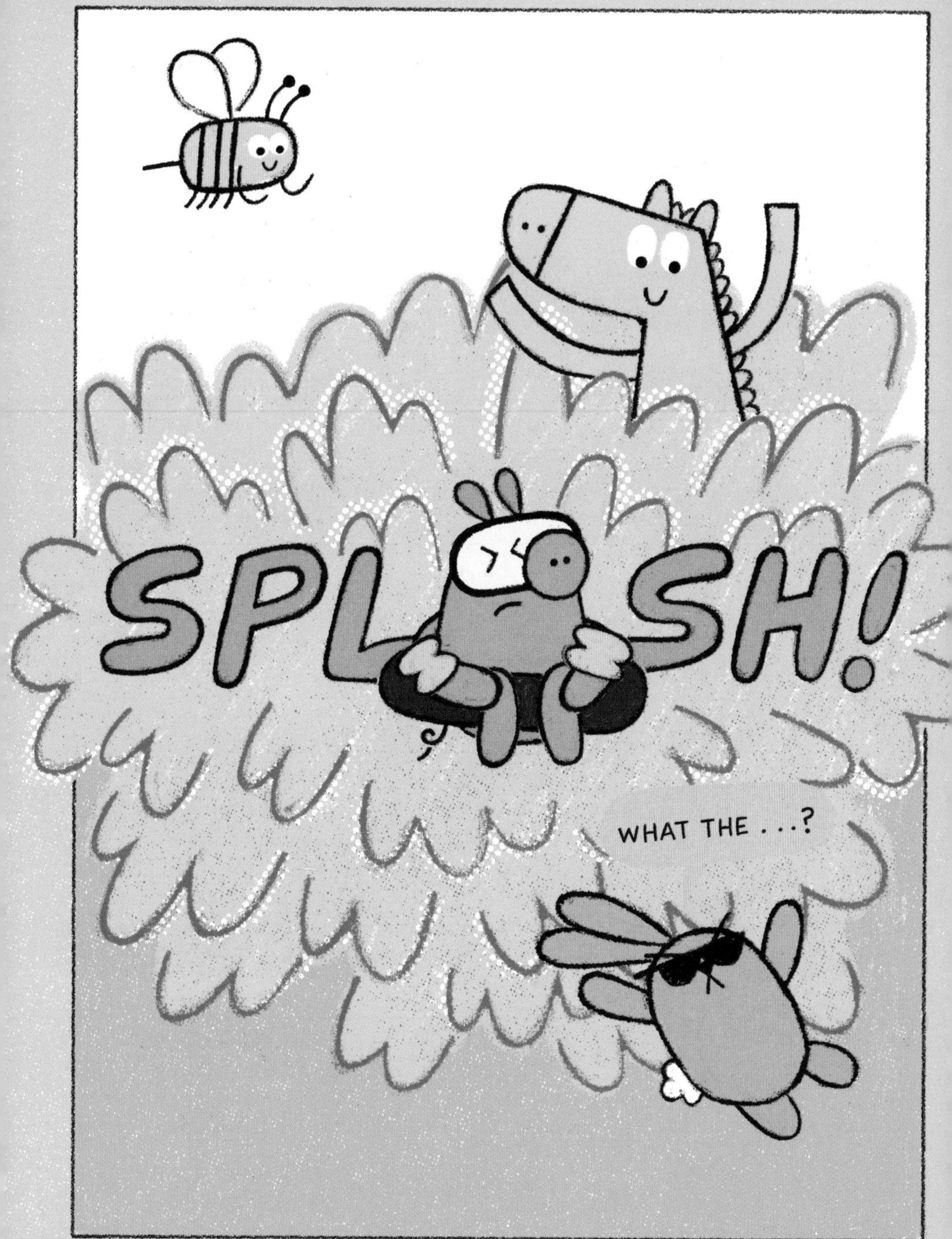
SPLASH!
WHAT THE . . .?

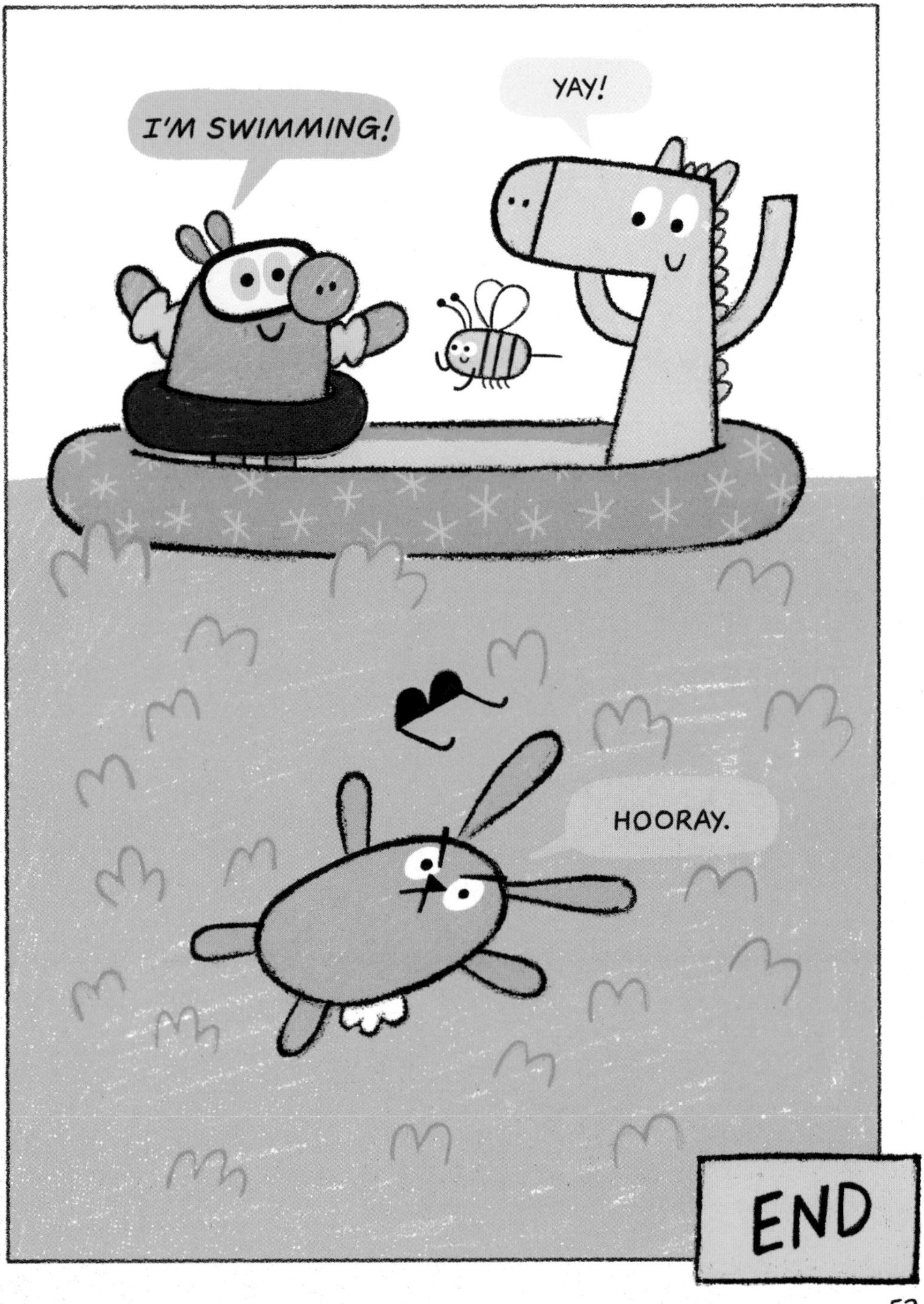
I'M SWIMMING!
YAY!
HOORAY.
END

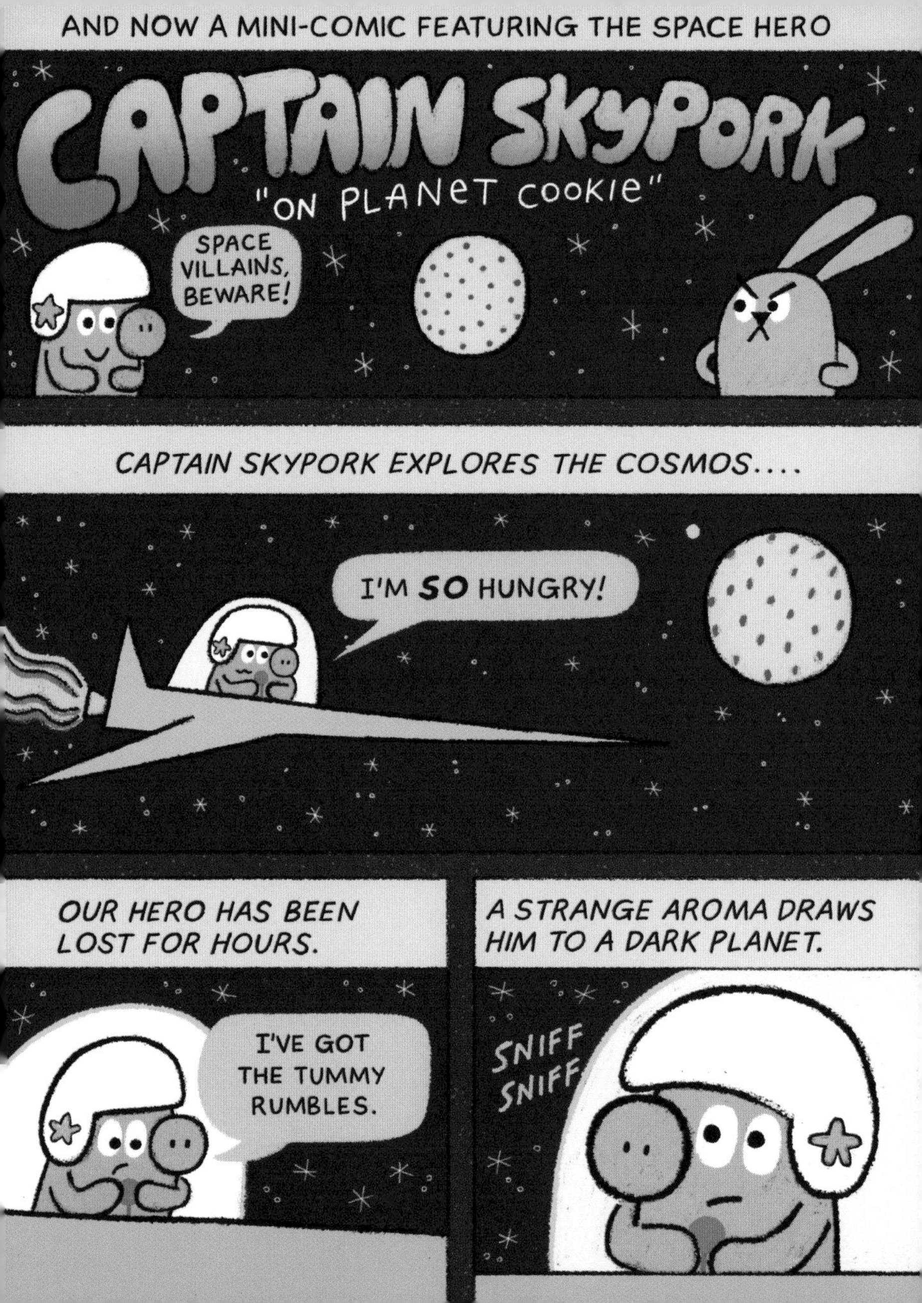
AND NOW A MINI-COMIC FEATURING THE SPACE HERO
CAPTAIN SKYPORK
"ON PLANET COOKIE"
SPACE VILLAINS, BEWARE!
CAPTAIN SKYPORK EXPLORES THE COSMOS....
I'M SO HUNGRY!
OUR HERO HAS BEEN LOST FOR HOURS.
I'VE GOT THE TUMMY RUMBLES.
A STRANGE AROMA DRAWS HIM TO A DARK PLANET.
SNIFF SNIFF

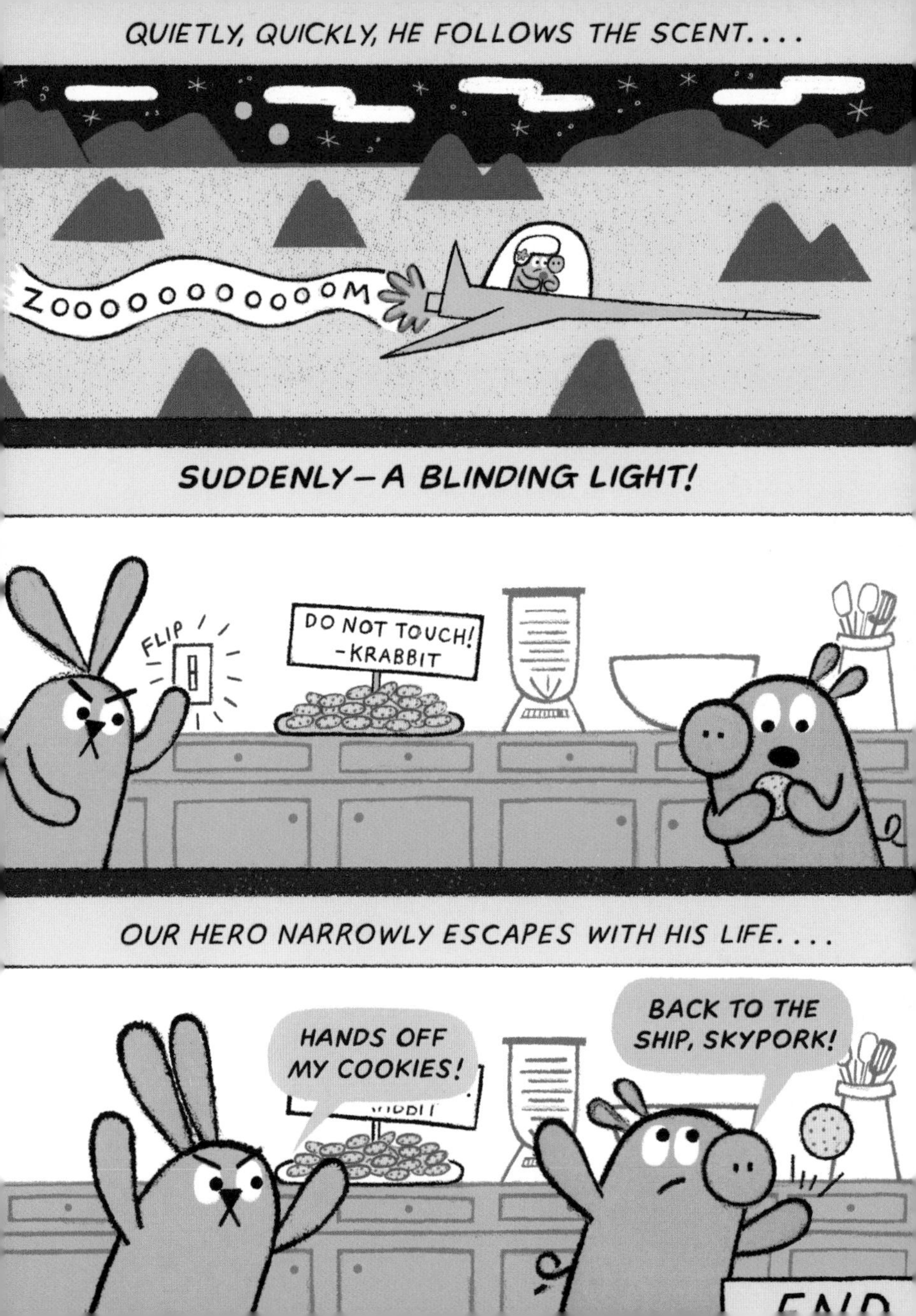
QUIETLY, QUICKLY, HE FOLLOWS THE SCENT. . . .
ZOOOOOOOOOOOM
SUDDENLY—A BLINDING LIGHT!
FLIP
DO NOT TOUCH!
-KRABBIT
OUR HERO NARROWLY ESCAPES WITH HIS LIFE. . . .
HANDS OFF MY COOKIES!
BACK TO THE SHIP, SKYPORK!

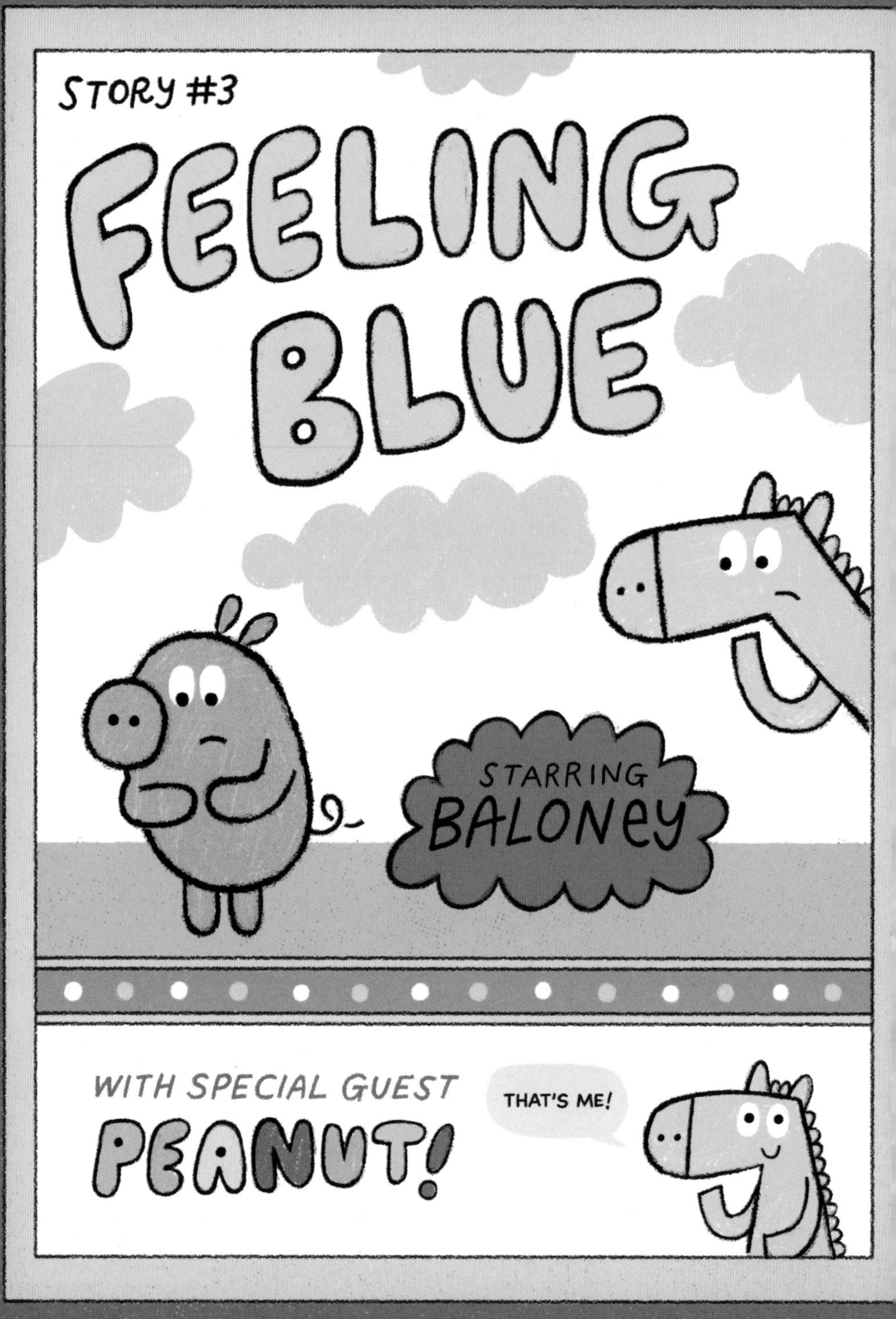
STORY #3
FEELING BLUE
STARRING BALONEY
WITH SPECIAL GUEST
PEANUT!
THAT'S ME!

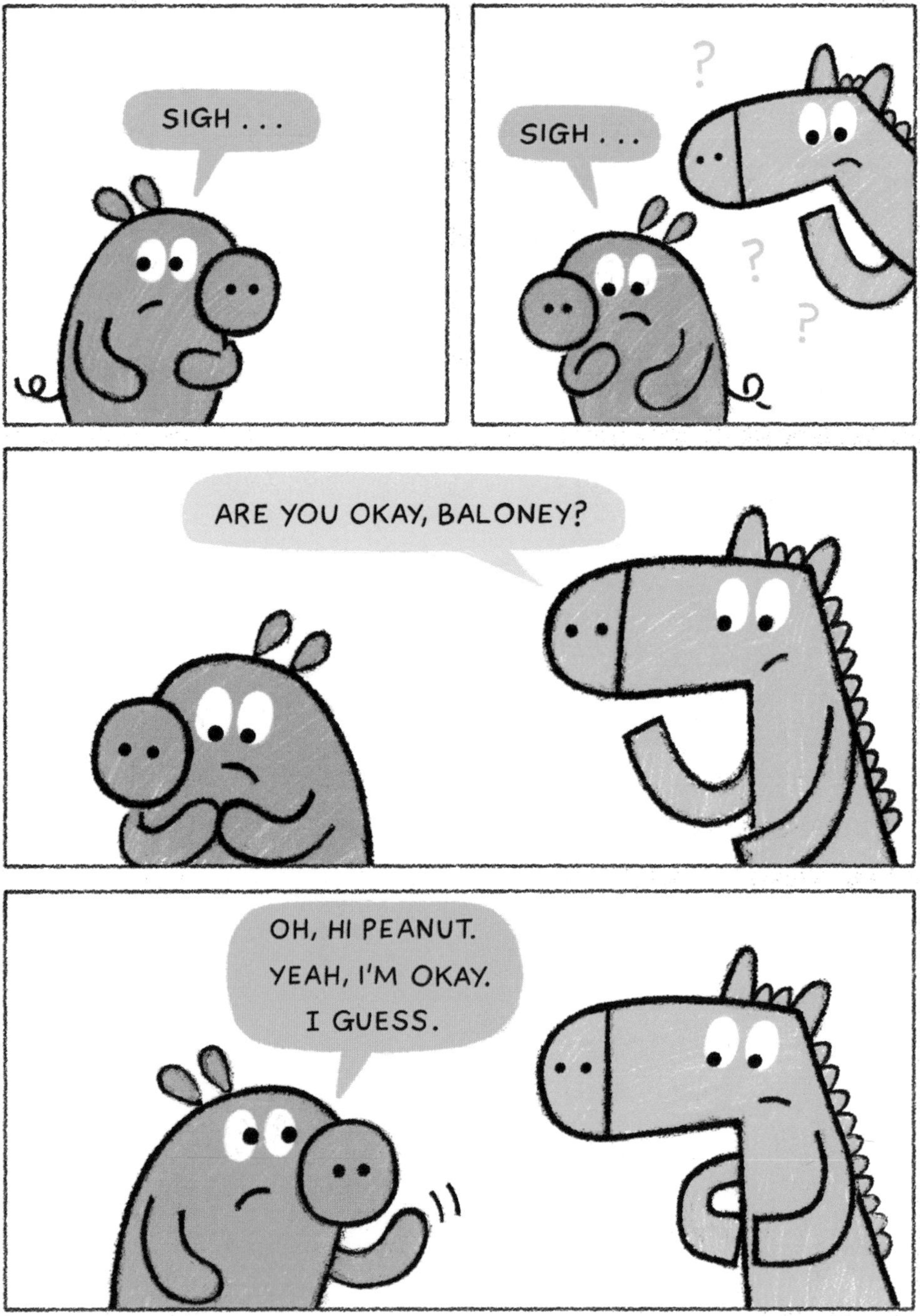
SIGH . . .
SIGH . . .
?
?
?
ARE YOU OKAY, BALONEY?
OH, HI PEANUT.
YEAH, I'M OKAY.
I GUESS.

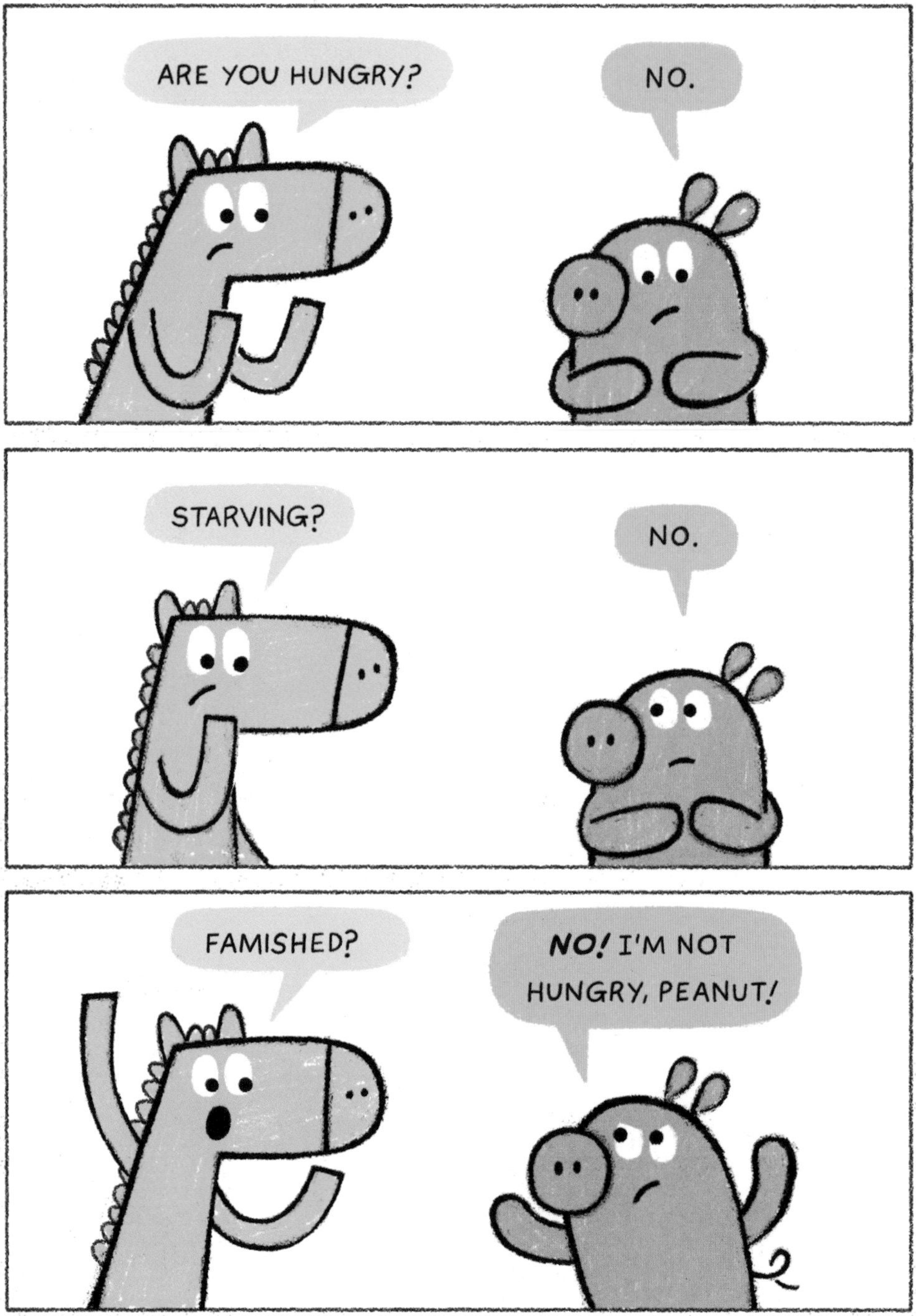
ARE YOU HUNGRY?
NO.
STARVING?
NO.
FAMISHED?
NO! I'M NOT HUNGRY, PEANUT!

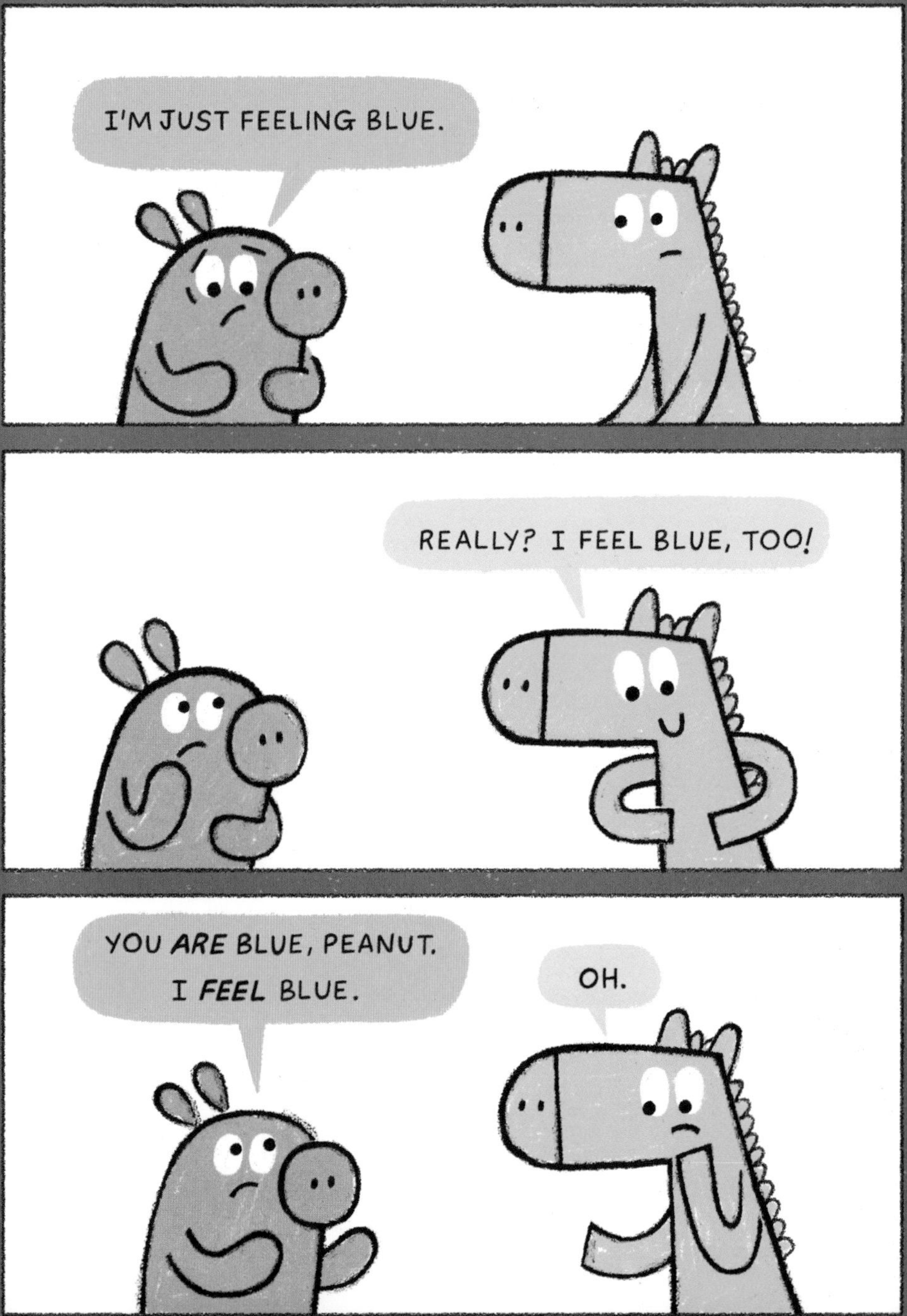
I'M JUST FEELING BLUE.
REALLY? I FEEL BLUE, TOO!
YOU *ARE* BLUE, PEANUT. I *FEEL* BLUE.
OH.

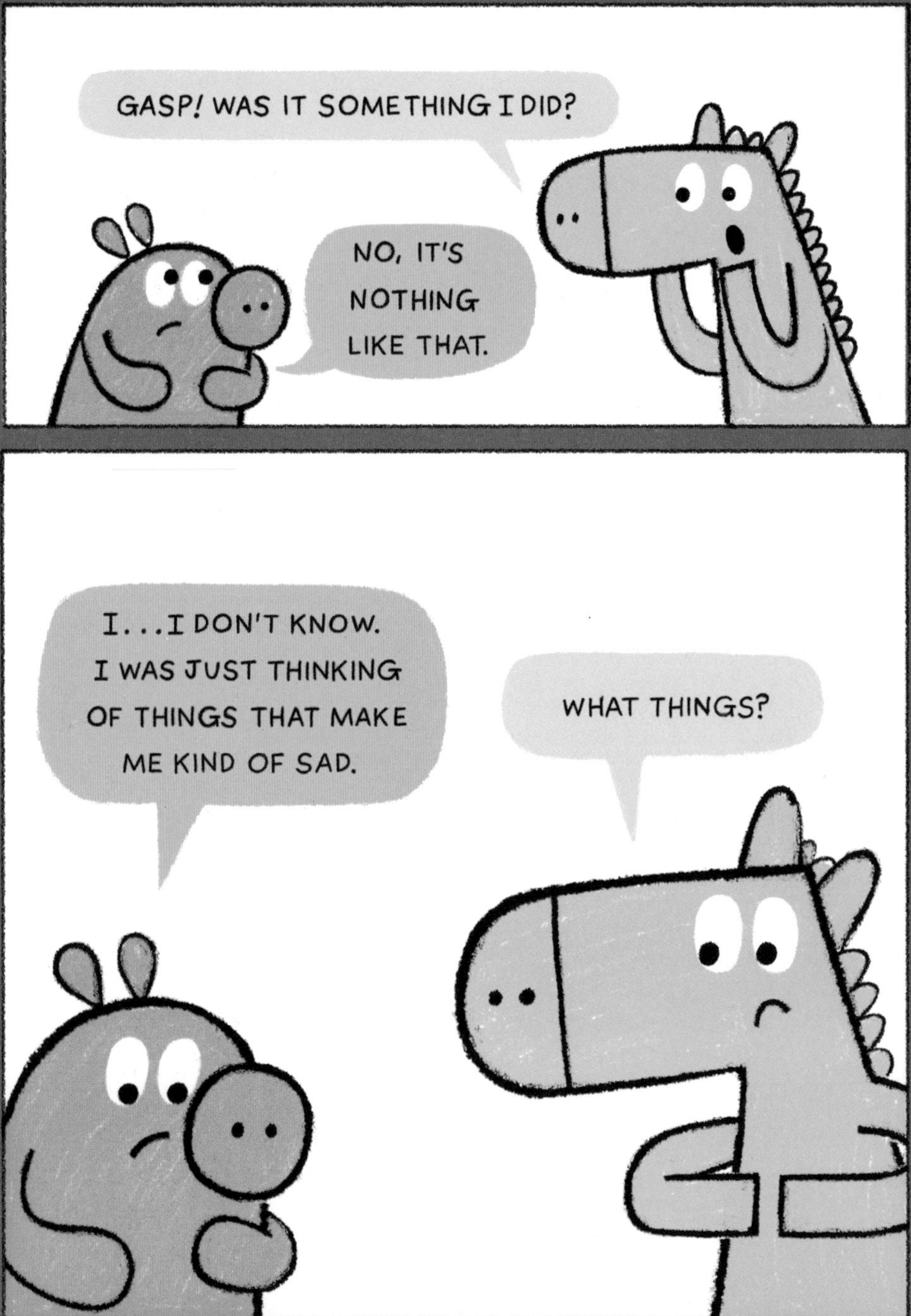
GASP! WAS IT SOMETHING I DID?
NO, IT'S NOTHING LIKE THAT.
I...I DON'T KNOW. I WAS JUST THINKING OF THINGS THAT MAKE ME KIND OF SAD.
WHAT THINGS?

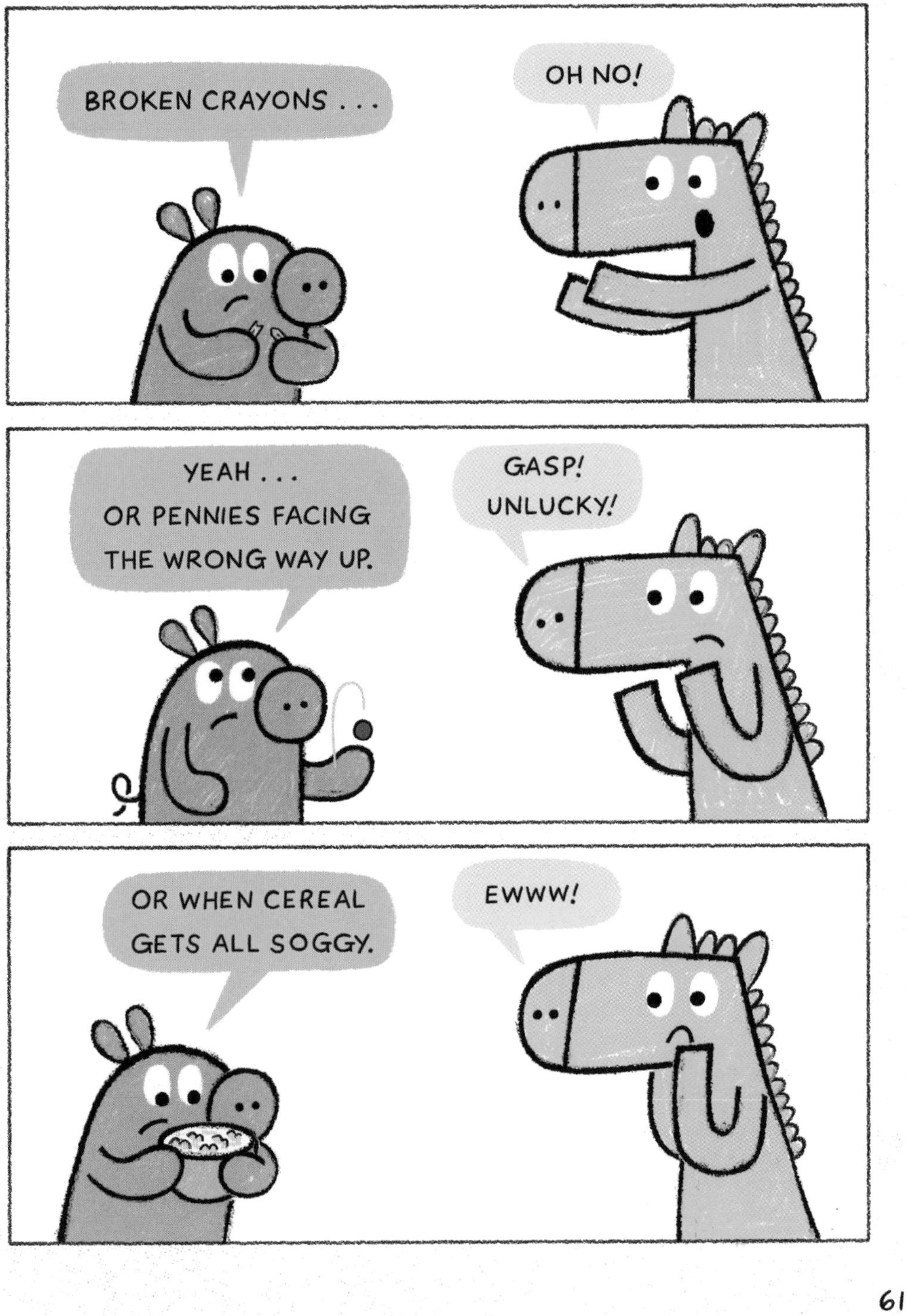
BROKEN CRAYONS . . .
OH NO!
YEAH . . .
OR PENNIES FACING
THE WRONG WAY UP.
GASP!
UNLUCKY!
OR WHEN CEREAL
GETS ALL SOGGY.
EWWW!

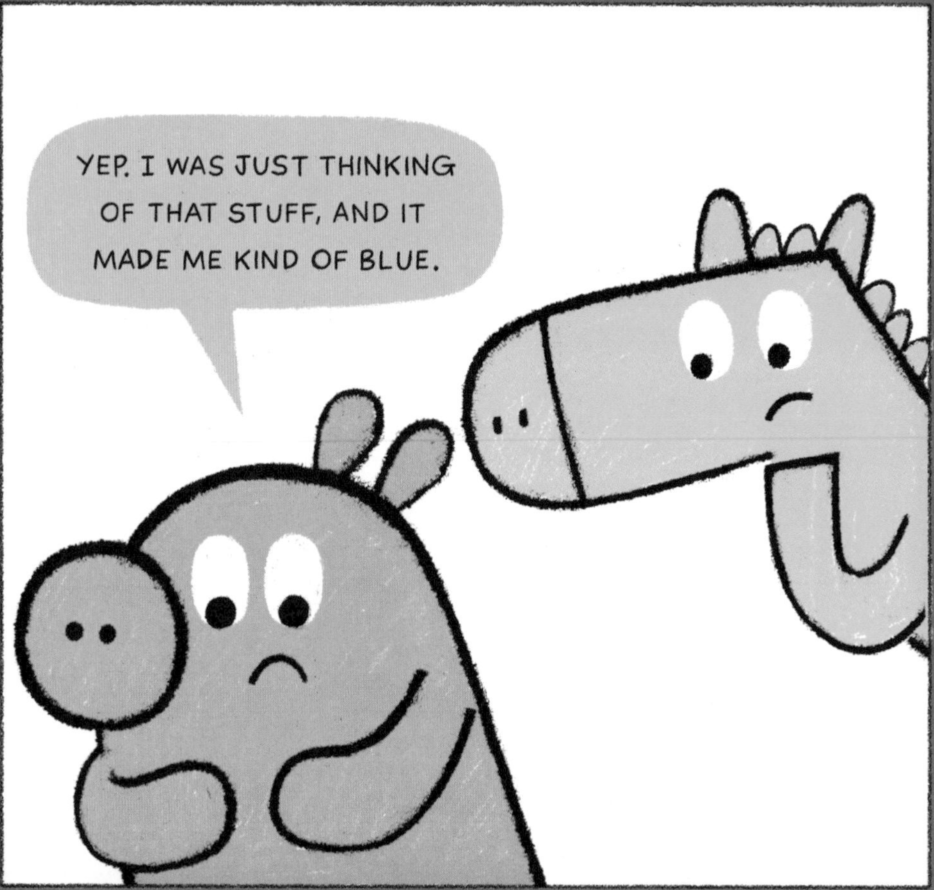
YEP. I WAS JUST THINKING OF THAT STUFF, AND IT MADE ME KIND OF BLUE.

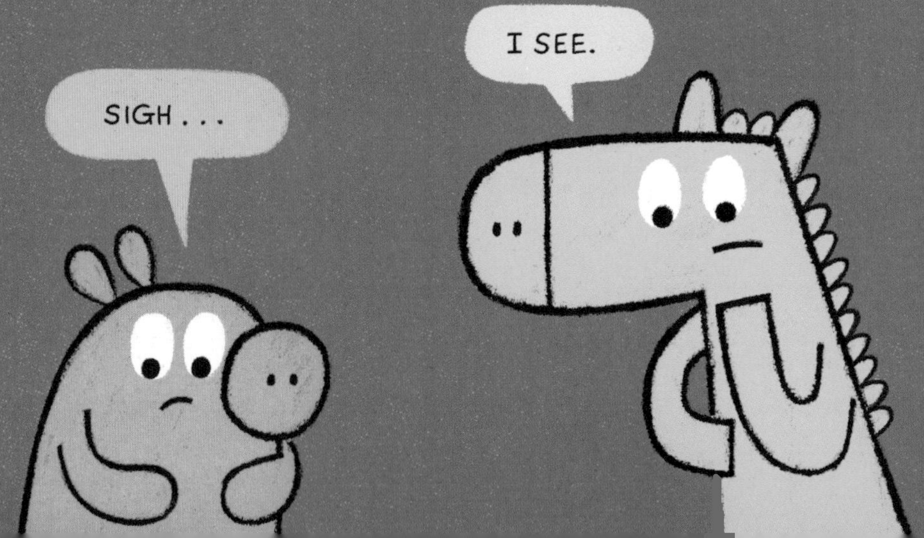
I SEE.
SIGH . . .

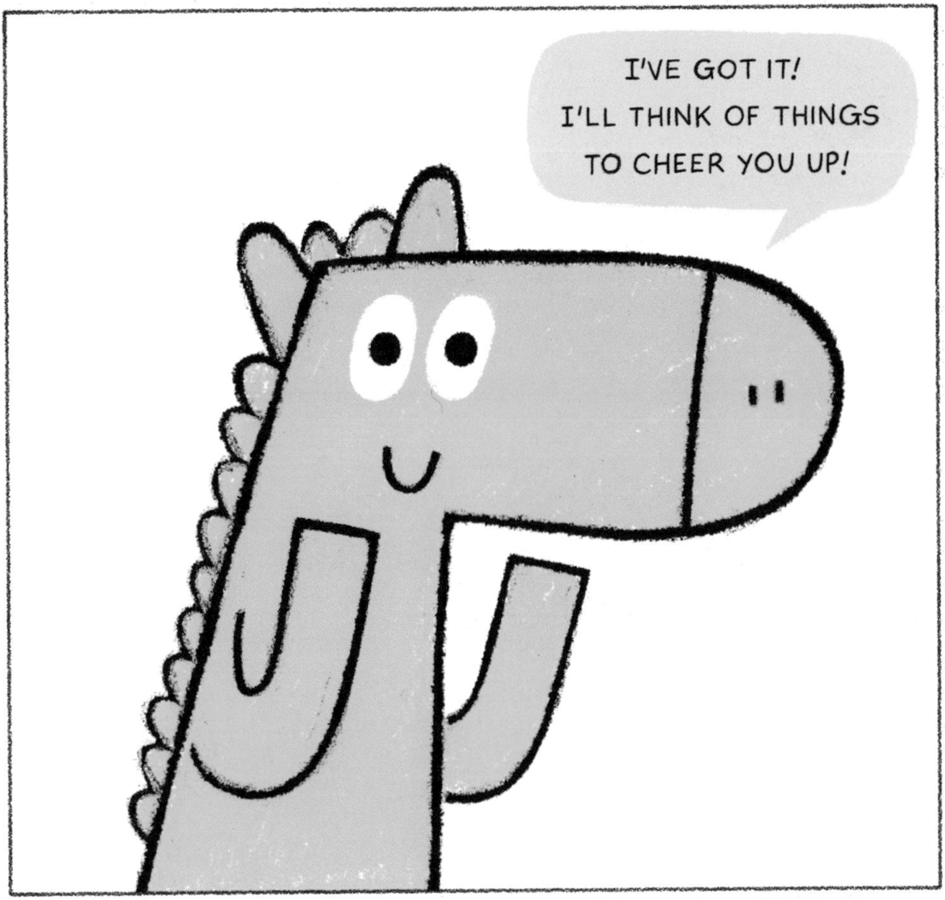
I'VE GOT IT!
I'LL THINK OF THINGS
TO CHEER YOU UP!

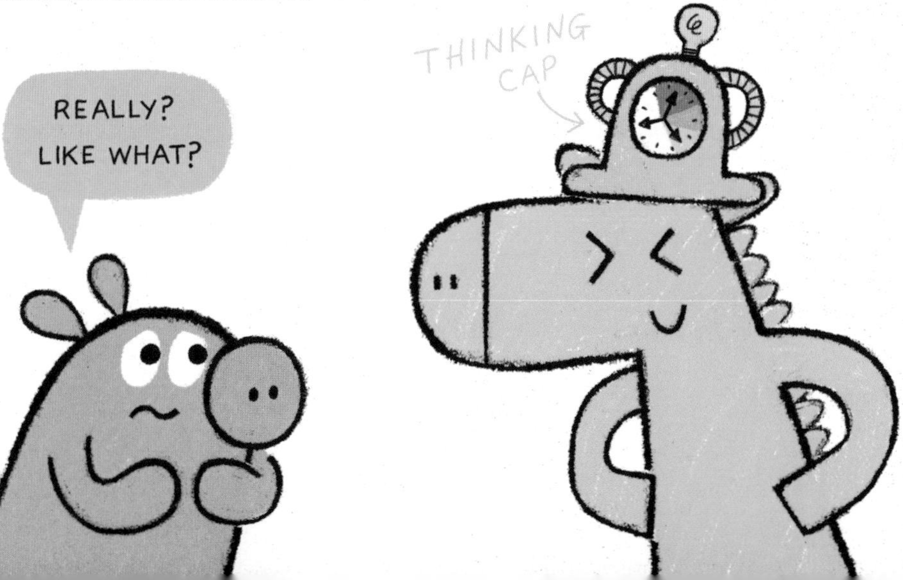
REALLY?
LIKE WHAT?
THINKING
CAP

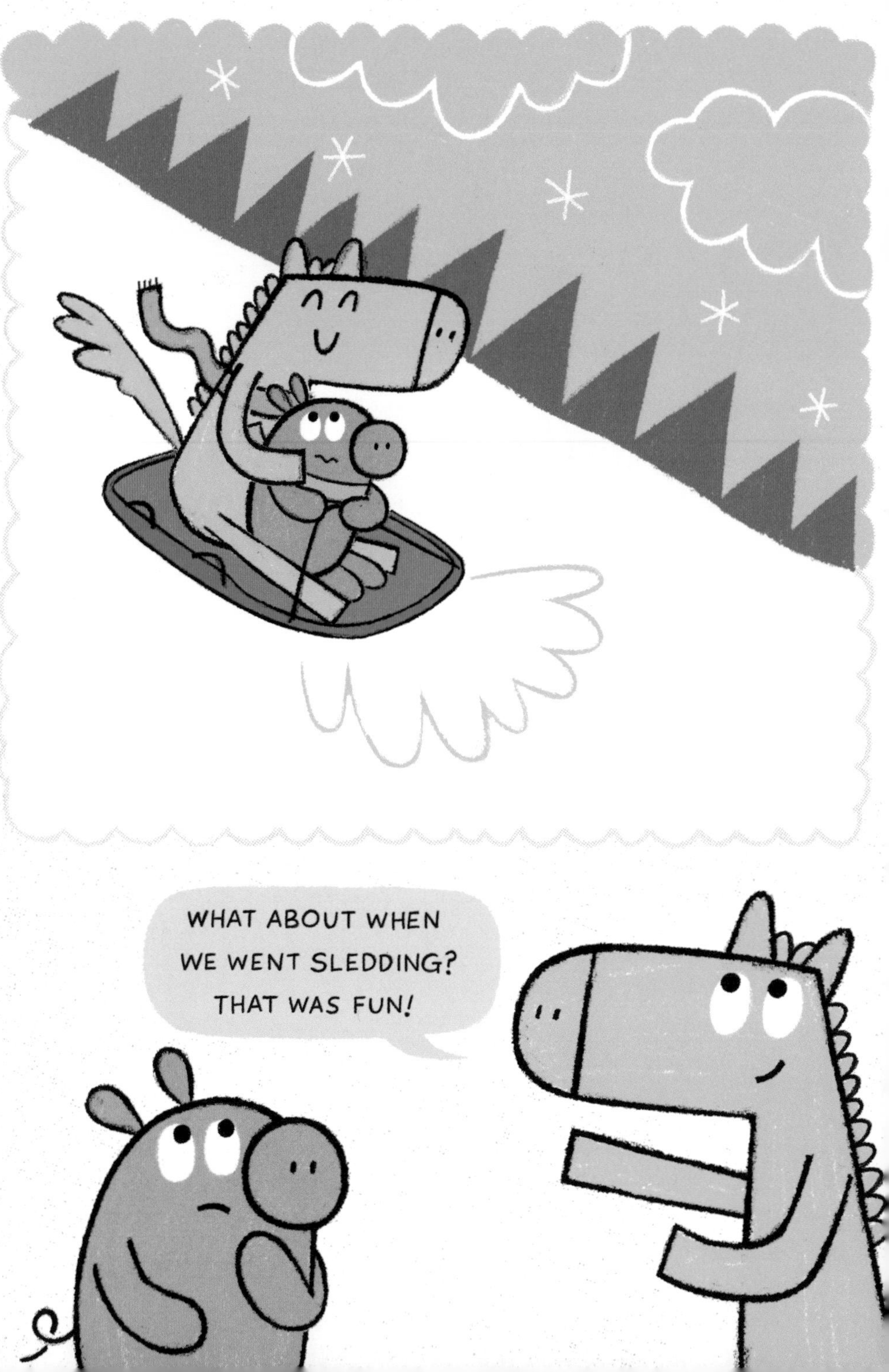
WHAT ABOUT WHEN WE WENT SLEDDING? THAT WAS FUN!

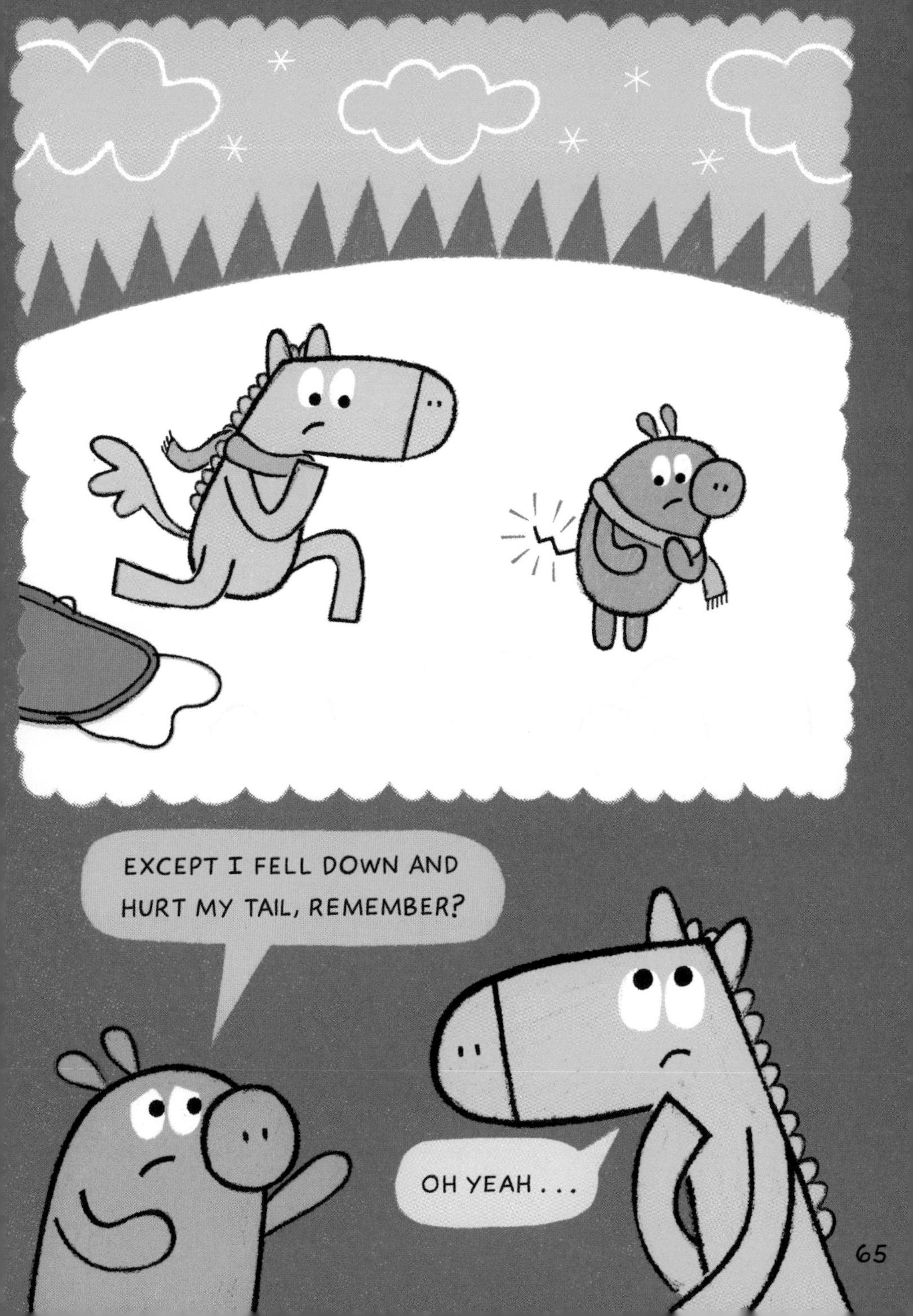
EXCEPT I FELL DOWN AND HURT MY TAIL, REMEMBER?
OH YEAH . . .

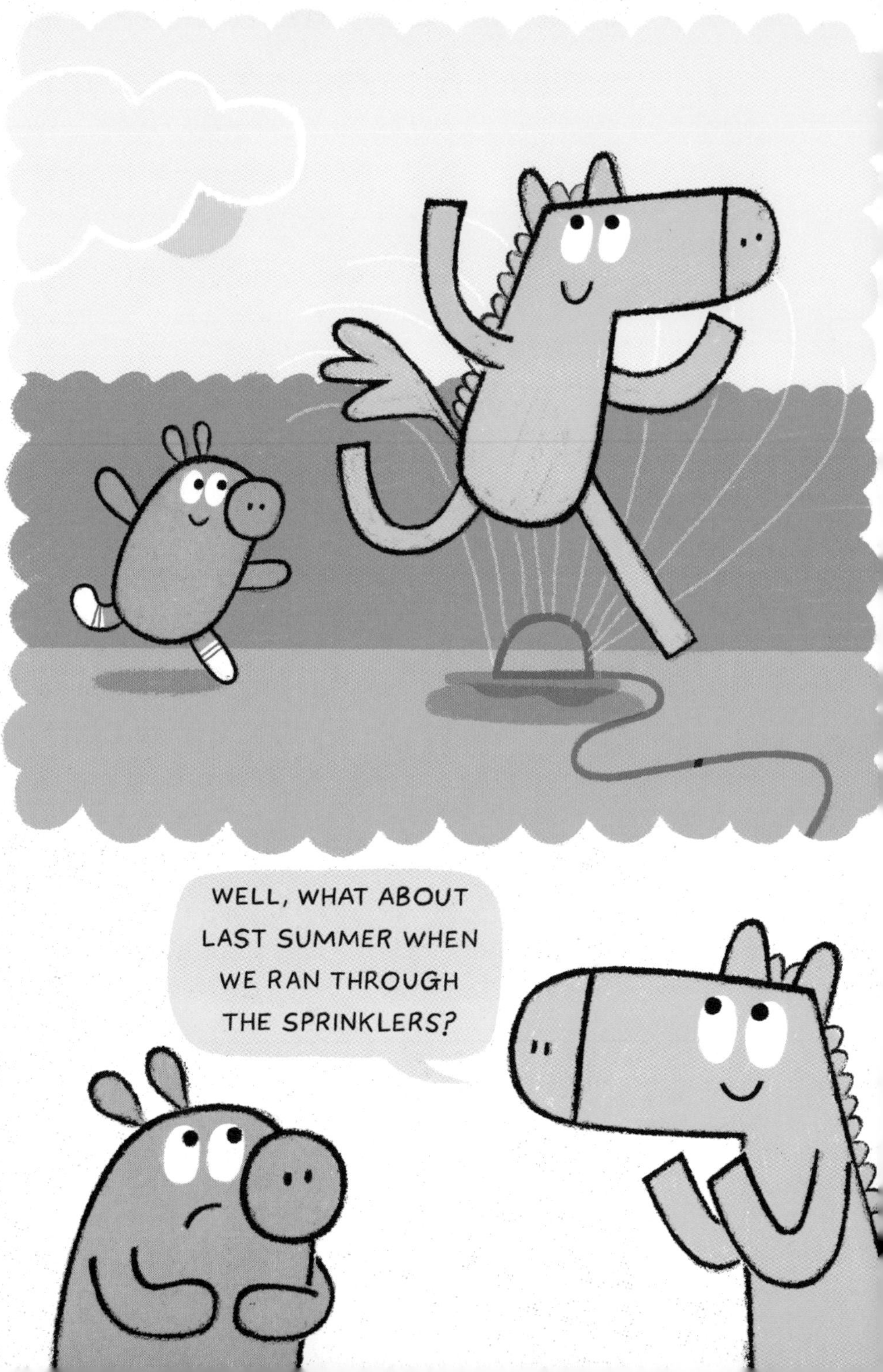
WELL, WHAT ABOUT LAST SUMMER WHEN WE RAN THROUGH THE SPRINKLERS?

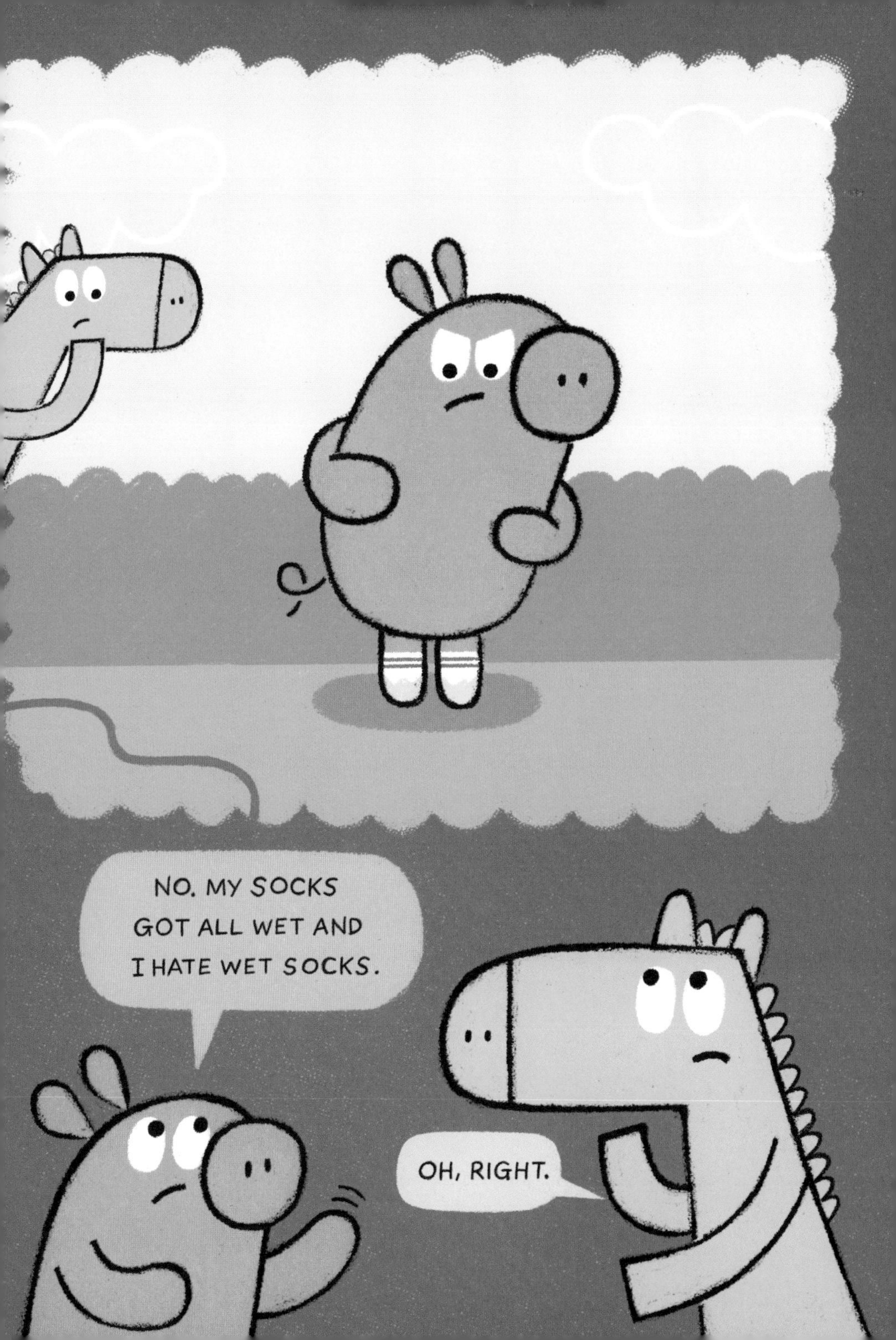
NO. MY SOCKS GOT ALL WET AND I HATE WET SOCKS.
OH, RIGHT.

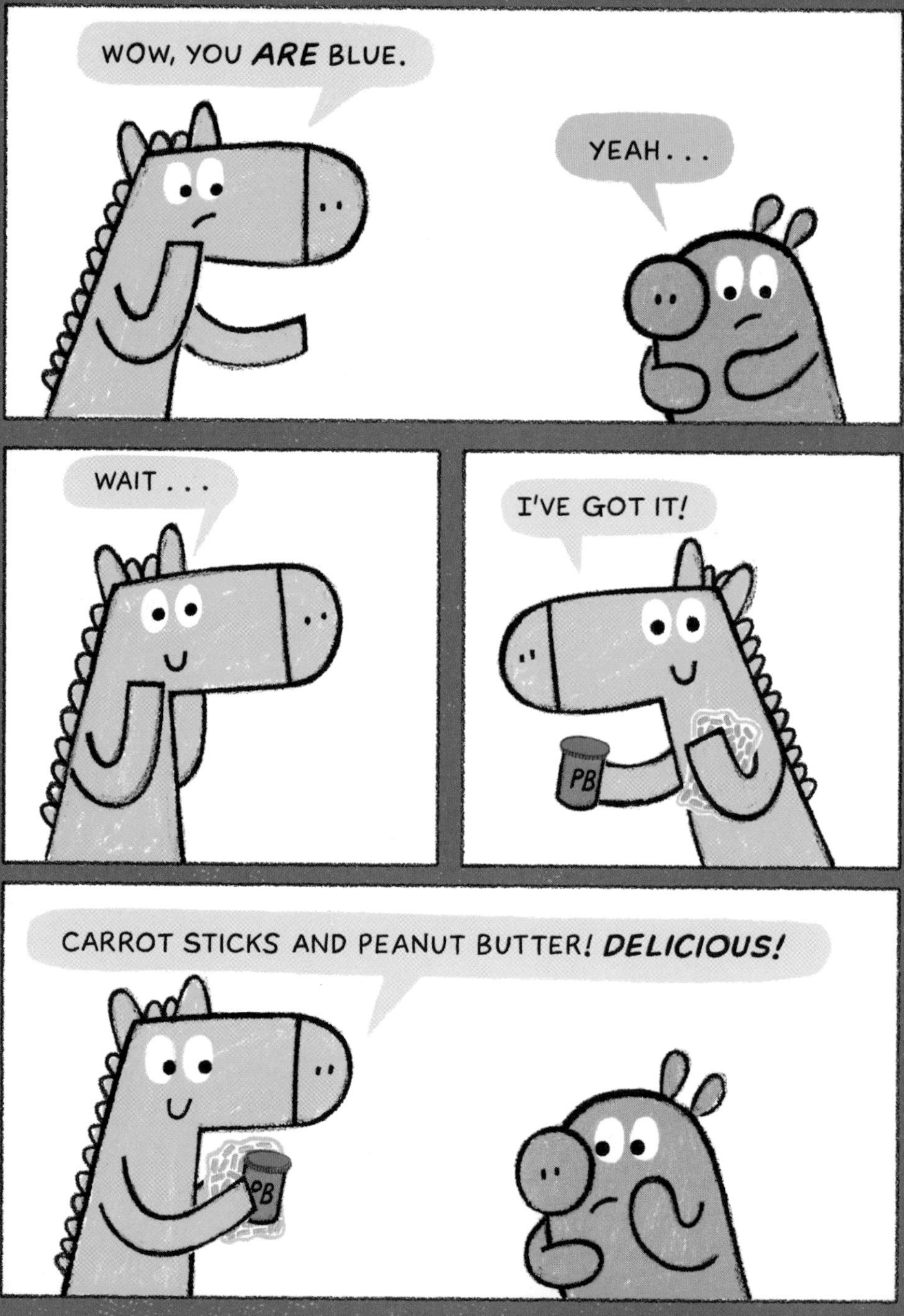
WOW, YOU ARE BLUE.
YEAH...
WAIT...
I'VE GOT IT!
PB
CARROT STICKS AND PEANUT BUTTER! DELICIOUS!
PB

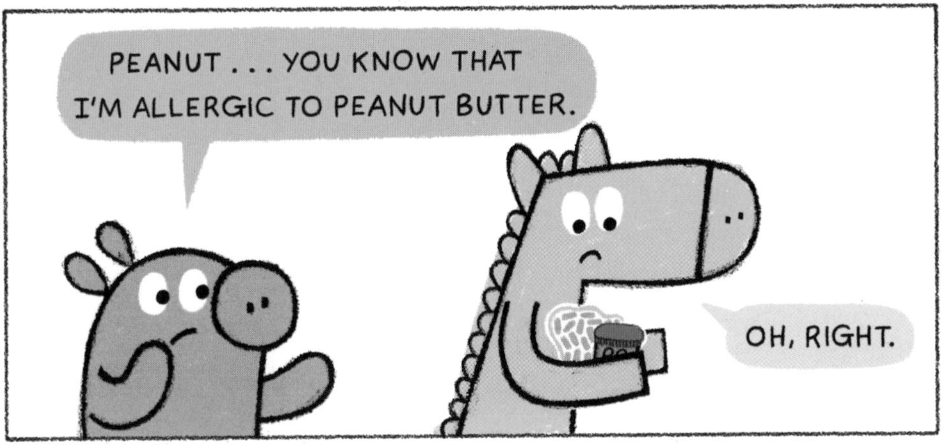
PEANUT . . . YOU KNOW THAT I'M ALLERGIC TO PEANUT BUTTER.
OH, RIGHT.

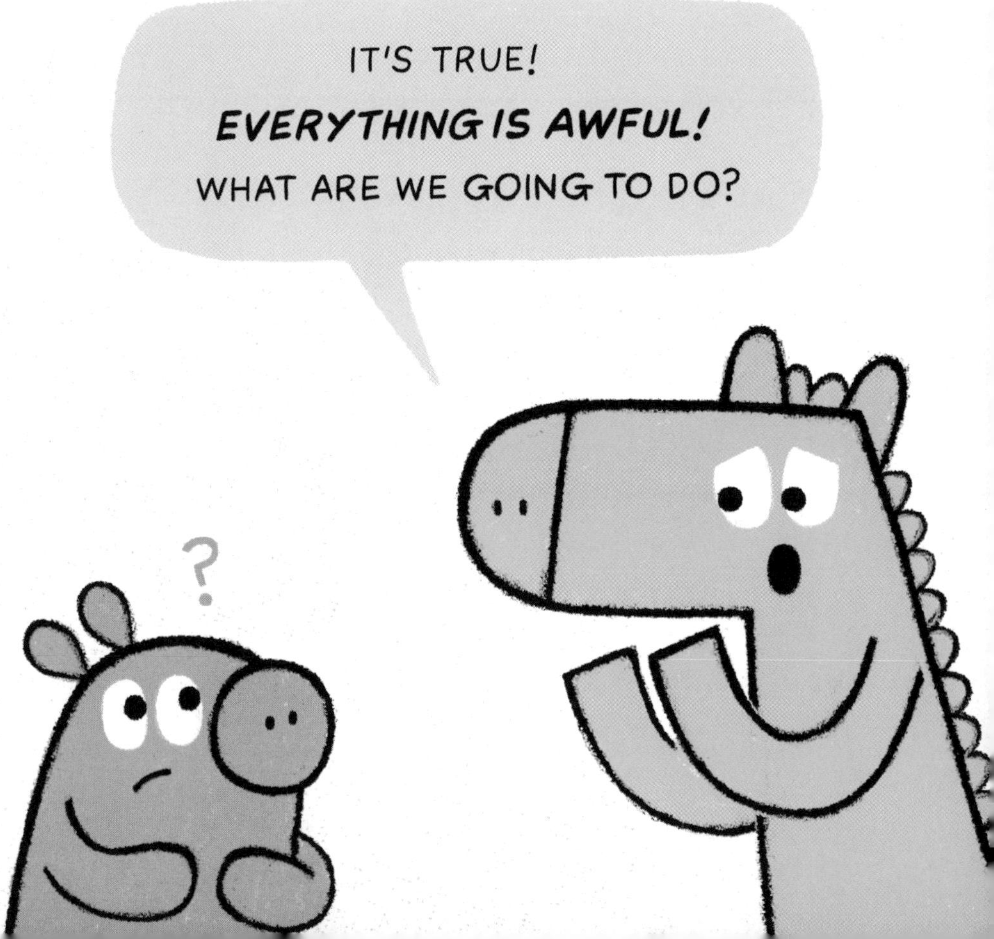
IT'S TRUE!
EVERYTHING IS AWFUL!
WHAT ARE WE GOING TO DO?
?

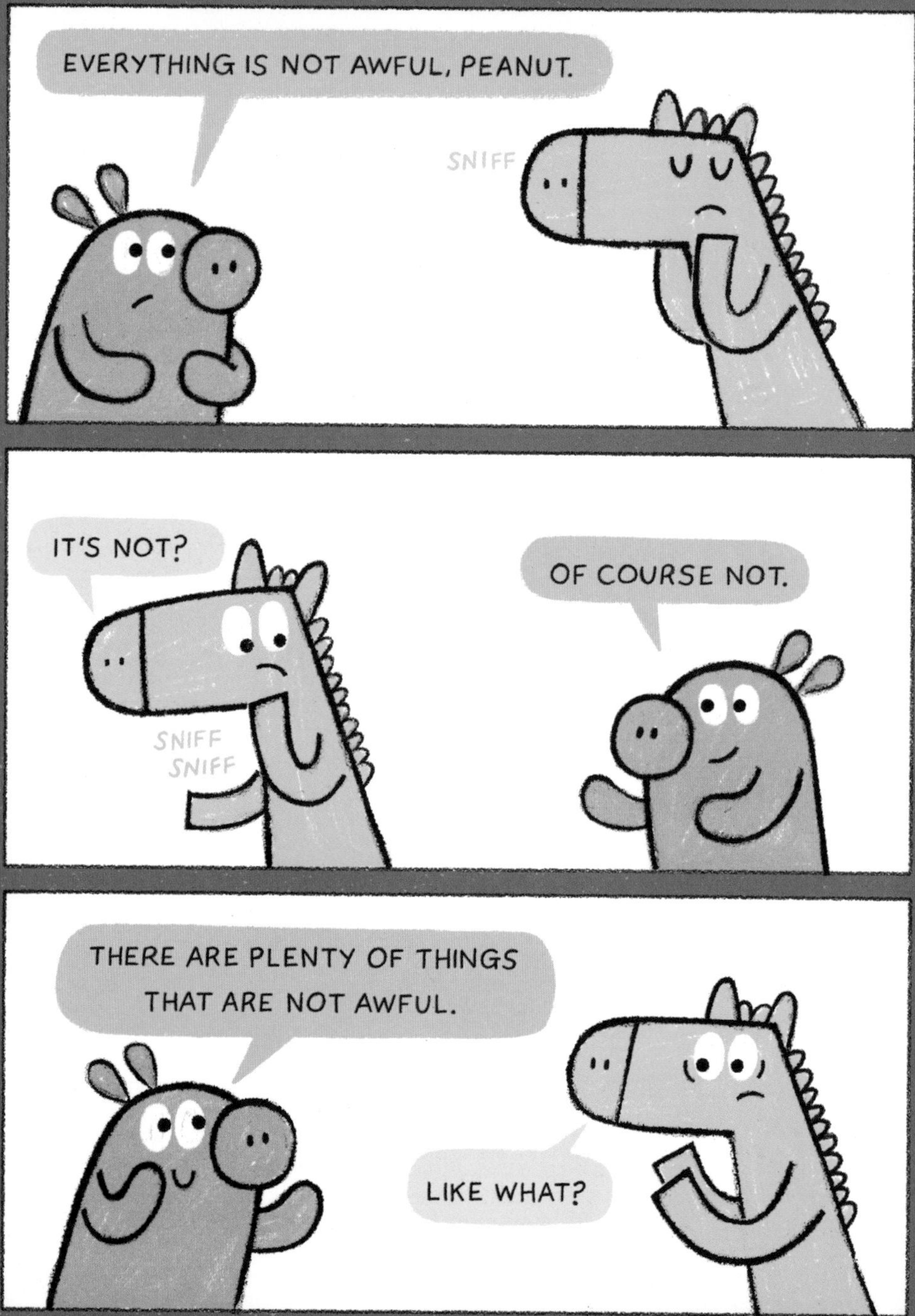

EVERYTHING IS NOT AWFUL, PEANUT.
SNIFF
IT'S NOT?
SNIFF
SNIFF
OF COURSE NOT.
THERE ARE PLENTY OF THINGS THAT ARE NOT AWFUL.
LIKE WHAT?

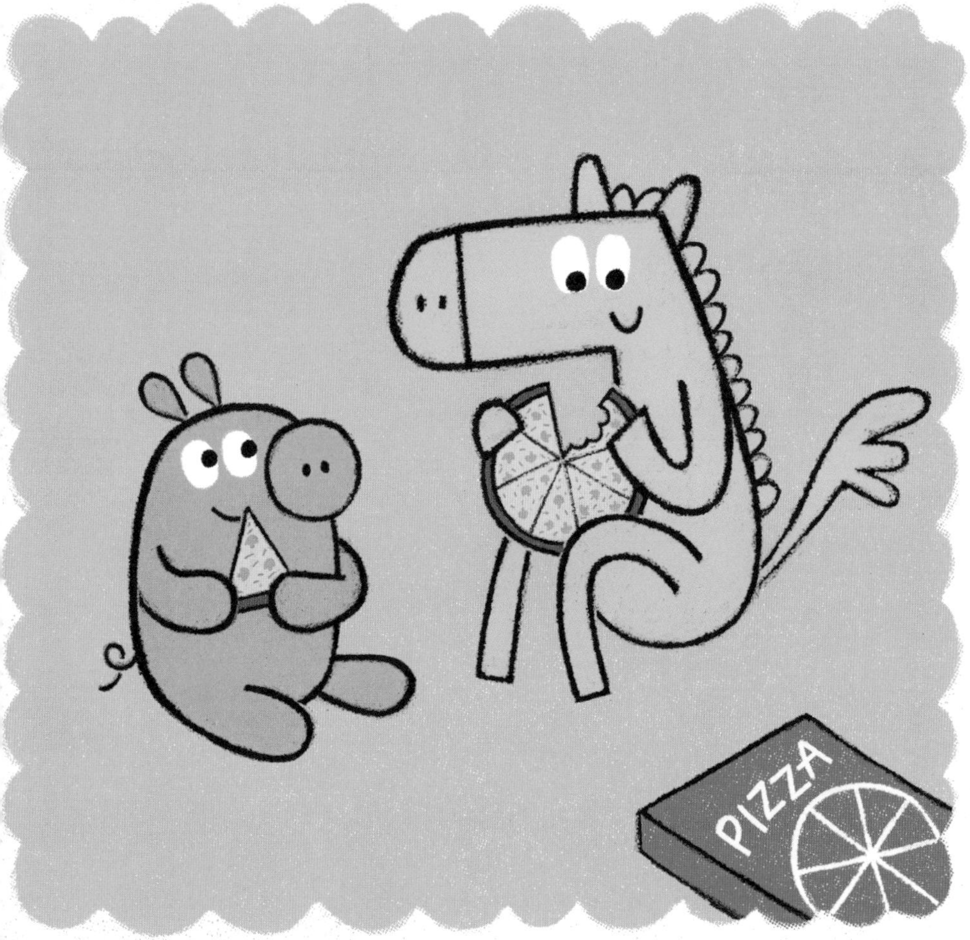
PIZZA

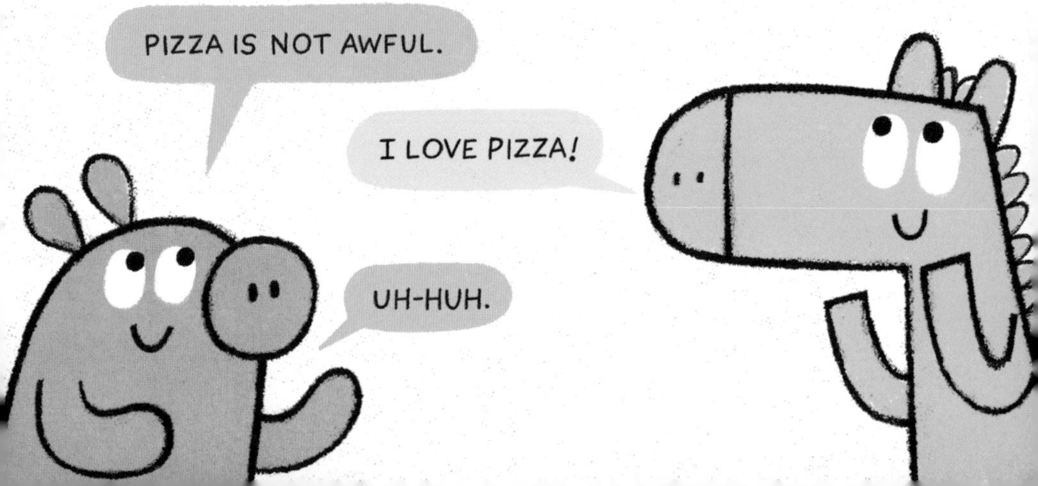
PIZZA IS NOT AWFUL.
I LOVE PIZZA!
UH-HUH.

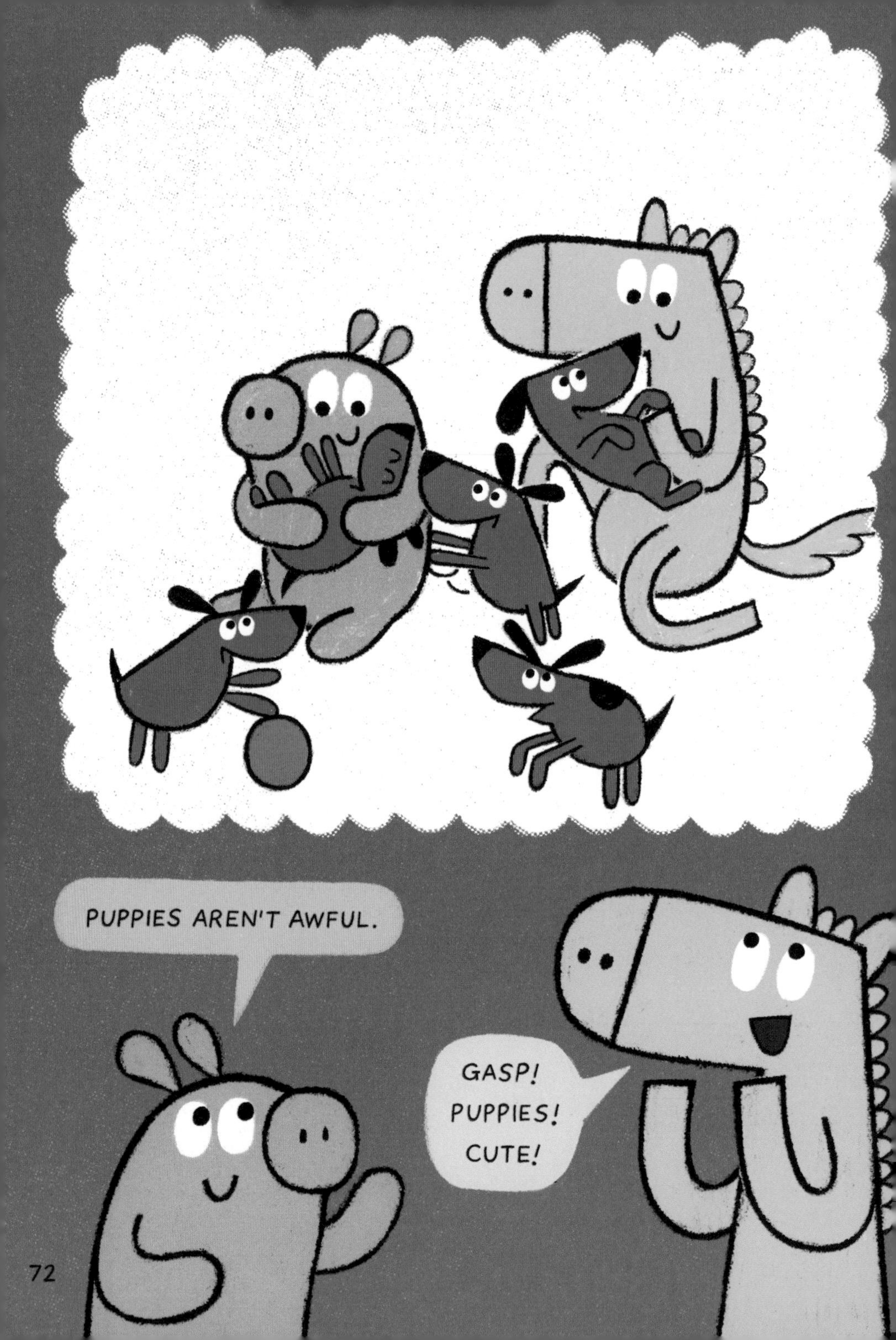
PUPPIES AREN'T AWFUL.
GASP! PUPPIES! CUTE!

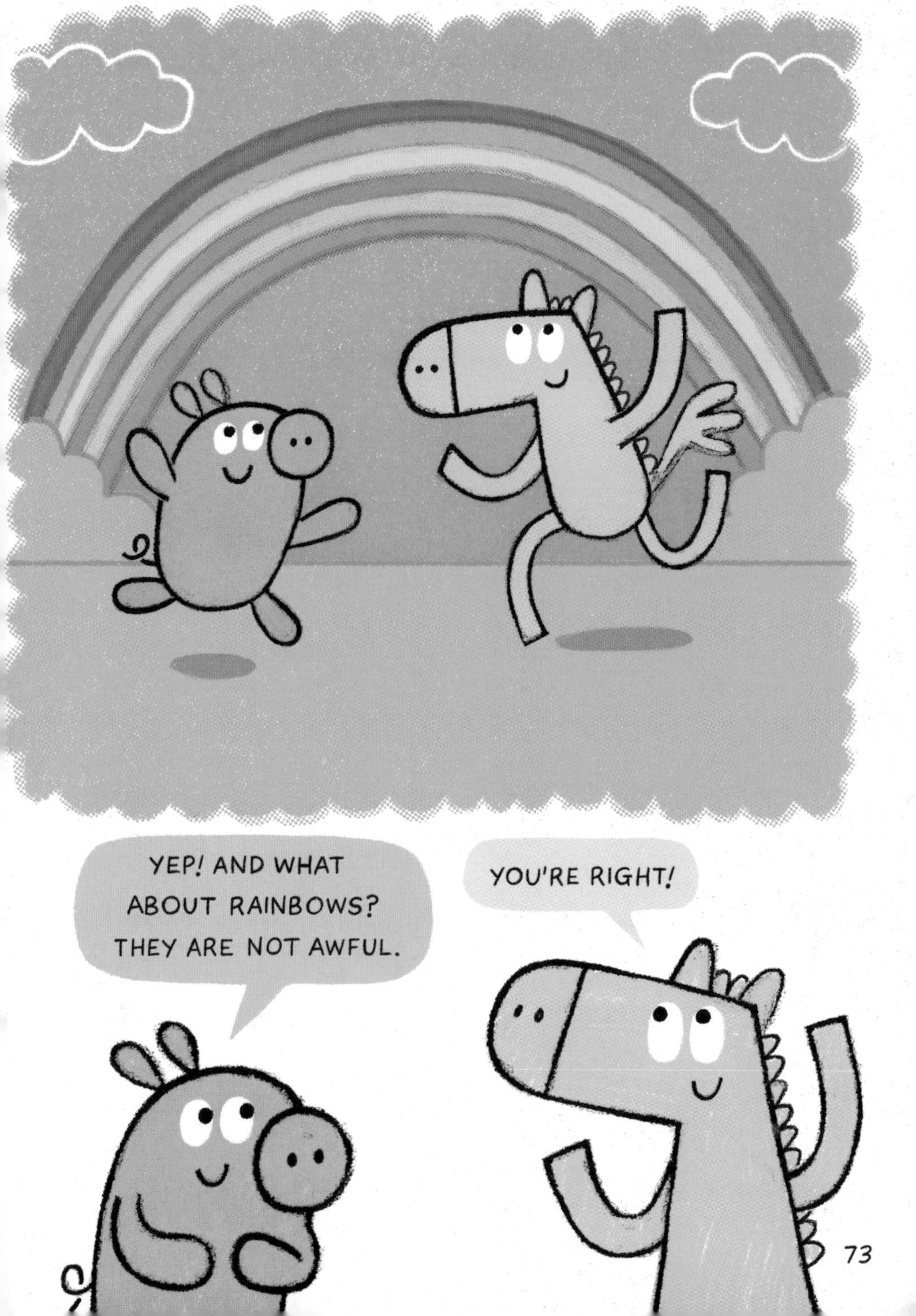
YEP! AND WHAT ABOUT RAINBOWS? THEY ARE NOT AWFUL.
YOU'RE RIGHT!

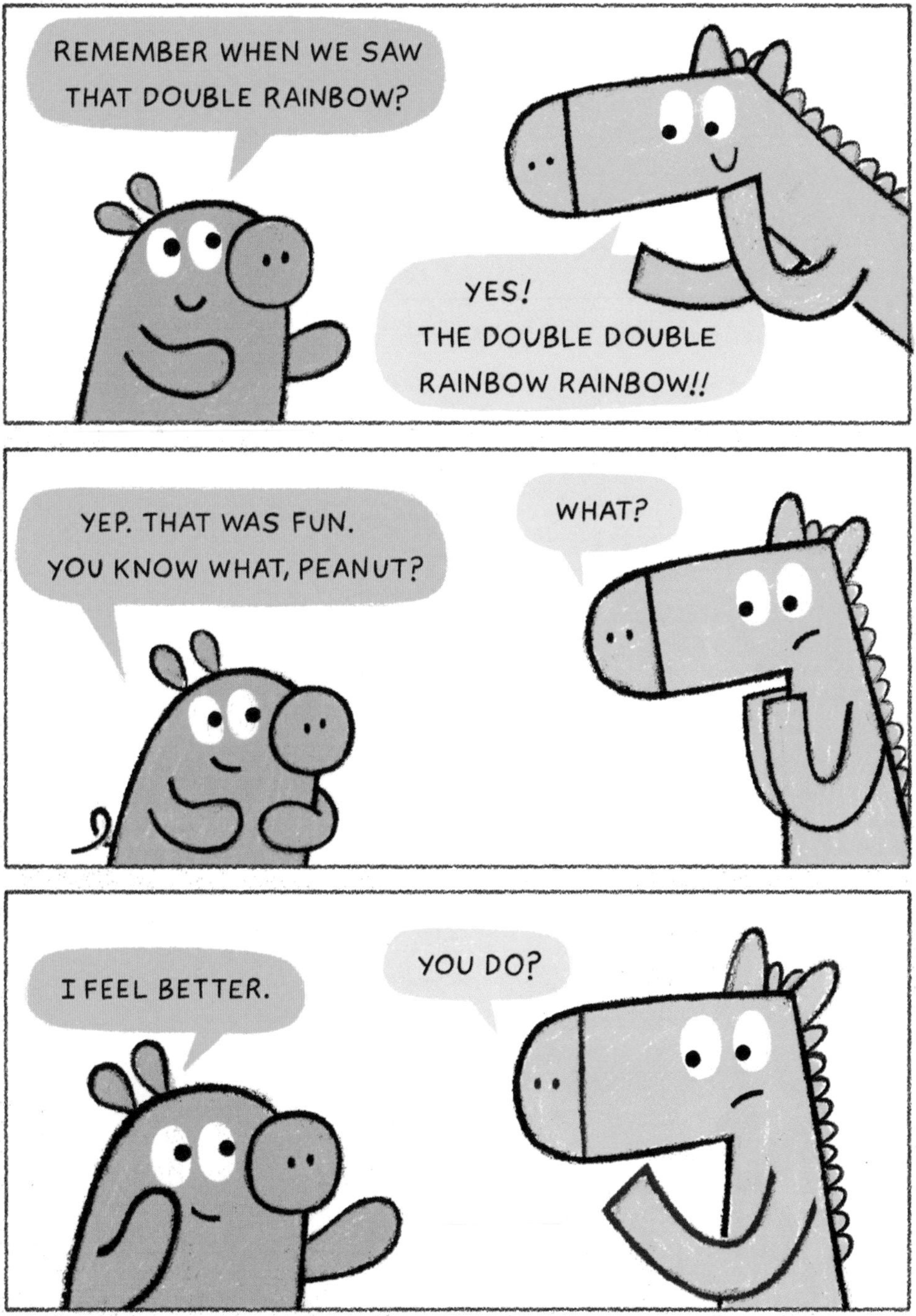
REMEMBER WHEN WE SAW THAT DOUBLE RAINBOW?
YES! THE DOUBLE DOUBLE RAINBOW RAINBOW!!
YEP. THAT WAS FUN. YOU KNOW WHAT, PEANUT?
WHAT?
I FEEL BETTER.
YOU DO?

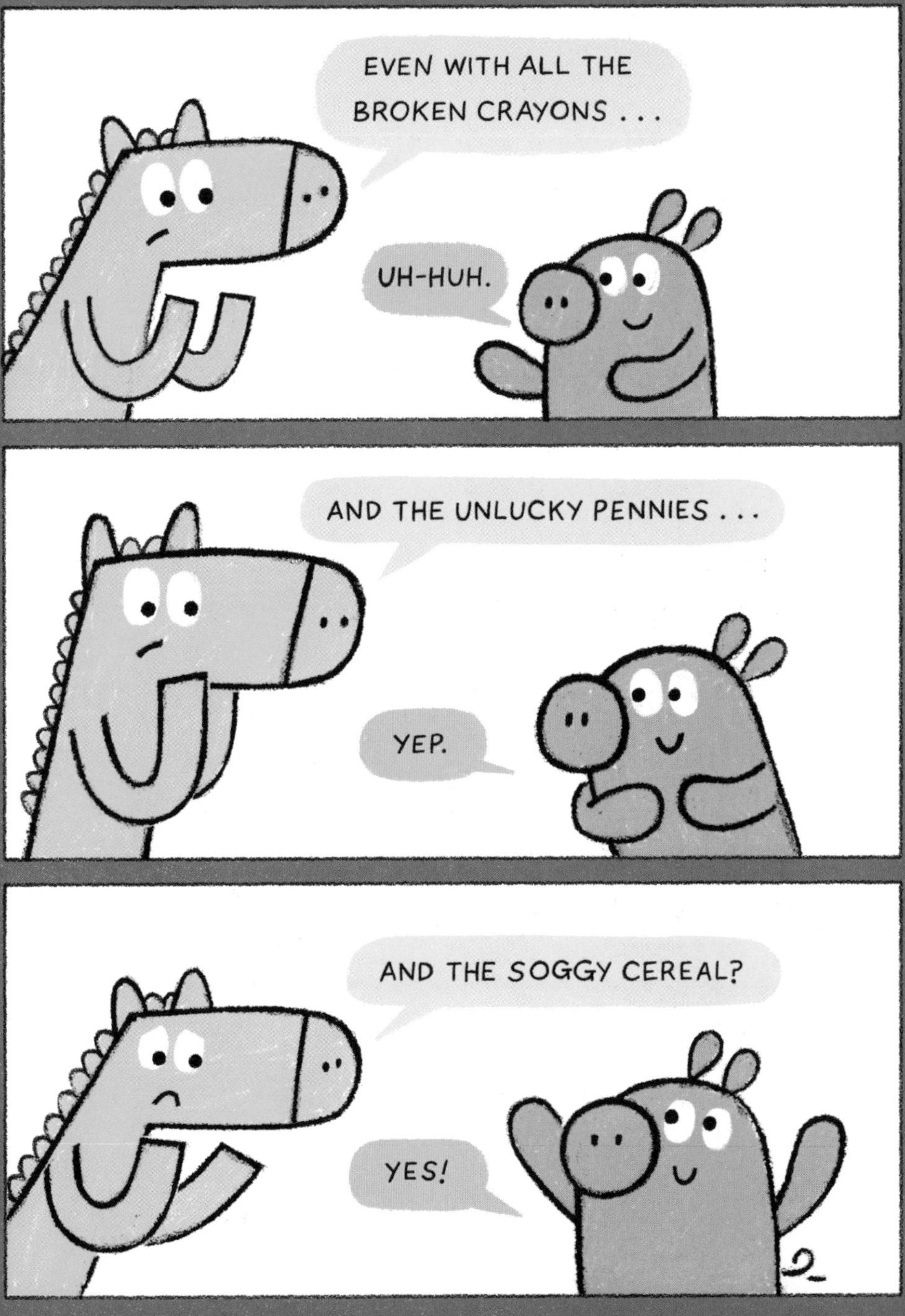
EVEN WITH ALL THE BROKEN CRAYONS . . .
UH-HUH.
AND THE UNLUCKY PENNIES . . .
YEP.
AND THE SOGGY CEREAL?
YES!

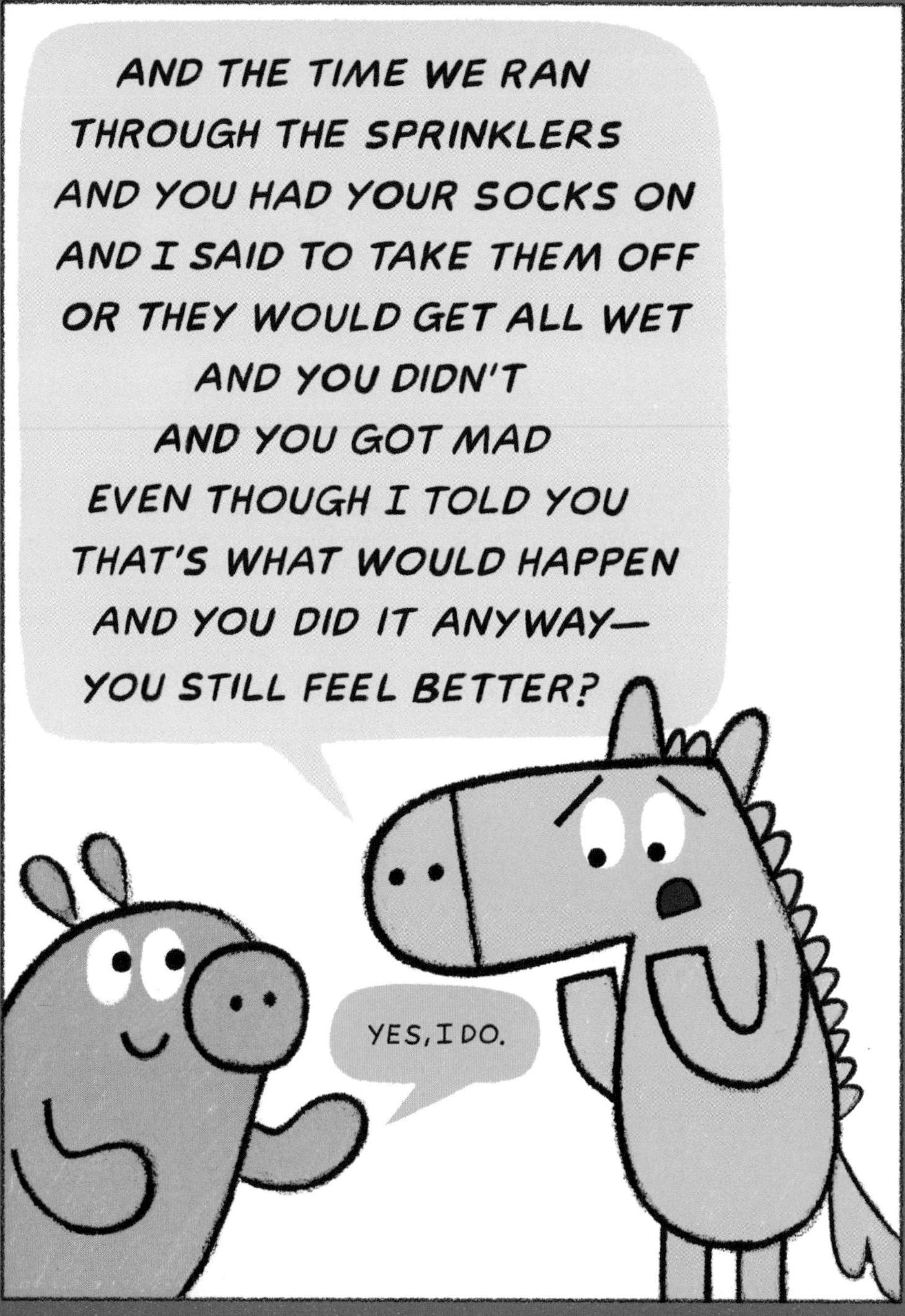
AND THE TIME WE RAN THROUGH THE SPRINKLERS AND YOU HAD YOUR SOCKS ON AND I SAID TO TAKE THEM OFF OR THEY WOULD GET ALL WET AND YOU DIDN'T AND YOU GOT MAD EVEN THOUGH I TOLD YOU THAT'S WHAT WOULD HAPPEN AND YOU DID IT ANYWAY—YOU STILL FEEL BETTER?
YES, I DO.

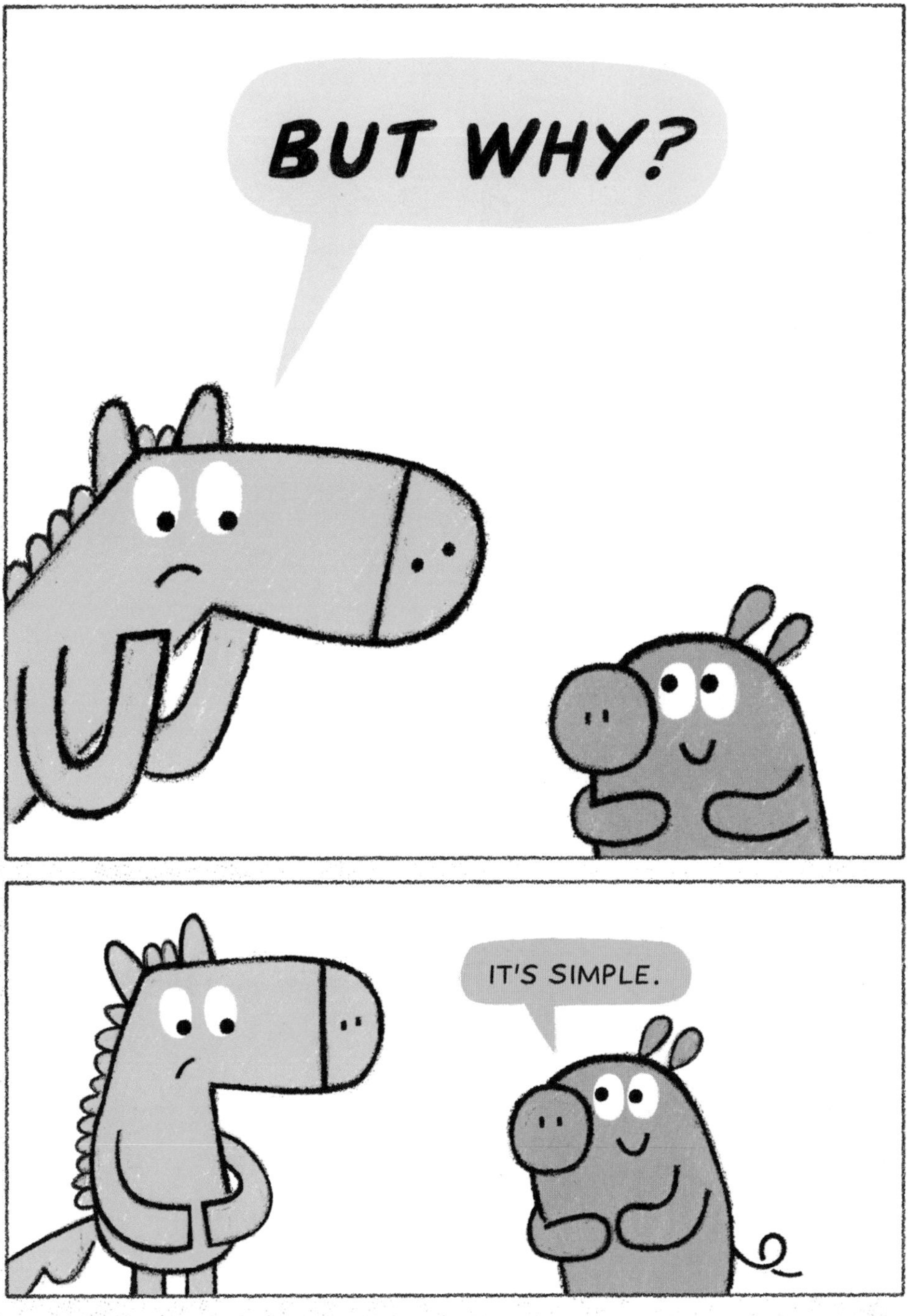
BUT WHY?
IT'S SIMPLE.

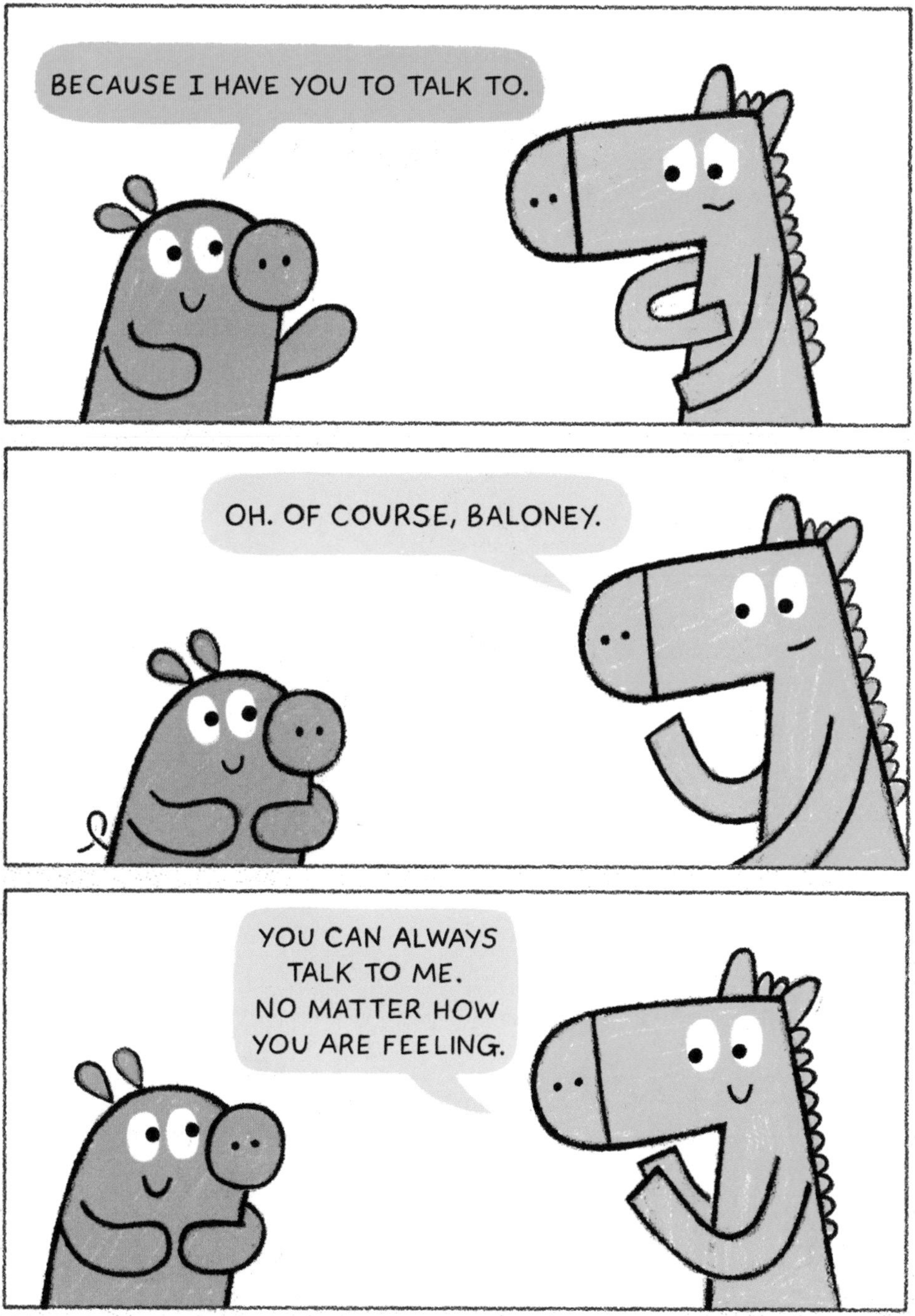
BECAUSE I HAVE YOU TO TALK TO.
OH. OF COURSE, BALONEY.
YOU CAN ALWAYS TALK TO ME. NO MATTER HOW YOU ARE FEELING.

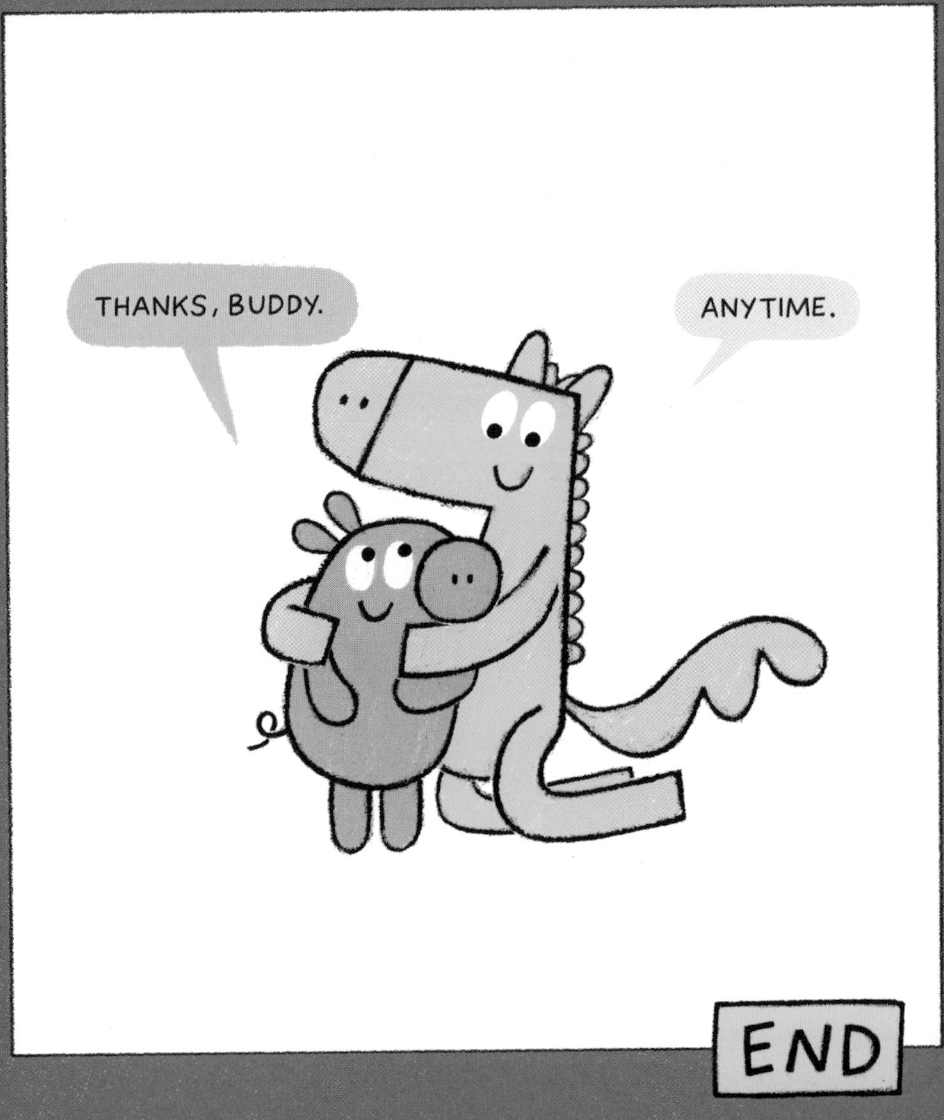
THANKS, BUDDY.
ANYTIME.
END

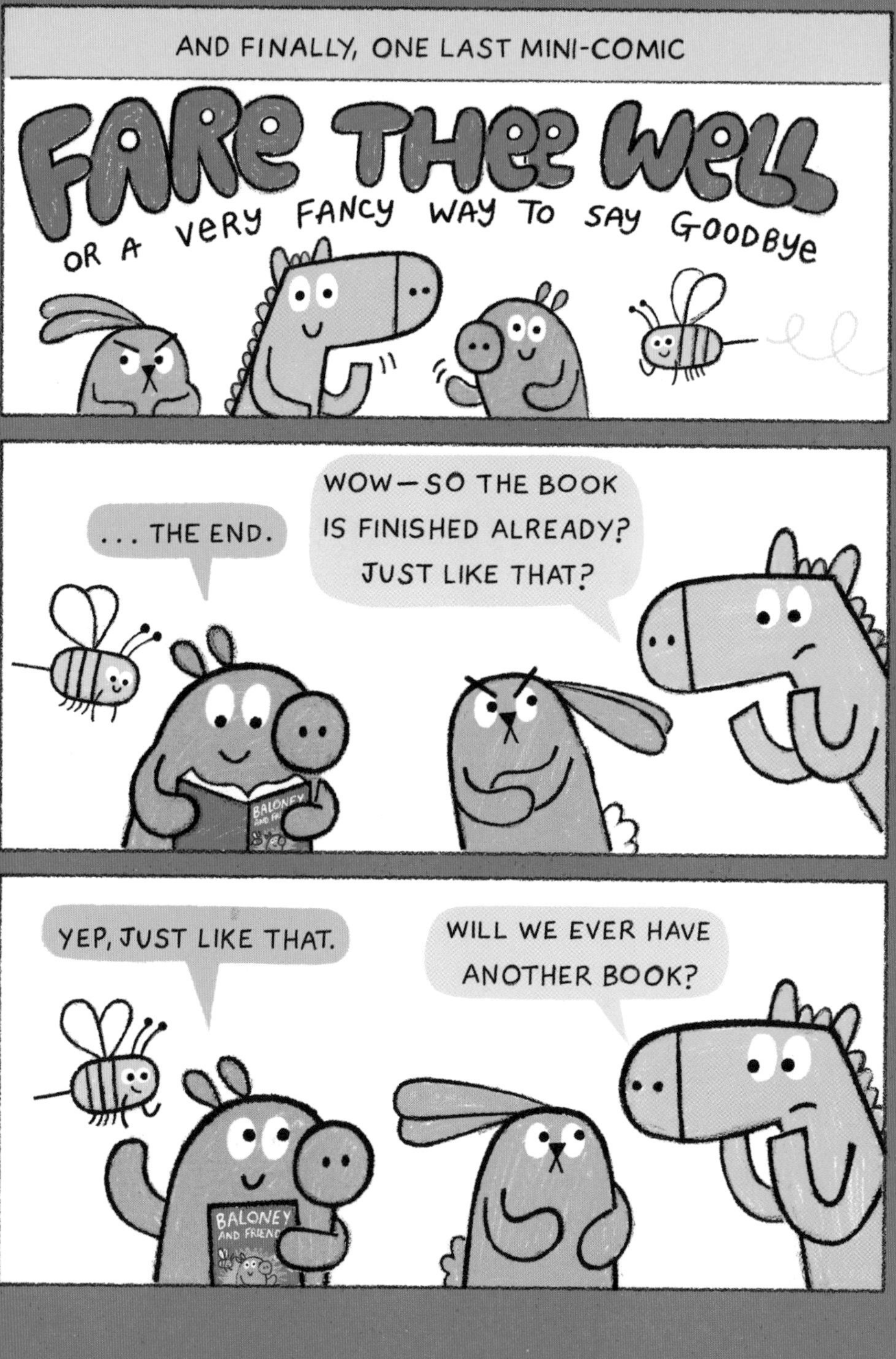
AND FINALLY, ONE LAST MINI-COMIC
FARE THEE WELL
OR A VERY FANCY WAY TO SAY GOODBYE
... THE END.
WOW—SO THE BOOK IS FINISHED ALREADY? JUST LIKE THAT?
YEP, JUST LIKE THAT.
WILL WE EVER HAVE ANOTHER BOOK?

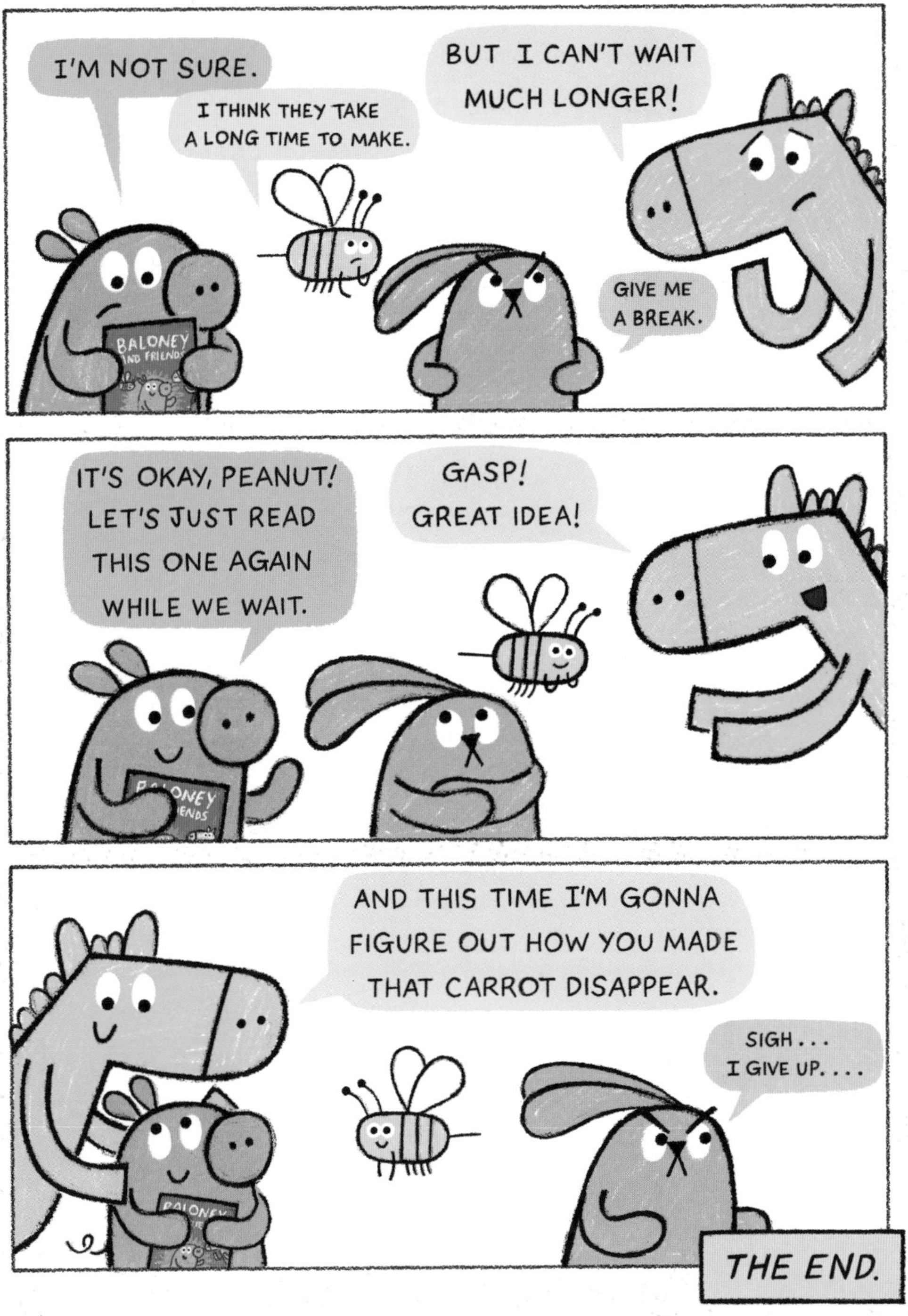
I'M NOT SURE.
I THINK THEY TAKE A LONG TIME TO MAKE.
BUT I CAN'T WAIT MUCH LONGER!
GIVE ME A BREAK.
IT'S OKAY, PEANUT! LET'S JUST READ THIS ONE AGAIN WHILE WE WAIT.
GASP! GREAT IDEA!
AND THIS TIME I'M GONNA FIGURE OUT HOW YOU MADE THAT CARROT DISAPPEAR.
SIGH . . . I GIVE UP. . . .
THE END.

YOU CAN

DRAW BALONEY

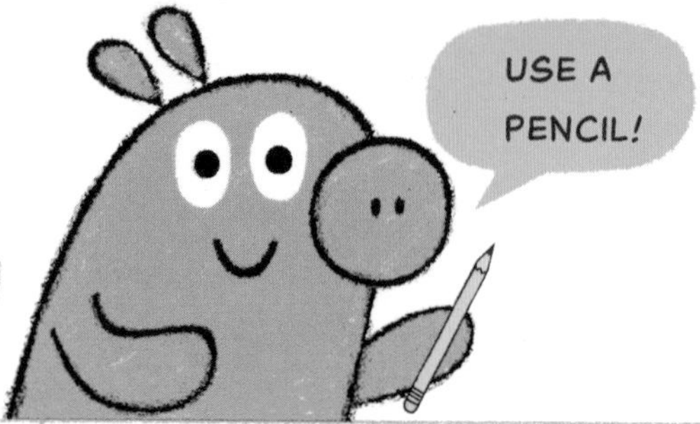
USE A PENCIL!

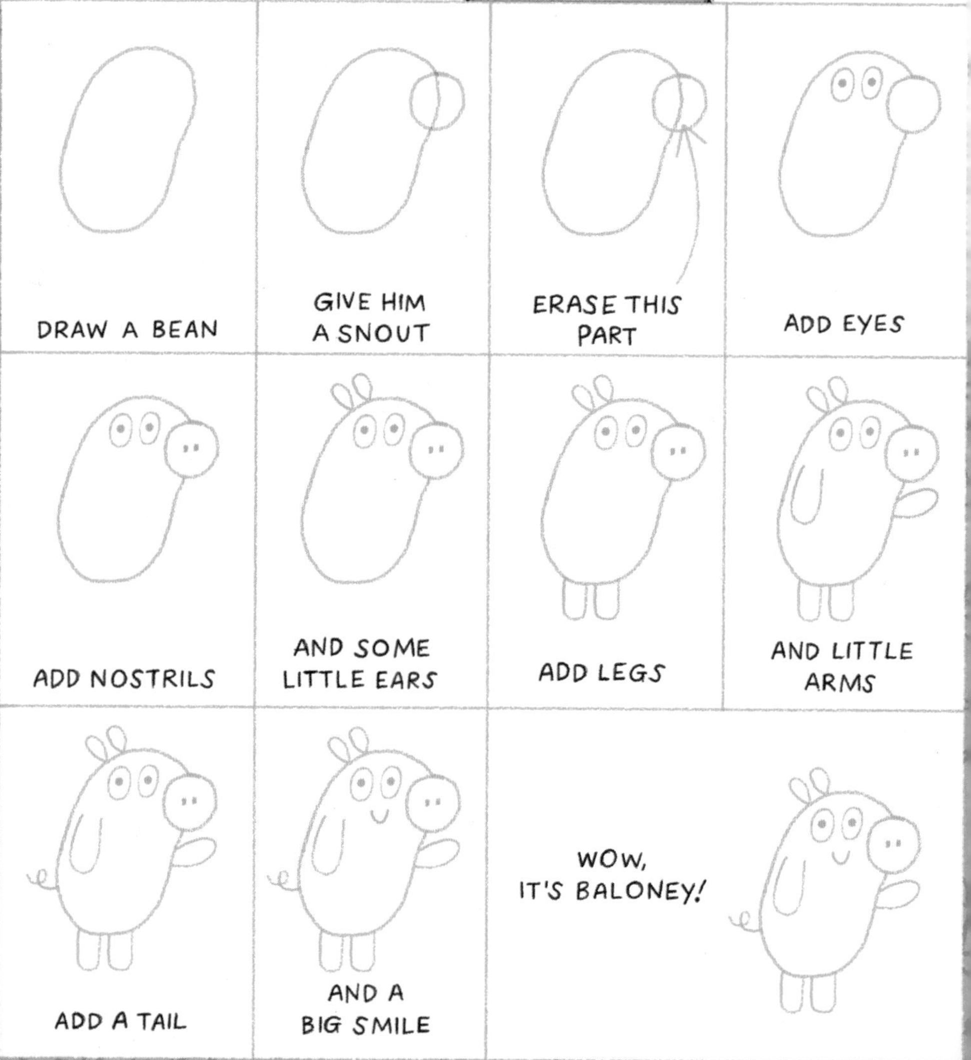
DRAW A BEAN
GIVE HIM A SNOUT
ERASE THIS PART
ADD EYES
ADD NOSTRILS
AND SOME LITTLE EARS
ADD LEGS
AND LITTLE ARMS
ADD A TAIL
AND A BIG SMILE
WOW, IT'S BALONEY!

AND DRAW PEANUT TOO!

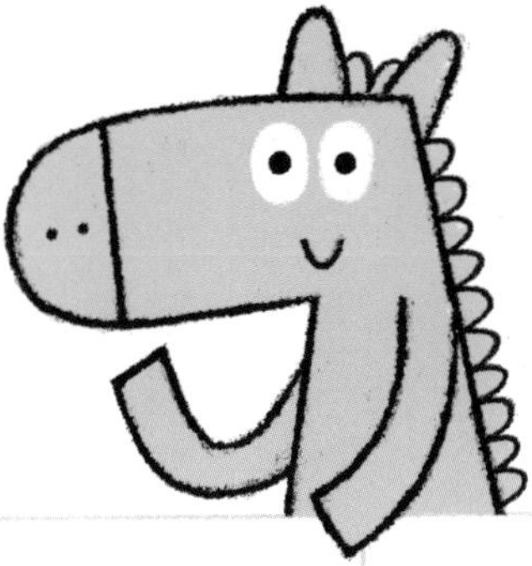

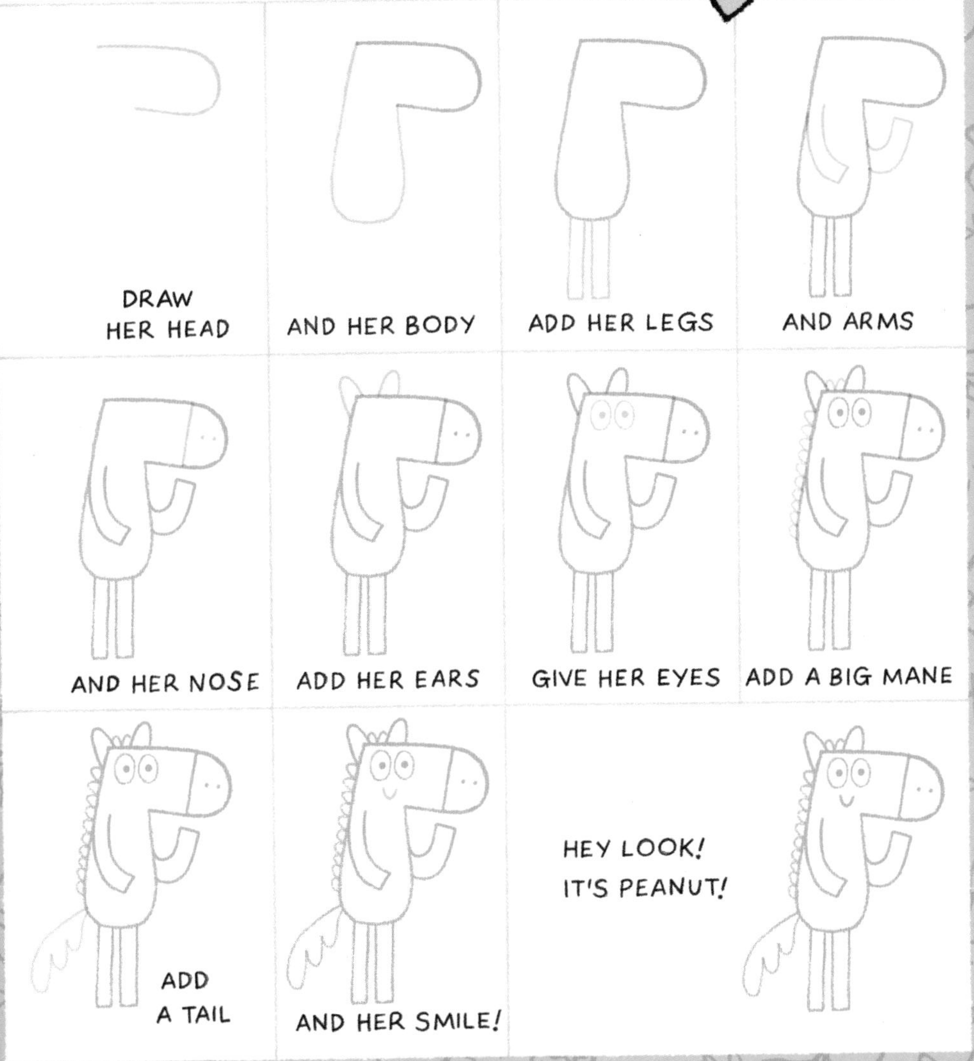
DRAW HER HEAD
AND HER BODY
ADD HER LEGS
AND ARMS
AND HER NOSE
ADD HER EARS
GIVE HER EYES
ADD A BIG MANE
ADD A TAIL
AND HER SMILE!
HEY LOOK! IT'S PEANUT!

DON'T FORGET TO

DRAW BIZZ

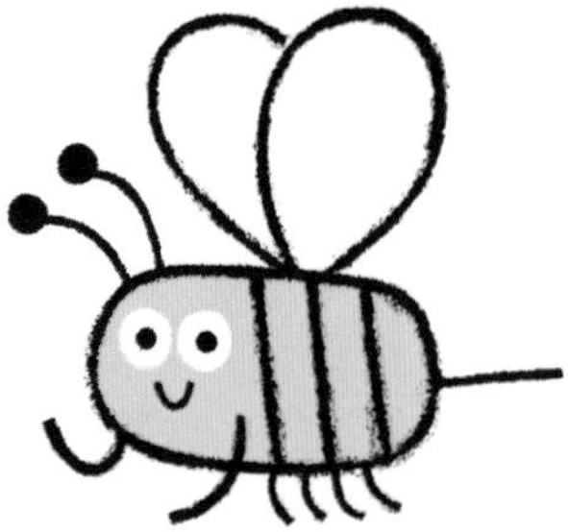

DRAW AN OVAL

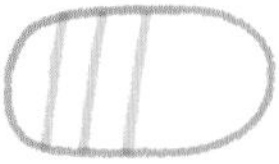

ADD STRIPES

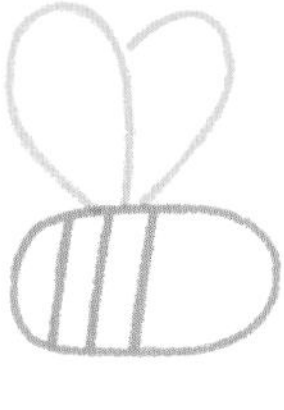

AND SOME WINGS

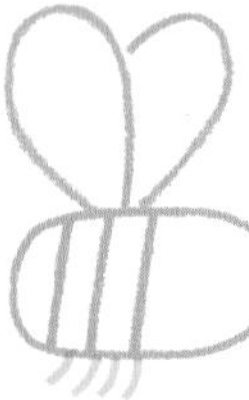

AND SOME TEENY LEGS

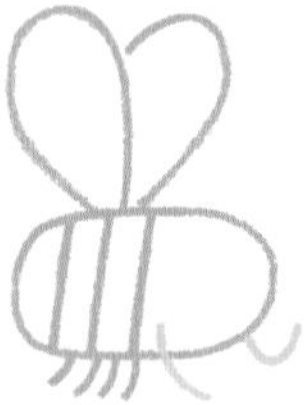

GIVE HER TWO ARMS

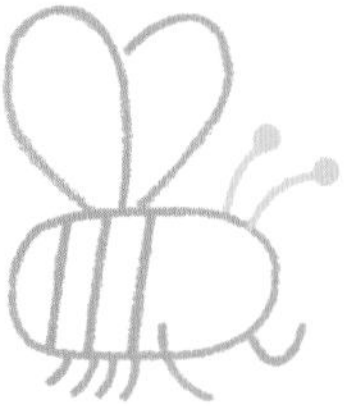

AND TWO ANTENNAE

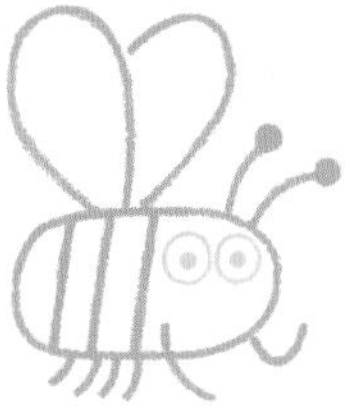

GIVE HER SOME EYES

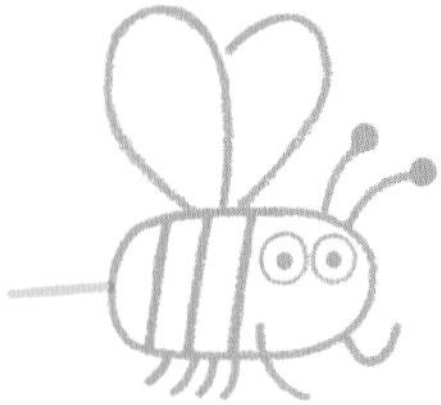

ADD HER STINGER

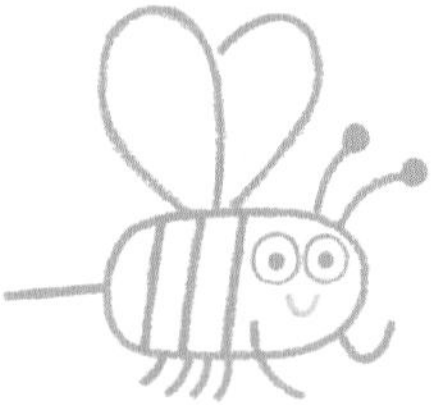

AND A BIG SMILE!

AND THAT'S BIZZ!

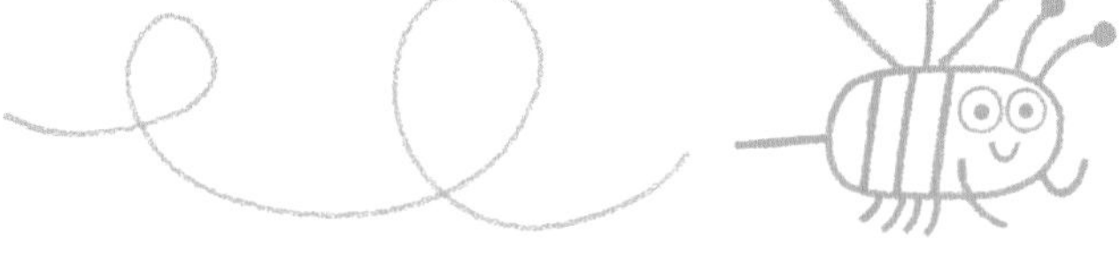

AND, YEAH, I GUESS YOU MIGHT AS WELL

DRAW KRABBIT

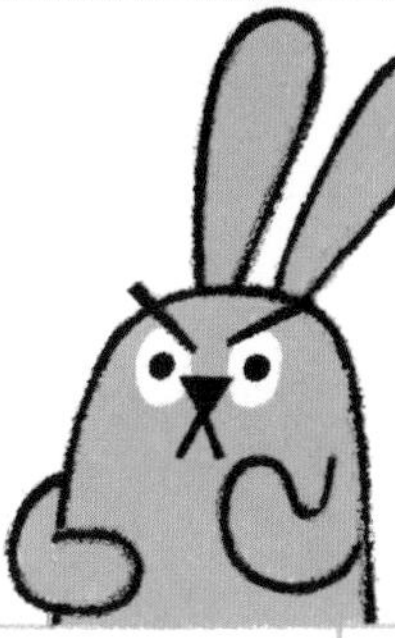

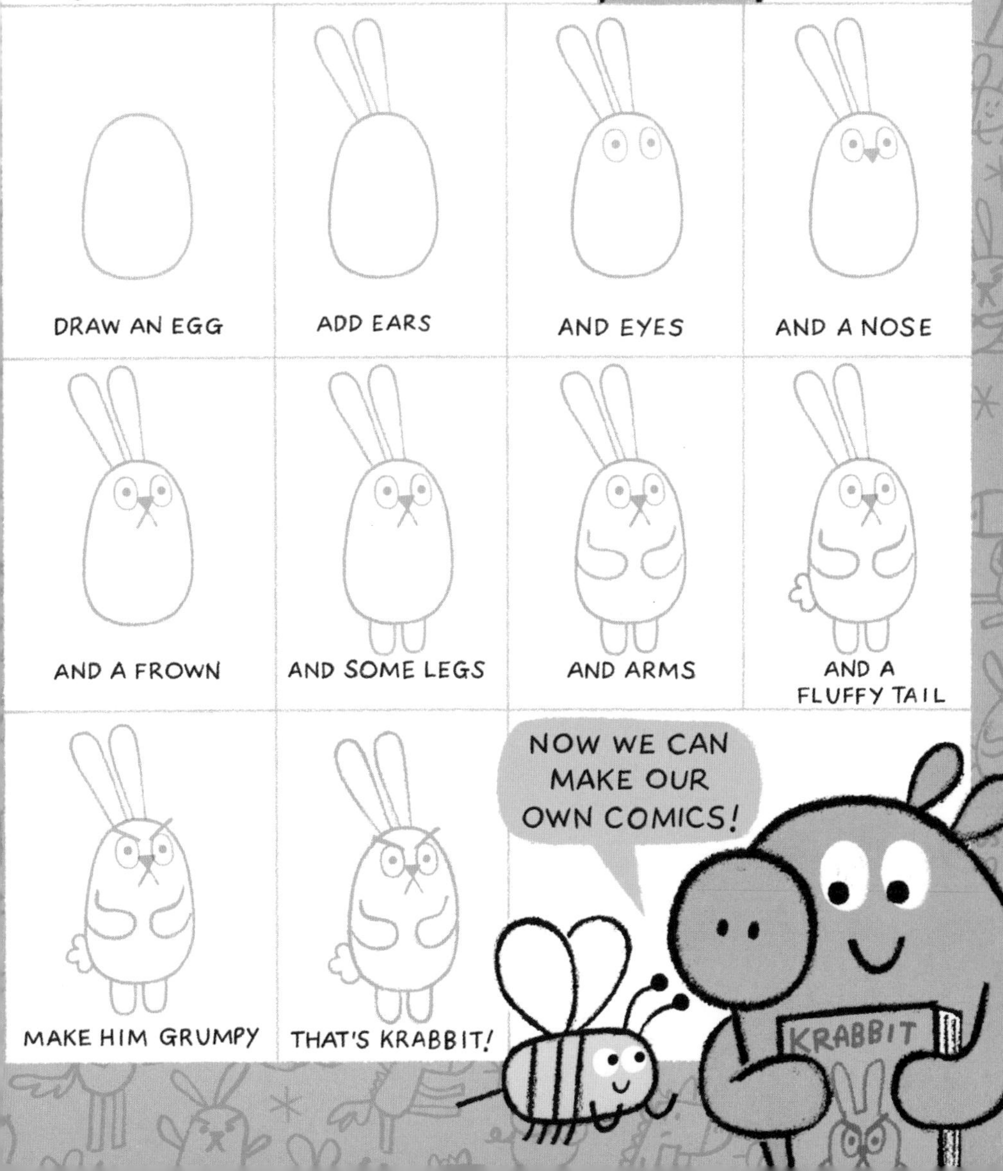
DRAW AN EGG
ADD EARS
AND EYES
AND A NOSE
AND A FROWN
AND SOME LEGS
AND ARMS
AND A FLUFFY TAIL
MAKE HIM GRUMPY
THAT'S KRABBIT!
NOW WE CAN MAKE OUR OWN COMICS!
KRABBIT

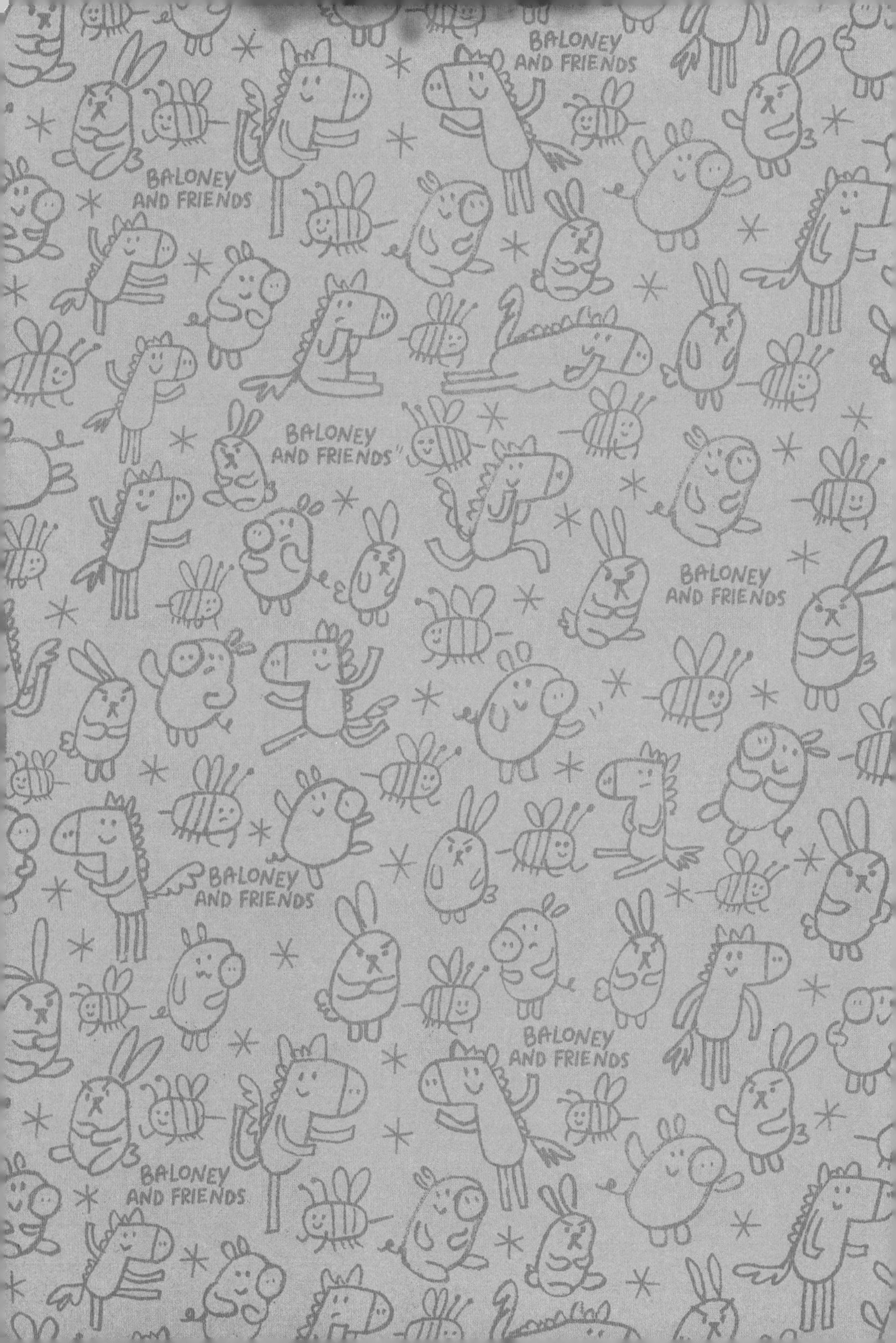
BALONEY AND FRIENDS
BALONEY AND FRIENDS
BALONEY AND FRIENDS
BALONEY AND FRIENDS
BALONEY AND FRIENDS
BALONEY AND FRIENDS
BALONEY AND FRIENDS

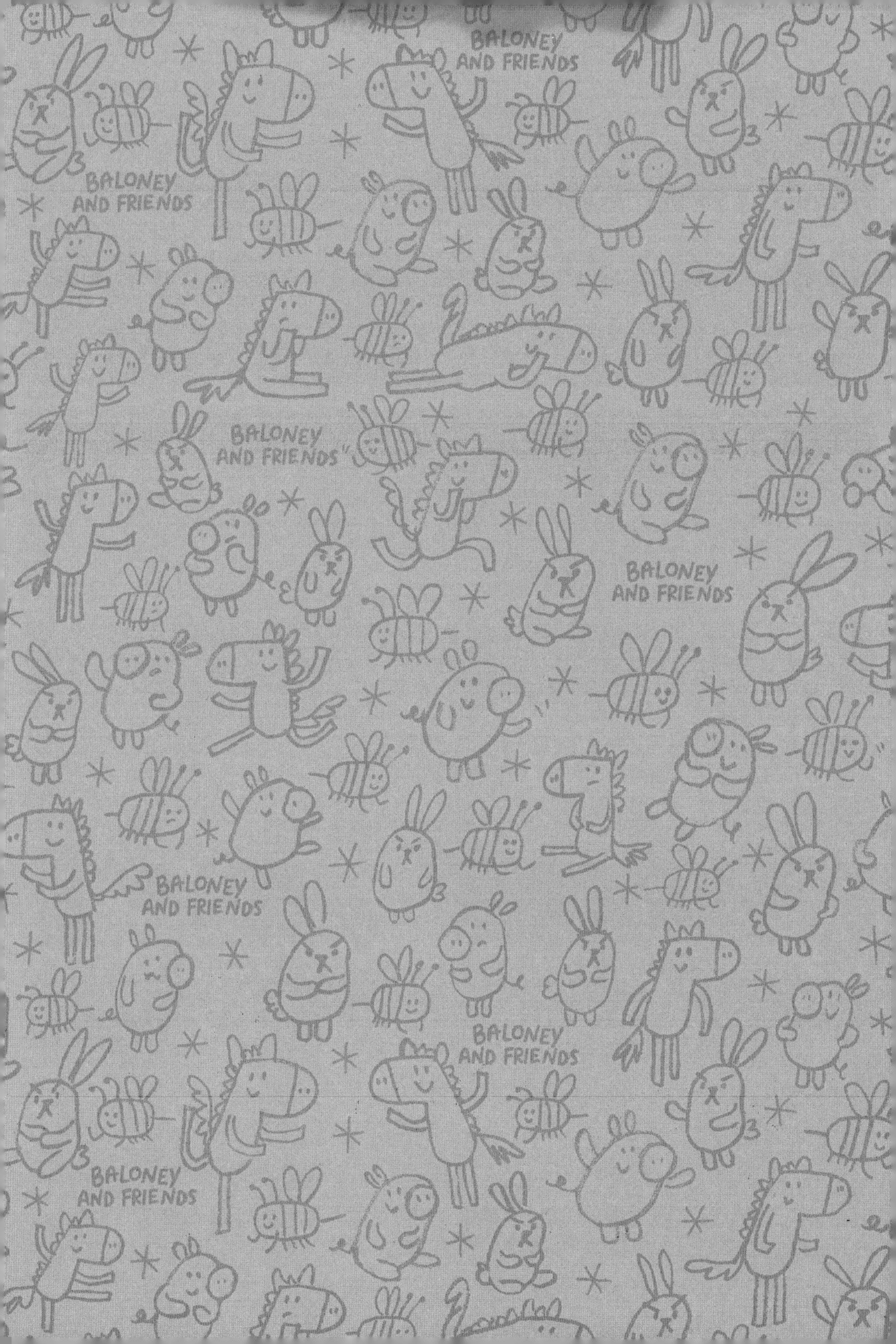
BALONEY
AND FRIENDS
BALONEY
AND FRIENDS
BALONEY
AND FRIENDS
BALONEY
AND FRIENDS
BALONEY
AND FRIENDS
BALONEY
AND FRIENDS
BALONEY
AND FRIENDS

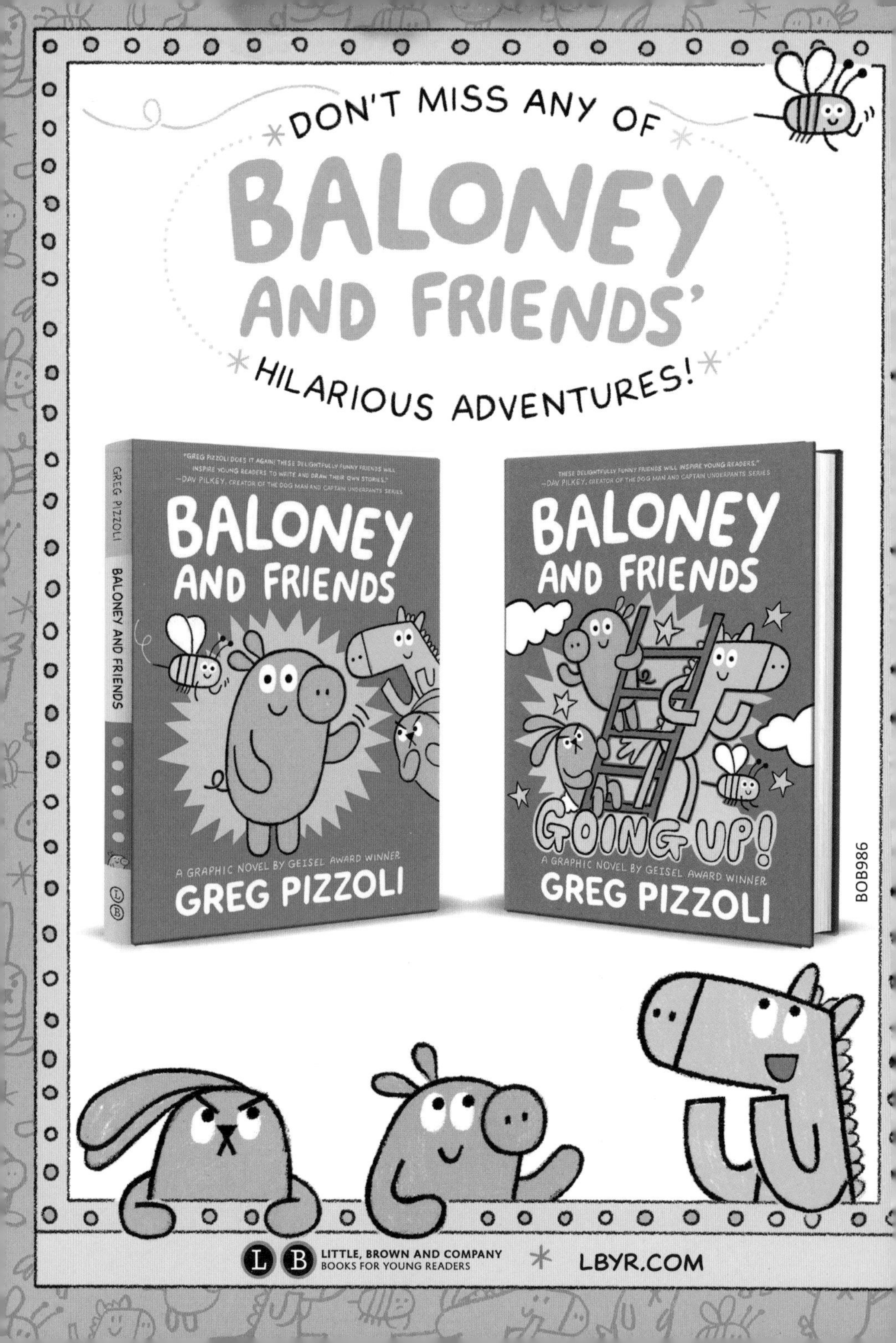
DON'T MISS ANY OF
BALONEY AND FRIENDS'
HILARIOUS ADVENTURES!
"GREG PIZZOLI DOES IT AGAIN! THESE DELIGHTFULLY FUNNY FRIENDS WILL INSPIRE YOUNG READERS TO WRITE AND DRAW THEIR OWN STORIES." —DAV PILKEY, CREATOR OF THE DOG MAN AND CAPTAIN UNDERPANTS SERIES
GREG PIZZOLI
BALONEY AND FRIENDS
BALONEY AND FRIENDS
A GRAPHIC NOVEL BY GEISEL AWARD WINNER
GREG PIZZOLI
"THESE DELIGHTFULLY FUNNY FRIENDS WILL INSPIRE YOUNG READERS." —DAV PILKEY, CREATOR OF THE DOG MAN AND CAPTAIN UNDERPANTS SERIES
BALONEY AND FRIENDS
GOING UP!
A GRAPHIC NOVEL BY GEISEL AWARD WINNER
GREG PIZZOLI
BOB986
LITTLE, BROWN AND COMPANY
BOOKS FOR YOUNG READERS
LBYR.COM